Rain on Your Wedding Day

Curtis Edmonds

SCARY HIPPOPOTAMUS BOOKS

Trenton, New Jersey

http://www.scaryhippopotamus.com

for Olive
(who never saw sunshine)
(or heard the patter of rainfall)
or felt the chill of a crisp autumn breeze
(or much of anything, really, except for)

LOVE

that goes on forever

Blessed are those who mourn,
for they shall be comforted.
— MATTHEW 5:4

1

My daughter Alicia called me once a year on Christmas Day. I would hear from her late in the afternoon when she was driving back from wherever she had spent the holiday. That was the extent of our relationship. There would come a time, I knew, when she would decide not to call me, and that would be the last I would ever hear from her. I didn't want that to happen this year.

When Alicia called me, I could hear the hum of the asphalt in the background. "Merry Christmas, Daddy," she said.

"Merry Christmas to you. Where are you calling from?"

I asked, because Alicia moved around a lot. She'd gone to three different colleges and four different master's programs, and she'd taught at many different campuses in her career. The last time I'd talked to her, some months back, she was teaching sculpture at Rutgers. For all I knew she'd already moved somewhere else.

"We're driving up I-95 right at the moment," she said.

I thought about asking who was in the car with her, but stopped myself. "That would put you where, around Trenton?" I asked. Alicia's mother had moved back to Philadelphia after the divorce. If Alicia spent the holiday with that side of the family, she would be on her way back north toward New Brunswick.

She laughed—her mother's laugh, short and breathy. "Not that part of I-95. We're in Georgia, a little ways south of Savannah."

I was confused for a moment until I figured out a possible explanation. "Are you working at the art college now?" I couldn't think of another good reason for her to come back home to Georgia.

"Not you too," Alicia said. "Toby has been teasing me about wanting to move down to Savannah this whole trip. But we're happy in New Jersey. For now."

"Oh." I had no idea who Toby was, but I was glad to hear she was happy.

"Granddaddy has been ill, so Aunt Valerie threw the big Christmas party this year. Her fourth husband has a house on Jekyll Island. You remember Jeff, her son? He and his wife came down from Philly with their three teenaged boys, and they were *so* impressed that you used to play for the Eagles. They wanted to drive up and meet you in person to get your autograph."

I felt the old, familiar, horrible chill I always got around my ex-wife's family. "I don't think that would be such a good idea," I said.

"Quit worrying, Daddy. I know you want to be left alone. But I found an old photo of you online. Will Morse, number seventy-seven, in that Kelly-green uniform. I printed it so you could sign it for them."

"Well, all right," I said. "Put it in the mail." It had been thirty years since anyone had wanted my autograph.

"I can do better than that. I can drop it by the cabin. We're staying in Atlanta tonight, and then we're driving up to Blue Ridge to see you tomorrow afternoon."

I hadn't seen Alicia since the divorce, since I left Atlanta, since I moved up to our old vacation cabin in the North Georgia mountains. That was almost five years ago.

Alicia is my daughter, and I love her. I tried not to let her absence bother me. Whenever she talked to me, it always seemed to bring up bad memories. I didn't want that for her. I wanted her to be happy. If talking to me made her unhappy, then silence was a price I was

2

willing to pay. It didn't make sense that she would want to go out of her way to come see me after all this time.

"I don't want to put you out," I said.

"Daddy, I came all the way down here. I sat through Christmas with crazy Aunt Valerie. Don't you *dare* say no."

"Of course not," I said. "I would be glad to see you, sweetie. It's a little bit of a surprise, that's all." I took a sip of hot tea, hoping that it would help steady my voice.

"I know this is short notice. But it's a good surprise. Trust me."

"Well, all right then," I said. "I'll cook something. What time are you going to be here?"

"Around two, if that works for you?"

"That's fine," I said. "You need directions?" I couldn't remember the last time she'd been to the cabin, and it's not the easiest place to find.

"Don't be silly, Daddy. I never get lost. See you tomorrow."

"See you tomorrow."

I looked around the cabin, trying to figure out what I could do in the next twenty-four hours to make the place presentable. The living room needed a light dusting, and the small stain on the Navajo rug would come up with a little effort. I had time to get a head start on my laundry. I am not much of a housekeeper, but thirty years of living with my ex-wife had taught me at least to pick up after myself. Cleaning was a way for me to stay busy and to keep my mind from constructing scenarios about why my daughter was coming to visit.

It was late in the evening before I was able to get to a stopping place. I fixed myself the biggest, blackest cup of coffee I could manage. I went out onto the back porch of the cabin and stood on the weathered planks for a long moment. The skyline was gray in the gathering darkness, but I could still see the headlights on the Appalachian Parkway in the valley below. A cold front was making its way south, and a stiff wind was blowing.

The mountain is quiet most days, but the wind gives it a voice. It stirred up the piles of dead brown leaves and rustled through the pine needles. I depend on the calm and the silence of the mountain, and the relentless December wind was an unwelcome intruder.

I breathed the cold air in deep to clear my head. *Who was Toby? Why were they in Georgia? Why did Alicia want to see me after all this time?* The wind didn't have any of the answers, not that I expected it to. I didn't have all that much in the way of answers myself.

I had a wife and four children, but I lost all of them. Danielle and I had one son who died of meningitis in 1979 when he was just a few months old. Alicia had an older sister named Francesca, who died in the fall of 2005 after a car accident. She had a younger sister, Trixie, who died five months later.

I was the only one who was with Trixie when she died. I drove her to the hospital. She whimpered in the backseat the whole way, lost in pain and anguish. Everyone blamed me for her death and they had every right to. No one stood by me then, not Danielle, and not Alicia.

I have lived a long life and have lost most everything I once cherished. I have spent the better part of the last five years alone, in my cabin, a long way from the outside world but far too close to my memories and fears. The loose threads of my relationship with my one surviving daughter were all I had to cling to. If there was any chance at all to bring her back into my life, even for a little while, I wanted to take it, whatever it might cost me.

2

The next morning, I had breakfast at the restaurant where I always eat on my weekly trip into town. The usual two waitresses were working. I got the pretty one for a change.

"Looks like I'll be taking care of you today, Mr. Morse," she said. "Coffee?"

"Sure, Margie."

"You know what you want? You must have the menu memorized by now."

From the other waitress this would have been sarcasm, but Margie was young and blonde enough that it wasn't. All I knew about her was that she was local and had been working there only a couple of years.

"French toast with a side of bacon," I said.

"Good choice. Get that right out for you."

I was about halfway through breakfast when Margie slipped into the other side of the booth. "How was your holiday?" she asked.

"It was very nice. Thanks for asking." Margie was about the only person in town I could have a friendly chat with, so I always made the effort to be pleasant and upbeat.

"You're usually not in here for breakfast."

"I have a little bit of shopping to do. My daughter and her friend are visiting from New Jersey." *Friend* seemed the safest thing to call Toby for the time being.

"I'm glad. You seemed a little sad and lonesome when you came in here last time."

"I'm fine," I said. I didn't want Margie to worry about me. "I'm just a little anxious, that's all. I didn't expect to be quite this busy."

"Tell me about it. I am so glad Christmas is over. My daughter is three and she was all excited, the way I used to be, but it's hard when you have to be Santa Claus."

I mopped up a stray drop of maple syrup with a wedge of French toast. "What did you get her?" I asked.

"Well, she wanted a baby brother, but I told her that wasn't happening. So I got her a doll, with a little bottle and everything. It's so hard to buy for kids that age, you never know what to get."

"I imagine not," I said.

"Of course, look who I'm talking to. You oughta have a ton of grandkids."

"No. I don't."

"Sorry. You'd said your daughter was coming up," she said, "so I kind of assumed. Is she your only child?"

I have never learned how to answer questions like this. I lie sometimes, but I hate doing that. It seems disloyal not to mention my other children, even in passing. I have nothing else to give Francie and Junior and Trixie but my loyalty. They are my children and always will be. To lie and say that they were not here, that their lives did not matter, would be a betrayal of the burned-out ashes of my love for them. I cannot betray them. I cannot turn my back on the remnants of that love. I have nothing else.

"No," I told Margie. "We had other children, but they passed away."

"Oh, no," she said. "I didn't know. I am so sorry."

"It was a long time ago," I said, although it didn't feel that way.

She placed her hand on mine for a second, and then pulled back.

"I'll get your check."

It was a short walk from the restaurant to the grocery store. I got what I needed for the side dishes, and then found a nice ham and put it in the cart. On Christmas and Easter, I always used to make ham baked with a Coca-Cola glaze. I hadn't made it in years, but the recipe wasn't hard, and I thought Alicia would like it. I got halfway to the register before I asked myself whether it was the right thing to get, which was another way to ask myself whether I knew my daughter at all anymore.

I hadn't seen Alicia since right after the divorce, a few months after Trixie died. It was the last time I set foot in our old house in Buckhead. Danielle had dumped everything she thought I might want downstairs and left it for me to sift through. She barricaded herself upstairs and had some fat goon in a deputy sheriff's uniform sitting on the staircase to make sure I didn't go up and try to talk to her.

Alicia's car was parked out front with a U-Haul trailer attached. You could tell it was her car because of all the campus parking stickers on it—although now most of them said "Faculty." I guessed she was upstairs with her mother, maybe gathering up the few little-girl possessions she still had left in the house.

Danielle had the house on the market. Neither of us could stand to live there any longer. She was headed back to Philadelphia to stay with one of her sisters. I was living in a tiny apartment in Midtown. It was within walking distance of Coca-Cola headquarters, where I had worked since I quit the NFL. I needed only another couple of months at work to maximize my pension, and then I would leave Atlanta for good.

It was a blistering July day, and I was worn out from carrying boxes to my truck. I went into the kitchen for something cold to drink. There wasn't anything in there but a six-pack of Pepsi. I hate Pepsi. I assumed Danielle put it there to annoy me. I didn't care. I opened a can and drank it anyway.

Alicia came halfway down the back staircase. She had her hair drawn back in a rubber band, like she did when she was twelve. She was wearing a dark-blue T-shirt that said "WOLVERINES" on it.

"Mom wanted me to tell you she was sorry about having the deputy here to watch you," she said.

"I don't want you in the middle of this," I said. "She shouldn't use you to deliver messages. If she has something she wants to tell me, she should come down here and tell me."

"She wanted me to tell you that having him here wasn't her idea. Her lawyer thought it up, so the deputy could…you know."

"Know what?" I asked.

"If you said something about Trixie, then he could testify in court."

I went to the refrigerator and got another can of Pepsi. I put the cold can on the back of my neck, more to give me a minute to compose what I wanted to say than anything else.

"I know it's hard for you to understand, and I know it's hard for your mother to accept. But your sister killed herself. If there was anything I could have done to change what happened, I would have, but it's too late. There's nothing else I can say that will change that or make it better for anyone."

"I know," she said. "And I know you wouldn't ever do anything to hurt her, not on purpose. But I'm not the one you need to convince of that."

"I know your mother is unhappy with me. I know she blames me. Whatever I did or didn't do, I didn't mean to hurt her. I didn't mean to hurt you," I said.

"I understand that," she said. "But you did hurt her, bad enough that she's asking me for help. She's never done that before, not once."

"That can't be easy for you."

Alicia wiped something from her face that might have been sweat or might have been tears. "It's not easy. I've been here for three hours. I only came because she asked me to help pack, and she's not doing anything. She's sitting in the middle of Trixie's room. She was crying for an hour before you got here, and now she's sitting there just staring at the wall. I don't know what to do."

"I'm sorry, sweetie. I appreciate you helping take care of her. You've been a good daughter for her these past months."

Alicia sat down on the stairs. "I thought you did it. I thought you killed her, at first. I know you loved her, I know you cared about Trixie, but it was so hard on you and Mom, having to watch her, and having her lash out at you all the time. When I heard that she died, and that you'd been arrested, I was so angry, just like Mom was. Like most people were."

When Trixie killed herself, I didn't just lose my daughter. I lost my freedom, at least for a while. I lost my marriage, not that it was that much of a surprise. But I hadn't been prepared to lose Alicia, not least because it meant that I would have to deal with my grief and shame alone.

"I know you were hurt, and I know you were angry," I said. "I'm not asking you to set aside your feelings. I just hope that, someday, maybe we can be a father and a daughter again."

"I want that too. And maybe, someday, we can have that kind of relationship. And I know it's not fair to you that Mom is asking me to take her side in this. But she needs me now."

I knew Alicia was right, even though I hated to admit it. Her mother needed her. We'd both gone through a horrible ordeal, but I'd wounded Danielle more deeply than anything that had happened to me.

"It's all right. I understand. If you're going to take sides, you made the right choice," I said.

She brought the end of her hair around and chewed on it, like she had when she was nine. "I want to know that you're still on my side."

"I am. I always will be."

I wanted to hold her, but I could see she didn't want that. I wanted to tell her everything would be all right, but it would have been a lie. She went back upstairs and stayed there, and I went back to my work.

I stood in line at the grocery store, staring at the ham in my shopping cart. Alicia could have turned vegetarian; young women were doing that more often now. She could ask me uncomfortable questions about whether it was free-range pork from a local farm. She could have allergies or be on a special macrobiotic diet—she might bring her own food, for all I knew.

Then there was Toby, the boyfriend—assuming that was who he was. I didn't think that Toby was a Jewish name, but it was possible, and if he was, he might not eat pork. He could even be a vegetarian. Living in New Jersey, he might never have heard of sweet potatoes. Well, they could fill up on macaroni and cheese if they wanted to.

"You're here early," the woman behind the counter said.

"I'm cooking for my daughter. She's driving up from Atlanta." I felt an unfamiliar paternal rush go through me, something I hadn't felt in years.

3

I was in the kitchen when I heard the knock at the door. My head was deep inside the refrigerator, checking to see if I had enough cream cheese for the corn casserole. I managed not to bump my head on the top shelf. I closed the door of the fridge and opened the front door, expecting to see my daughter for the first time in five years.

It wasn't Alicia. It wasn't anyone I knew.

"Hi, there," she said.

"Hi."

She was tall. That was the first thing I noticed. The second was that she had what my father's generation would have called platinum-blonde hair. It was piled up on her head in artistic disarray, or perhaps that was what it was meant to look like. She looked maybe ten years younger than me, but I wasn't good at guessing people's ages. She had a kind face, one that looked a little puzzled at the moment. It was probably how I looked too.

"Excuse me; I'm sorry to disturb you," she said. "But is this Falcon's Ridge? I mean, is that the name of the cabin?"

"It used to be called Falcon's Perch." The outfits that rent cabins out to tourists always give them some fanciful name.

"What is it called now?"

"I don't call it anything," I said. "It's just my house."

"Oh, dear," she said. "I have been driving around in circles the last hour, hoping that I was getting close, and now I have no idea where I am. I will have to drive all the way back to Atlanta and turn around just to get reoriented."

She was wearing an ankle-length parka, suitable for a hunting trip in the Arctic, and heavy gloves. It wasn't all that cold out, so I figured she was cold-natured. "If you want to come inside for a minute, I can take a look at your directions and try to get you on the right road."

"Under normal circumstances, I would have to decline to enter a strange man's home. But these are not normal circumstances."

I helped her take off her coat, and it turned out that she wasn't as tall as I'd thought—she was wearing knee-high boots with absurd heels. *Women and shoes*, I thought. She handed me a sheaf of paper with the directions, and then went over to the fireplace, putting her hands as close as she could get without them turning into charcoal. "I hate cold weather," she said. "There's nothing good about it. Human civilization started in Kenya because the weather was nice."

"You came up from Atlanta?" I asked.

"I live in Midtown," she said. "My friend Beth has a cabin up here. Her husband took her to Barbados for the holiday, and she let me borrow it while they're gone. It's nice and warm in Barbados. Not that I'm jealous or anything."

"Have you been to their cabin before?"

"A couple of times," she said.

"So you know that it's on the lake."

"That's what I've been looking for the last hour."

"The lake," I explained, "is on the other side of the highway. All this is mountains up here. You must have made a left coming off the highway when you should have made a right."

"One wrong turn, and I get confused. Are you cooking something? It smells very nice."

"I'm cooking a ham."

She gave me a disapproving look. "Why would you cook a whole ham?" she asked. "That seems wasteful for someone who lives alone.

You do live alone, right? Wait. I'm sorry. That was kind of a personal question."

"I'm expecting my daughter and her friend in a few minutes."

She turned from the fire, as though it had just suddenly gotten twenty degrees hotter. "Your daughter?" she asked.

"You sound surprised."

"Well, no. I mean, I shouldn't be. Of course you have a daughter."

There was a crunch of gravel just then, the sound of Alicia's car pulling into the driveway. That was followed by a banging noise when she slammed the car door, and a couple of sharp sounds that I couldn't place, but were what you'd expect to hear if you gave the front quarter panel a good kick or two.

"That would be her," I said.

"Oh, goodness. I hope this isn't awkward for you," she said. "I should go."

"Under normal circumstances, you'd be welcome to stay a little longer. But these are not normal circumstances."

"I understand. Thanks for your help."

"Don't mention it," I said.

"I'm Dot. Dot Crawford. Nice to meet you."

"Will Morse," I said. I worried for a minute that she might recognize my name. If she did, it didn't affect her at all.

"I'll get out of here. I hope you have a nice time with your daughter."

"Thanks."

"Maybe I can make it up to you sometime," she said.

"Don't worry about it," I said. "I hope you have a nice time using your friend's cabin."

"I have papers to grade and a whole morass of notes to organize. It's going to be miserable. You have no idea."

I saw Dot out the door, and she hurried to her car. If Alicia saw Dot leave, she didn't seem to notice—she was sitting on the trunk of her car, yelling something indistinct into her cell phone. *Good for her*, I thought. Alicia had always been a little unwilling to speak her mind or defend her own side in an argument. Her sisters were

13

always in some operatic quarrel with their mother, but Alicia shied away from conflict when she could. I suspected that this was at least in part the reason for her transient lifestyle; it must have been easier for her to pack up and leave than deal with things. I was glad to see her stand her ground for a change.

There wasn't a passenger in the car, so I assumed she was yelling at Toby. I guessed that he had elected to stay behind in Atlanta. That was probably what they had argued about, but it could have been anything. On a long enough road trip you could spend hours battling over the most trivial thing—who was in what movie when, how many RBIs Dale Murphy hit in his career, whether the universe was balanced on the back of a turtle or not.

This argument didn't sound trivial. I could catch snatches of words, and most of them were things like "bastard" and "jackass." I went back into the kitchen to check the ham.

Alicia came in as I was turning the green bean casserole around in the lower oven. She was wearing a leather jacket that was long in the sleeves. It looked like she had gained a little weight, not that I was fool enough to mention that. I wiped my hands on a dishrag and gave her a hug.

"You OK?" I asked.

"Yeah. Give me a minute."

"Have a seat." She would tell me about Toby when she was ready. "You want anything to drink?"

"Got a Coke?"

"A Coke, you say? Might have heard of that once."

"You must have enough in the fridge to drown a medium-size giraffe."

I got out a can and poured it for her. "That was your grandfather's joke. It's nice to see it passed down to the younger generation."

"Thanks, Daddy."

"Catch a lot of traffic in Atlanta?"

"A little around Cobb Galleria—great big, huge mobs of people at the after-Christmas sales. Not like up here."

"Nothing like up here."

14

"That's what I tried to tell Toby. We had some good times in this cabin, didn't we? Mom always took us on those long hikes in the fall to collect leaves."

"I remember," I said.

"Hikes that always seemed to coincide with some football game being on."

"You figured that out, I see. But when you got back, I always fixed you hot chocolate and let you stay up late and play Monopoly."

"I know. I remember. It was always nicer here than it was at home. I guess that's why you decided to move here."

I could have stayed in Atlanta. I lived there for thirty-five years. I knew people. I had favorite restaurants. But I got to the point where I broke down in tears every time I passed Piedmont Hospital. I couldn't get a slaw dog at The Varsity without people whispering. People I'd worked with for years suddenly wouldn't look at me when they talked to me. So I left.

I could have gone back home to Alabama, but I don't have any family there anymore, and all the places I ever lived have been bulldozed by time and avarice. I could have started over in San Diego or Seattle or San Juan, where nobody knew me and nothing reminded me of anything. But I'm too old for a change like that.

I live here, where I have the best memories of my daughters when they were alive and happy. The mountain is quiet and beautiful, but that's almost beside the point. We had a lot of good times here and very few bad ones. Loneliness is not too steep a price to pay for that.

"Hey, can you hold still a second?"

"OK," I said.

Alicia pulled a smallish rectangle of black plastic out of her jacket pocket and held it up. "I'm going to take a couple pictures and send them to Toby."

"If you like."

She snapped a picture of me and took some shots of the living room, with the fireplace and the big-screen. "I'm going to text him the pictures —you can do that now with these phones."

"So I gather."

"Of course, here I am, talking to the last person in America without a cell phone."

"No, you're not," I said. "I bought one of those prepaid phones they sell at the 7-11. I keep it in my glove compartment in case my truck breaks down on the highway."

"Well, then, I take it back," she said. "You're clearly up-to-date with the latest gadgets."

"You get a little gray hair and people think you can't work technology anymore. I go to the library in town, sometimes, and there's always some volunteer asking me if I need help to use the computer."

"Nice to see that old age hasn't made you cranky yet. Do you know the number? I can put in my contacts."

I had the number written down on a scrap of paper in my wallet, and I told it to her as she entered in to her phone. Just as she finished, her phone chimed a familiar sound that I couldn't quite place. "The *Law & Order* sound," she explained. "Means Toby texted me back."

"Is he a lawyer?" I asked, not without some apprehension.

"No, he just likes the show. Here's the deal. Toby got out of the car when I stopped for gas at the Conoco in Blue Ridge and wouldn't get back in. He finally got bored with being stranded, I guess. I need to drive down there and pick him up."

"I'll be glad to see him. If you're hungry, I can have dinner on the table by the time you get back."

"He'll like that," Alicia said. "Dinner, I mean. I don't think he'd act like such a jackass if he had something to eat."

"What made him get out of the car?" I asked, and then I kicked myself for asking. I didn't want to be inquisitive, but it seemed an odd place for him to bail out.

Alicia jammed the phone in her pocket. "He didn't believe me," she said. "I told him that this was a nice cabin with a great view and that I'd been up here a hundred times."

"So you sent him the pictures."

"Toby is a city boy. We started driving up here, and he sort of freaked out once we got past Marietta. I think he thought that this place had a dirt floor and that there was a moonshine still out back."

"Well, you better go get him then, before he gets caught by the revenuers."

"OK, Daddy." She got up and kissed me on the cheek. "I'll be right back."

I didn't think Toby was scared of the Georgia countryside. I didn't imagine that any normal young man of Toby's generation—assuming he was about Alicia's age—would be all that worked up about a nice drive on a paved highway up to the Appalachian foothills to a vacation cabin with central air and a hot tub.

If Toby was scared of anything, he was scared of me.

And not with the normal meet-the-parents fear. If Toby was smart enough to date my daughter, he was smart enough to do his due diligence. He'd looked me up on Google or Wikipedia or something. There were ten thousand stories on the Internet that said that I'd killed Trixie and gotten away with it. That would scare most people.

4

I shouldn't have worried about Toby's eating habits. He turned out to be one of those tall, stringy people who can put away amazing quantities of food without ever gaining an ounce. He downed three slices of ham and half the green bean casserole before he came up for air.

"This is amazing, Daddy," Alicia said, and then elbowed Toby, who was shoveling in a heaping spoonful of sweet potatoes.

"Fantastic," he said. "Delicious."

"Glad this is such a hit."

Toby paused to swallow a chunk of ham that could have been part of an excellent sandwich. "The glaze is delicious. What's in it?"

"Coke and brown sugar. Nothing fancy."

Toby glanced around the kitchen, which was decorated—if you could call it that—with Coke-related memorabilia. "Never would have guessed."

"Daddy worked for Coca-Cola for thirty years. Hence the dish-towels and the tin signs and the saltshakers."

"Wow. So, like, does this mean you know the secret formula?"

"Not a word of it," I said. Everyone always asks about the secret formula, and everyone always thinks they're being clever when they ask. The truth is that soft drinks, like people, are more alike than we think.

"Disappointing. I know there's vanilla in there, and citrus, and what I think is the stuff they put in Earl Grey tea, but I can't figure out the rest of it."

"Toby," Alicia explained, "is a foodie."

"Does that mean you're a chef?" I asked.

"It means he eats. A lot. This is a light snack for him. You know Rutgers is famous for the Fat Darrell sandwich, right?"

"Now that you mention it, yes. I saw it on the Paula Deen show once. It had chicken fingers, mozzarella sticks, French fries and marinara sauce on a roll."

"That's not the best one," Toby said between mouthfuls of green bean casserole.

"Whatever. Toby goes through those two or three at a time."

"They're good. Are there any rolls?"

"I can get you some bread."

I tried not to have any preconceptions about Toby, but it was getting hard. Judging by the stubble on his chin, he was in his early thirties—about Alicia's age, as I'd guessed. But he didn't seem to be anywhere near grown up. He had a shaggy mop of black curls and was wearing a gray Rutgers sweatshirt that was about two sizes too big on his rangy frame. Despite the cold weather, he was wearing the kind of leather sandals that would have gotten you thrown out of most of the bars I had frequented in college. His eyes were as dark and as empty as the night.

I put the loaf of bread on the table; Toby took two slices and started sopping up the juice from the ham, clearing up some more room on his plate. "So you're at Rutgers?" I asked. I didn't have any clue what he did for a living besides eat.

"Yeah. Sorry. I don't get to eat this good most of the time."

"Starving student?"

"I used to be. I got my doctorate two years ago, so now I'm a starving professor."

"Toby teaches in the music department," Alicia explained. "Freshman music appreciation and an online course on the intersection of jazz and popular music."

"Do you play an instrument?"

"I do theory," he said.

"So, in theory, you play an instrument."

Toby ate one last slice of ham and wiped his mouth. "I play guitar a little, but I'm not any good. I'm an ethnomusicologist."

"Oh."

"Toby knows everything about regional variations in pop music."

"Regional variations," I said, not wanting to stumble over how you pronounced *ethnomusicologist*.

"Toby, do the thing you do, with the albums. It's amazing, Daddy. It's like he's psychic."

Toby stacked his knife and fork on his plate and folded his hands. "I hate showing off. It's a cheap stunt. A parlor trick."

"But you do it so well, sweetie."

"If Mr. Morse is up for it, fine. It does explain what I do."

"Call me Will," I said.

"OK then. Will. Basically, I get some demographic information from you, and then I come up with a list of five albums I think you might have lying around. Most people have at least two or three. You have a stack of CDs or something?"

"In the office," I said. "They're in a wire-mesh box."

"Excellent. You're how old?"

"Sixty-three."

"That means you were born in what, '48? Graduated high school in '66?"

"Yeah."

"And you grew up in the South."

"I was born in Dothan, Alabama. We moved to Montgomery when I was six. I went to school there."

"The civil rights era. Hey, you would have been there when the church blew up."

"What?"

"The Klan bombed a black church. It was a big deal. Spike Lee did a documentary about it."

"You mean the bombing at the Sixteenth Street Church."

"Yeah."

"That happened in Birmingham."

"Yeah! Birmingham, Alabama," he said confidently.

"I'm from Montgomery," I said, rolling off the syllables one by one, as you would do for a slow child. "Not Birmingham. Birmingham is an hour and a half north."

"Oh. Yeah. You did say that. Sorry. Then you went to college where? Alabama?"

"I didn't go to Alabama. I went to Auburn."

"And you played football."

"A little bit." I'd been a three-year starter, selected for the all-Southeastern Conference team my senior year. I was drafted by the Philadelphia Eagles in the seventh round in 1971. I started dating Danielle in the middle of my rookie year. We got married after my second year in the league, a few weeks before I got traded to Atlanta. I spent the next two years as a backup for the Falcons, and when they released me, I landed a job with Coca-Cola. "It was a long time ago."

"Yeah, that's why I wanted to ask you. I read this *New York Times* article once about the whole Alabama football thing—I mean, I think it was an article. Maybe it was a book. This guy went out and tailgated at a bunch of football games, and wrote about it."

"I know which book you're talking about. Didn't read it."

"Anyway, it was all about this guy named Bear Bryant, who was supposed to be this awesome figure or whatever. What was he like?"

"I don't know. I laid eyes on the man only three times in my life, and he was on the other sideline. Everything that I've heard said he was a son of a bitch."

"Wait, didn't you play for him?"

"No."

"I thought he was the coach for Alabama."

"That's right. But I told you already, I went to Auburn. Don't you listen?"

"Daddy. Relax. You're turning purple," Alicia said, looking concerned.

I opened my mouth but then closed it. I did what the doctors had told me to do when I got worked up over nothing. I started flexing my toes, back and forth, and then started flexing my ankles—a relaxation technique, they called it, but it was more to get my mind to concentrate on something else besides what was causing the emotional response. So this Toby, my future son-in-law—why else would Alicia bring him here?—didn't know the difference between Auburn University and The University of Alabama. It wasn't the worst thing to ever happen.

"So, wait. Do, like, Auburn and Alabama play each other in football?"

Alicia got up and grabbed Toby by the hood of his sweatshirt and half-dragged him out the kitchen door and onto the front porch. "Quit being a jackass," she said as she slammed the door. I couldn't catch the rest, except that it was loud and one-sided, and there was a "you're embarrassing me" in there somewhere. I flexed my knees for a minute and then I got up and started to clear the table. I didn't need Alicia to stand up for me, but it was nice to see.

I put the few last scraps of ham in a storage bag and put the roasting pan in the sink with water to soak off the residue. Enough of the green bean casserole was left to save, and I was rummaging around for a plastic storage container when they walked back in.

"I wanted to say, there, um, Mr. Morse."

"Call me Will."

"Will. I'm sorry for what I said. I was nervous and not paying attention." Alicia poked him in the ribs. "And I was a jackass, and I'm sorry."

"That's fine, then. Sit down, and I'll make you some coffee, if you drink coffee."

"I thought I could help do the dishes or something."

"You thought wrong. This is the South, and you're company. We don't make company do the dishes; it's rude."

"Sorry. Again."

"I'll do the dishes, Daddy. You go show Toby those CDs."

5

We went into my office, which I hadn't had time to straighten up at all. It had been a guest bedroom back in the days when we had guests. When I moved in for good, I put my desk and a computer in there. All my files and the World War I research stuff I was working on was stacked everywhere. I had a big shelving unit on the back wall, and the CDs sat on a top shelf. I grabbed the box and set it on the desk.

"So you're going to guess what's in here," I said.

"Yeah. Look, we don't have to do this."

"Alicia says you're an expert. And they don't give away PhD's at Rutgers, do they?"

"They don't give them away anywhere. But I didn't get mine there. I went to Wisconsin for undergrad, and then grad school at Northwestern."

"Doesn't matter. Give it your best shot. Show me what you've got."

"It's a stunt, like a cold reading. I know what the most popular albums were in a given year in different genres, and then I make educated guesses based on that."

"If it's a good stunt, you ought to be able to pull it off even if I know what's coming."

"Yeah. Um, Alabama means Hank Williams, but he died when you were, what, five?"

"Drank himself to death in the backseat of a Cadillac. It's at the museum in Montgomery."

"Right. I'm going to say Hank Junior, though. *Major Moves*—that was the album that had the *Monday Night Football* theme. Alan Jackson, *A Lot About Livin'*, and Randy Travis, *Storms of Life*. And we're in Georgia, so let's go with Charlie Daniels, *Million Mile Reflections*. Mainstream, traditional country, on the conservative side. I'd go with older albums, but they're more likely vinyl."

"That's four."

"I know. I try to do a wild card for the fifth. Let me think a second. Not Neil Young."

"No."

"Not Lynyrd Skynyrd."

"This is the part that's like a cold reading. You're trying to get me to give something away by guessing."

"OK, you got me. I'm going to say one of the Mel Tillis greatest hits records."

I hadn't thought about Mel Tillis for twenty years. "How come?"

"He had that 'Coca-Cola Cowboy' song. You would have liked that."

"Well then. Not bad, for a stunt."

"How'd I do?"

"Oh for five." I handed him the box.

"Jane's Addiction," he said, flipping through the discs. "A couple of Hole albums, which means Courtney Love. Evanescence. Slipknot. R.E.M.?" He picked up that one and examined it. "Let's see…yeah. 'Everybody Hurts,' I forgot that was on *Automatic for the People*. Indigo Girls. System of a Down. *Jagged Little Pill*, of course. Oh, the She Wants Revenge album. Local color. Nice."

"Not what you expected."

"No. Based on this selection, I would have to say that you were a young woman, past college age."

"Why a woman?"

"Because of the Indigo Girls. A man would have Rage Against the Machine or Nine Inch Nails. But Indigo Girls—has to be female. And, given the amount of Courtney Love music in here, it was someone with extreme emotional issues."

"Fair enough."

"So they're not yours. I do notice that a couple of them have 'Property of Alicia Morse' written on them. Having said that, I know what Alicia listens to, and this isn't representative. The other thing I notice is that the newest of these was released five years ago. That gives me a good idea who these belonged to—used to belong to, I mean."

"They were my daughter Trixie's."

He put the CDs back on the shelf and sat down in my swivel chair. "When Alicia said we were driving up here, she told me a little about you, and I looked the rest of it up. About Trixie, I mean."

"You shouldn't believe everything you read."

He ran his hands through his thick mop of curls. "I don't know what you did or didn't do. I think it still bothers Alicia."

"I know it does. It still bothers me. It was a horrible thing that happened to our family, and I'd rather not talk about it."

"I understand that, but you understand why I'm concerned."

"It's not any of your business. Even if it was, nothing I could say would bring her back, anyway. I wish it could, but it can't."

"That's such a cop-out. Nothing can bring back the dead. That's not a reason to do or not do anything now," he said.

"How about this. I want to look forward, not backward. I would rather concentrate on the daughter I have than the one I don't. I suggest you do the same."

Toby pushed back in the chair, leaning it farther back than I realized it went. "Yeah," he said. "That's a good idea."

"So what did you do to make Alicia so pissed off at you? It's not like her."

"Look, no offense, but I didn't want to come up here. We had a long drive yesterday, and I'm tired. Not to mention I've been stuck in South Georgia with her mom and all her aunts and uncles for a solid week. I want to go home, that's all."

Even the ignorant and obnoxious among us deserve sympathy. "You've been dealing with my ex-wife's family for a week? Good Lord, son."

"Are they always that way?"

"What, like you want to punch somebody every five minutes for being a rich, stuck-up East Coast smartass?"

"Yeah."

"Let's go see if Alicia made some coffee. I'll pour a shot of Maker's Mark in there for you. You could use a stiff drink."

6

I signed the photo Alicia had found of me wearing the Eagles uniform, which showed me looking younger than I had ever managed to feel. We talked for a few minutes about safe subjects, like the small bit of remodeling I'd done since moving up here. "When did you put in the dishwasher?" Alicia asked.

"Right before I moved in."

"We never had a dishwasher in here before," Alicia explained to Toby. "We had to wash all the dishes by hand."

"Washing dishes helps build character," I said.

Alicia was sitting in the den, on the couch across from my armchair, with Toby's head in her lap. The whiskey had made him a bit sleepy.

"So did you just decide that you'd built enough character?"

"Something like that," I said. I was glad that she was teasing me, glad that the conversation wasn't all stiff and formal and sad. She'd probably gotten enough of that from seeing her mother's family, though.

"Unless … wait a second. Did your mystery woman ask you to put in the dishwasher?" Alicia asked.

"Mystery woman?" I had no idea what she could be talking about. Outside of Margie the waitress and a couple of people at the library, I hadn't so much as talked to a woman since I moved up here.

"The blonde woman in the blue Honda. She left just as I pulled in the first time."

"Oh, her. I'd never seen her before today," I explained. "She got lost and needed directions. It happens sometimes."

"She looked very familiar. I can't place her; I didn't get enough of a good look at her. But she definitely looked familiar. Are you sure you don't know her?" she asked.

"I have no idea who she is. She said she'd borrowed a friend's cabin over by the lake, and she'd gotten lost. I showed her where the right road was."

"So you're not seeing anyone," she said. I couldn't tell if she was relieved or disappointed.

"I'm not. But I'm fine. You don't need to worry about me. I have everything up here that I need."

"Oh, I don't think you have everything you need," Alicia said.

"I think so. Big-screen TV, hot tub, propane grill. Everything a growing boy needs."

"Maybe you still need a couple of things." She nudged Toby's shoulder, and he lifted his head up with a start.

"Huh? What?" he grunted.

"Would you be a dear and go to the car and get the presents for Daddy?"

"Oh. Sure." Toby shuffled into the kitchen and out the door.

"You're going to have to forgive Toby. He's had a rough week. He's usually a sweetheart. I think he's ready to go home."

"Does he have a home?" I asked. "I mean, do you have a home? In New Jersey?" I was curious as to whether they were living together, but didn't want to ask her straight out.

"I think so," she said. "For now, anyway. Sometimes you have to pick a place and settle down."

"It's nice to hear you say that."

Toby came back with two boxes, a large square one and a smaller flat one. "The little one first," he said.

I unwrapped the flat box, taking care not to damage what was inside. It was a wedding invitation in a nice silver frame:

ALICIA BORDEN MORSE
AND
TOBIAS DAHLGREN
REQUEST THE PLEASURE OF YOUR COMPANY
AT THEIR WEDDING
SATURDAY, APRIL 30
AT 6:00 P.M.
THE PALACE AT SOMERSET PARK
RECEPTION TO FOLLOW

"So you've set a date," I said, trying to keep the surprise out of my voice. "That's ... that's something. I hope it turns out to be a nice day for you."

"What makes you say that, Daddy?"

"Well, you know, with the weather and all."

"That's what you say to someone when you're not planning to be there."

"Well, I know you'll take a lot of pictures, and there'll be a video, I guess."

"You're coming," she said.

"Yeah, we really want you there," Toby said stiffly. It was a good thing he was an ethnomusicologist; he would have starved to death as an actor.

"I'm not saying I wouldn't like to come. But have you talked to your mother about this?"

"Mom is not in charge of this wedding," Alicia said, biting off every word.

Oh, Lord Jesus, give me strength. I wasn't a praying man anymore, hadn't been for a long time, but there are no atheists in foxholes. Alicia had about as much chance of imposing her will on her mother in wedding-related matters as I had of fitting into my old Eagles uniform, which is to say, not much.

"I know you're in charge. You should be. I support that. But your wedding day is your special day, and if I go, it'll get ruined. You know that. Somebody's going to say something or do something, and it'll all end in tears. It's better if I don't go."

Alicia sank down on the couch, and Toby put a cautious arm around her.

"I know how you feel," she said. "I know you don't want to go."

"I want to go," I said.

"Then go."

"I want to go, but it's better if I don't."

"It's not better for me. I want you there. I know what Mom thinks, but I don't care. She can put up with it for one day, for me. I want you to be there. That's all that matters."

"Why?"

"Because you're my father, and I want you to be there."

I didn't buy it. There had to be another reason, something she wasn't telling me. It could have been something simple. Maybe she'd gotten crossways with Danielle—knowing Danielle, she likely had—and she was inviting me out of spite. That would make it even more important for me to stay home, not least because it would keep me out of Danielle's way. If anything could ruin Alicia's wedding day, it would be a big fight between me and her mother, and I didn't want any part of that. As much as I loved my daughter and wanted to be a part of her life again, I didn't want to take that risk.

But I suddenly realized there was one thing I could do—something I could give her, at any rate—to be a part of her wedding.

"We have a long time to make a decision about that," I said. "In the meantime, if you'd like your present, it's in the little carved box over there by your elbow."

"You got me a present?" Alicia asked. "You didn't have to do that." She picked up the box and rattled it. "Wait a second. I made you this box. I gave it to you for Christmas, twelve years ago."

"I remember. It was a nice present."

32

She opened up the carved box, which contained a maroon velvet jewelry box. Inside the jewelry box, she found the two gold rings—one a plain band, and one set with a big square-cut diamond. Alicia hadn't been wearing an engagement ring, so I figured she'd be thrilled.

She sat there, openmouthed, for a minute, as though she were trying to divine the provenance of the rings by feeling their vibrations.

"These are Francie's rings," she said softly.

"They're your rings. Before that, they were my mother's. And they were her mother's before then; they came over from England. They're a little old-fashioned, and they could do with a cleaning, but they should be fine."

"You gave these rings to Francie at her engagement party. You told her where they came from. I remember talking to her about them afterward; she was excited, and I was jealous. I thought they'd been lost when she died."

"They weren't with her when she died. When she left to go back to St. Louis, she asked me to take them to the jeweler so they could be resized." Francesca, bless her heart, had fingers like veal sausages. "I was going to bring them with me and give them to her at the wedding. I didn't get them back from the jeweler's until after the funeral. It's the same box, even."

"I can't wear these, Daddy."

"I understand if they're too big, but you can get them resized."

"That's not what I mean," she said. "Just looking at these rings makes me think about Francie, and how she never got to wear them—how she never got to do anything, have a wedding or a honeymoon or…or anything like that. It's not fair to her for me to wear them."

"Of course it's not fair," I said. "But I think she would want you to have them. I know your grandmother would have wanted you to have them."

"They are very nice," Toby said. "And we don't have rings picked out yet."

"Toby, shut up."

Toby shut up.

"You don't have to make a decision right now about whether you want to wear them. But you should take them with you. You can get them cleaned and resized while you get used to the idea. If you decide you don't want to wear them, then you can put them in a box somewhere. When the time comes, you can give them to your daughter."

Alicia dropped the jewelry box on the floor and strode out of the room. She hit full speed in the kitchen, stopping only to open the door leading outside. It was a good thing. If the door had been open, she might have gotten all the way to Marietta on momentum.

Toby sat there, his mouth half-open, trying to make sense of the situation. "Um," he said at last.

"Don't just sit there, son. Go get her." I could have run after her myself, but I figured that was Toby's job now, and he had better get used to it.

"Yeah. Yes, sir. Um. What do I say?"

"Don't you know anything about women? Don't say squat. Go out there."

I picked up the box with the rings in it. I went into the kitchen and got out a can of Coke, poured it in a glass, and added some ice and a couple of ounces of Maker's Mark. I wanted to kick myself. If anyone knew about the destructive power of memory, it was me, and here I had gone and unleashed that on poor Alicia, ruining a happy moment for both of us.

Danielle was right. I shouldn't go to the wedding.

7

I took my drink out to the back porch and watched the cold north wind blowing through the branches of the trees. I didn't want to be where I could hear Alicia sobbing, because I was worried that it might start me crying too, and I couldn't have that. Part of that was the normal parental desire not to have your child see you crying, and part of it was that I wasn't sure that, if I started crying, I could stop again. One of the reasons I live alone, on my mountain, is that it's easier to handle situations where I start crying uncontrollably. I can lie down on my couch and wrap myself in my blanket and not embarrass myself in front of anyone else. I wanted to avoid that sort of outburst in front of Alicia and Toby if I possibly could.

I flipped open the little maroon box and looked at the rings. The diamond was an emerald cut, or that's what Danielle had said when I first showed it to her. I had no real idea how old it was. My grandfather gave it to my grandmother in England, right in the middle of the First World War. He had gotten dosed with poison gas somewhere along the line and had been sent back to one of the big convalescent hospitals to recover, and that's where he met my grandmother. It was not at all clear to her exactly how he had managed to procure such a large diamond on a private soldier's pay, and she never got the chance to ask him, because he was killed in Belgium not a year later. My mother brought it to Alabama when she left England with my father after the end of the Second World War, and she had kept it until her death.

Mother had wanted to give the rings to Francesca as a birthday present one year. I asked her not to, because I didn't want Francie to lose them or to have one of the younger children swallow them. Mother agreed to wait until Francie was older, but she died that next year and never got the chance to pass them down herself. I found them in the little house she was living in, up on top of a high shelf in a closet, in a box marked with Francesca's name.

I'd put the rings in the box Alicia had given me and left them in the living room for a reason. I figured Alicia would be the one to clean out my cabin when I was gone, and I knew she would recognize that box, and want to open it.

I drank the last of my drink and went back in the house to check on how Alicia was doing. She was loading a pod into the coffee machine.

"I figured I'd make a cup to go," she said. "It's a long drive back to Atlanta."

"That sounds like a good idea. Are you OK?"

"I'm fine. I'm sorry I ran out like that. It was a lot for me to deal with, all at once. I mean, I appreciate the gesture, honestly I do. I know what you were trying to do, but it made me feel so guilty and hollow inside all of a sudden."

"I know. I wish Francie was here to wear it. I know you do too. But she's not here, and Trixie isn't here, and I don't have anyone else left to give it to. It would mean a lot to me if you had it, to pass it on as an heirloom. That would be very important to me."

Alicia sat down at the kitchen table and took a careful sip of her coffee. "Here's the thing," she said. "I'm going to go soon. Toby's sitting out there in the car, and I think he's tired of waiting on me. We're going to drive back to Atlanta and fly back to Newark, and you're going to stay right here on this mountain. I'm going to get married, and you're not going to be there. Chances are, we're not going to see each other for another five years, unless I have the time to come down here, or you make the effort to come up and see us. Maybe we'll talk on the phone a little more often, but that will be it, as far as our relationship goes."

I wished I hadn't drunk that last bit of whiskey. "I know this wedding means a lot to you," I said. "It means a lot to me too. I would like to go. But you understand how difficult it would be for me to be there."

Part of it was the travel. I like sleeping in my own bed, where I know where everything is in case I wake up in the middle of the night after a bad dream. I don't like leaving my cabin. I do it once a week, and that's more out of habit than anything else.

I had no desire whatsoever to make the drive south, back to Atlanta. Even if I took the Perimeter around the city to get to the airport, I would still be traveling through the dangerous and familiar terrain of memory and regret. Making my way through the Atlanta airport and the Newark airport would be something of a physical challenge for me. The effort would take its toll, even before the stress of the rehearsal and the wedding and the reception.

But those were minor considerations, and we both knew it.

"I know you're worried about Mother," Alicia said. "I know she doesn't want you to come. She was unhappy when I told her Toby and I were stopping by here, and I understand why. Seeing you again would be hard for her."

I wasn't concerned about how Danielle might feel about me going to the wedding—she couldn't be any unhappier with me than she already was. I was concerned that she might spend the next few months making Alicia's life as difficult as possible, but Alicia was a grown-up now and she would have to learn how to handle her mother. What I wanted to avoid, at all costs, was the inevitable scene that would result if I showed up. Danielle was capable of throwing a very loud and very public fit, if she wanted to. I didn't think she would do that at the wedding, but it couldn't be discounted—and if she didn't do it herself, any one of her sisters would be glad to do it for her.

I wasn't too worried about anything Danielle or her family might throw at me, at least not for my own sake. If they wanted to belittle or humiliate me in some way, they would. But I didn't want my presence to embarrass Alicia, or mar her wedding day.

But that wasn't the whole of it. More than anything else, I was worried about myself, and how I would react, and whether or not I would be able to make it through a very stressful day without becoming an emotional wreck. It happens to me every so often— some sort of trigger, some sort of reminder, and I'll spend the next couple of hours wrapped up in my blanket, crying for no real reason. I could just see myself rolling on the floor of some fancy hotel ballroom, getting lint all over my tuxedo, and Alicia looking pitiable and helpless in her white dress. I didn't want to have something awful like that happen, and the simplest way to avoid that was to stay in Georgia and send a nice present.

"It's not just your mother," I explained. "It's a lot of things. It's not that I don't want to be there, and it's not that I don't care. I know it's a disappointment, but I don't see another way around it."

"Do you have more of these coffee pods?" Alicia asked.

"Up in the cabinet, over to the left."

She loaded another pod in the coffee maker, and got out another paper cup. "I need to send Toby a text to let him know I'm going to be in here another minute or two," she said.

"You could just go out and tell him," I said.

She fished her phone out of her pocket and typed a quick message. "Do you remember when we went to that wedding in Montgomery?" she asked. "I think it was one of your cousins."

"I can think of a couple of weddings in Montgomery. Was this the one where Trixie had the chicken pox?"

"That one. You took me and Francie, and Mom stayed home with Trixie. She didn't seem too unhappy about that, if I remember right."

"Your mother isn't really cut out for Alabama," I said. "It was a nice wedding, and we had a nice time, but it was a long time ago."

"I was twelve, and I was dancing with my daddy at a beautiful wedding, and I knew that's what I wanted for my wedding. Maybe that's selfish. It probably is. Maybe that's asking a lot of you, and I'm sure it is. And maybe I haven't been the best daughter for you, all this time," she said, and I could hear the catch in her voice when she said that.

"You've been a wonderful daughter," I said. "We haven't had a great relationship lately, but that's my fault. You shouldn't beat yourself up over that."

"It doesn't matter whose fault it is. When you come right down to it, you're my father, and I'm your daughter, and it would really mean a lot to me if you were there. Not just to give me away, not just to dance with me, but to be part of my family."

"I wish we could be a family again, sweetie," I said. "I just don't see how we can."

"Toby and I are starting a family—him, and me, and the baby. You can still be a part of that, if you want."

"Baby?" I asked.

She brought the end of her hair around and chewed on it. "I'm pregnant."

Of course she was. She'd gained weight. That's why she ran out of the house—not because I'd given her Francie's ring, but because I'd suggested she pass it on to her daughter. That's why she wanted to reconnect with me after all this time.

"That's wonderful, sweetie. How far along are you?"

"Just seven weeks. I wasn't sure I wanted to tell you before, but I am now. I told Mom, and she turned into a puddle."

"I'm not going to turn into a puddle," I said. That was more of a hope than a promise. Being a grandfather would be the best thing that had happened to me in a long time, and it was hard not to show how pleased I was at the prospect. "I'm glad for you, for you and Toby. Thank you for telling me."

"I want us to try to be a family again," she said. "That's why I want you to come to the wedding. I'll square it with Mom, I promise. You won't have to talk to her, even, if you don't want to. We can keep you two totally separated. I have the seating chart all worked out."

39

"It's been a long day," I said. "I can't make that decision today. I need to work it out in my own mind and decide."

"Is that the best answer I'm going to get?"

"It's the best answer I have to give you today."

She kissed me on the cheek. "Then I'll take it."

"Take this too." I handed her the jewelry box.

"Thanks. I'll figure out some way to make them work for me."

"That would make me very happy."

"I love you, Daddy."

"I love you too." We reached out for a hug, as awkward as it was heartfelt. "Be careful on the way back."

"I will."

"And take care of Toby. He needs taking care of."

"You get to know him a little better, you'll appreciate him. I know you will. He's cranky and ready to get back home."

"Do you love him?"

"With all my heart."

"Well, he's waiting for you. You better go."

She kissed me again and left, keys jangling in her hand. Toby was in the car, stretched out in the passenger seat. Alicia started the car, and the electric motor turned over. It was quiet enough that I could hear Toby ask her, "How many dead sisters do you *have*, anyway?" right before they pulled out onto the dirt road.

I went back inside and saw my other Christmas present, still sitting on the coffee table where I had left it. I opened it carefully; it was heavier than I expected, and I didn't want to drop it. There was a sturdy cardboard box underneath the wrapping paper, and I opened the flap.

The box was full of packing peanuts, so I took it into the kitchen and opened it over the trash can. I excavated the contents, trying to spill all the plastic fluff into the trash.

It was a football, smaller than full-size, made of beaten copper. The surface wasn't pebbled the way a real football was, but dimpled with subtle patterns, arrayed in whorls and spirals like a fingerprint. A brass plate on the base read:

BILLY RAY MORSE—#77
AUBURN UNIVERSITY 1968–1971

At the very bottom of the box was a printout of a website—from something called *The Daily Targum*, which I guessed was the Rutgers campus paper. The football in the box was a model of a big, thirty-foot sculpture they were putting by the south end of the Rutgers stadium.

The article quoted Alicia; she'd highlighted it for me:

"When they interviewed me for my job at Rutgers, they told me about this project. They asked me if I wanted to help build the sculpture, and I told them that it would mean a lot to me because my dad played college football. Every time we put a new piece of it together, I think about him."

I sank down on one of the kitchen chairs. I was crying like a pageant winner.

I shouldn't have been that choked up over a fifty-dollar metal football that wasn't much more than a come-on for a college fund-raising campaign. But I was.

You love your kids, you have fun with them, but what you want to know is whether your kids will make something of themselves—whether they will matter to the world at large. You want to know that all the work and love you put into parenting meant something, that it mattered, that it was important. And when your child dies, you don't just lose everything that child was, you lose everything he or she could have been or should have been.

I thought I had lost Alicia too, but now it turned out that I hadn't. She was alive, pregnant, getting ready for marriage, and working on a project that had a direct connection to that young man in a football uniform I had been. It wasn't pride alone, although I felt that. It was fulfillment, as welcome as it was unexpected.

I stayed in the kitchen a long while, waiting to get control over myself. When I was done, I opened the dishwasher and put everything back on the shelves. Then I went into the living room and switched on the TV. The NFL Network was showing a Saturday night game; the Buccaneers playing the Lions in Detroit. It was going to be a sorry matchup, but I turned it on anyway.

8

I woke up the next morning with my clothes on, sprawled out on the couch. The TV was still on from the night before. Rich Eisen and Deion Sanders were having some inane conversation about the Jacksonville Jaguars. I switched it off. I felt I had swallowed one of Deion's fur coats and it had rotted in the back of my throat.

I don't drink much, not anymore. Drinking alone has its hazards, and one of them is that you don't always know where you will wake up and what you will be wearing when you do. I was lucky I hadn't rolled off the couch or fallen asleep on the toilet or something else embarrassing.

Part of it is the alcohol, and I have worked hard to cut back on that. I don't keep beer in the fridge, for one thing. I drink whiskey, but only the expensive stuff—I am far too cheap to drink as much Maker's Mark as I would need to get drunk. The problem with the whiskey is that I don't enjoy the taste all that much, so I disguise it with lots of Coke, and the combination of the alcohol and the sugar does bad things to my bloodstream.

I went into the kitchen to fix myself some toast, but it looked as though Toby had eaten all the bread—my guess was that he had gone into the kitchen when I wasn't paying attention and fixed himself some ham sandwiches for the road. I always tried to make toast on Sunday because the English muffins I like come in a six-pack, so I have to have something different at least one day out of seven. I popped a muffin in the toaster anyway—I figured I could treat myself and go out for breakfast at the Waffle House in Ellijay on Thursday. It would be a nice break in the routine.

I was annoyed with myself for not getting in bed properly and then waking up so early. I try to keep myself to a routine—not a strict routine or anything, but something to keep the days from running into each other, to keep myself from sliding into the anarchy of timelessness. I tend to get up early, but I allow myself to sleep in on Sundays. This isn't only so I can stay up late and watch the Pac-10 games on Saturday nights, although that's a side benefit. So is sleeping through the NFL pregame shows. But the real reason is that long, drawn-out Sunday mornings leave me far too much time to be alone with my thoughts.

I finished my muffin and went out to the front porch. I turned on the water for the hot tub and waited for it to fill up enough so I could turn on the heater. I left the cover on so it would be good and hot by the time I got in.

The hot tub is mostly for spring and summer; I spend a lot of evenings soaking my sore legs, reading a book, with the Braves game on the radio in the background. There's something extravagant about running the hot tub in the winter, but it's a nice treat now and then. The big drawback is that, eventually, you have to get out of the thing, and that can be a miserable experience in near-freezing air.

It was a misty morning, cool but not frosty. All I could see were the trees closest to the cabin and the indistinct profiles of those farther out. The rest of the world was a distant rumor. In a few hours the fog would burn off, and the trees and the mountain on the other side of the valley would appear, and the sun would glint off the high-tension power lines. But not right then.

I opened the cover and tested the temperature of the water. It would do. I went back inside and got undressed and wrapped myself in a thick, brown robe for the short trip back outside. I put the robe on a hook I had installed for the purpose and climbed up onto the little staircase I had built on the side of the hot tub. I swung one leg over. The heat was bearable. I got the other leg inside and sank down into the water.

So there would be a baby, I thought. The genetic code would pass on to another generation. I would have a grandchild. A boy, or so I hoped. I wanted another baby boy to play with. I missed out on so much with Junior, who died of spinal meningitis when he was seven months old. I had all these plans—Falcons games, fishing trips, hiking the Appalachian Trail together—and they all burned up in his last fever. We held him those last few hours in that hospital bed, knowing that it was the end, thinking of all the things we wanted to do that would never be. And then he was gone. Yes, I wanted a baby boy again. I wanted that more than young knees or inheritances or having Danielle back again, loving me, looking after me. I couldn't have any of that, but I could hold Alicia's baby and give him back when he messed his diaper, as he would.

That would make it worth leaving the mountain now and again.

Whether it would be worth going to the wedding, however, I didn't know. I couldn't guess how many people would be there. It could run into the hundreds. The only thing I had to go on was the name of the facility, which was a palace. I had never been to a palace but doubted I would feel comfortable there. I would have to wear a suit, which meant I would have to buy a suit. I had a few in my closet, but they would hang on me like nobody's business. That would mean driving down to Atlanta, and I hated the thought of doing that. The alternative was going to Chattanooga, a town I didn't know well, or making the longer trek to Charlotte.

I trusted Alicia to keep me isolated from my wife's family. I knew Danielle would want to stay as far away from me as possible. Except that it wouldn't be possible, would it? There would be a photographer, and he would want us together for at least a few pictures. *Maybe we could stand near each other and not talk. That would be fine. I could manage that,* I thought. Then I snorted, amused with my own optimism. It was going to be a disaster. I knew that, and Danielle knew it too. Alicia didn't know it, but she would find out.

I flexed my knees, which responded to the warm water. I would need them to be in top condition for the long trip to New Jersey. Then the wedding—no telling how much I would have to stand around. And then there would be a dance, Alicia steering me around some dance floor, me trying hard not to stomp on her dress and tear it.

What bothered me more than anything else was that I would be alone. Not that loneliness bothered me much anymore, but it is one thing to be lonely on top of a mountain and another thing to be lonely in a palace, surrounded by people who I either didn't know or didn't much care for. Alicia would be the only one there who would so much as want to talk to me. I didn't know any of her friends now, and those friends who she'd had in Atlanta would know who I was and wouldn't want anything much to do with me. Or worse, they'd remember and be interested and ask questions. It would be uncomfortable, bordering on intolerable.

I sat for a long time, watching the steam rise from the tub and mix with the mist off the mountain. I took long, slow breaths, trying to force as much steam as I could into my lungs to get the passages open again. I felt the sweat start to trickle down my face, a sign that I should get out before I passed out. I turned over, floating for a minute, and then started to pull myself over the edge, taking care not to slip on the bottom of the tub. It was a long production, and I was glad to wrap myself up in the robe against the chill air when I got out. I decided to leave the tub open and go inside and get dressed.

I was walking back in the house when the idea hit me, harder and sharper than the cold air.

9

I met Sharon Walsh for the first time about four years previously, a year or so after I had moved to Blue Ridge. My toaster had burned out, and that meant a trip to the Walmart in Ellijay for a new one. North of Blue Ridge, the rain started coming down in sheets. It wasn't safe to keep driving, so I decided to find someplace to hole up until the weather cleared. I didn't want to go into any of the antique shops or diners, so I drove around a little bit. I saw the sign for the library and figured, well, why not. It was as good a place as any to kill a little time.

I walked in, found where they kept *American Heritage* in the periodicals, and sat down to read. I was deep into an article about the history of diet soda—a good piece, written by a Yale student, but a little naïve about consumer loyalty to the sugary stuff—when I felt someone's hand brush my knee.

"Hey, mister." He was a boy, about ten, African-American. "You looking at that?"

"This?"

"The paper." Someone had left the comics section of the Atlanta paper on the table next to me.

"Go ahead."

I went back to the magazine and was halfway through an article about poor Mary Todd Lincoln when I overheard a little snippet of a very quiet argument. I glanced up, and a young black woman was saying something to somebody at the circulation desk. The boy who had wanted the comics page was standing next to her, looking alternately bored and horrified. I didn't think anything of it, not even when the woman pointed in my general direction. I couldn't imagine that she was unhappy with me. I hadn't done or said anything.

The woman walked out, and I decided to stretch my legs a little. I put the magazine away and walked over to a window to see if the rain had stopped. It hadn't, but the worst seemed to have passed, and I could make it down to Ellijay if I was careful.

Sharon—I hadn't known her name at the time, of course—stopped me right before I walked out the door. "Excuse me," she asked, "but are you planning on using the restroom?"

I hadn't thought about it, but it sounded reasonable now that she had said something. "Yes. Why? Is it broken?"

"Oh, no. We ask that you don't, you know, camp out in there or anything."

"I wasn't planning on it. I didn't even bring anything to read."

"That's not what I meant. I mean, you know where the shelter is, right? If you need to bathe, that's where you should do it. We want to be welcoming, but our bathrooms aren't set up for taking care of personal needs and such."

"Do what?"

"Well—believe me, this is nothing personal, no reflection on you—but we've had issues with people using the library bathrooms as a locker room. I probably shouldn't bother, but you should know that there are other alternatives in town."

Now, there are some people who could have said that and meant it in a mean way. Maybe it's a Southern thing, but there's a nice way of telling someone he looks like a vagrant, and a mean-spirited and ugly way of telling him the exact same thing, and you wouldn't pick up on the difference if you hadn't grown up here. Sharon Walsh wasn't the type to be mean. She was tall, in her late forties, with straw-blonde hair cut in a way that was supposed to make her look young and innocent but didn't quite manage to do so. She wasn't smiling—she never smiled much—but she had a kind look on her face.

"I have a place to stay," I said. "I'll be a minute. I won't mess anything up."

I looked in the mirror while washing my hands, trying to see what Sharon had seen. It was my old face still, but my hair was shaggy and matted. I hadn't shaved in weeks, and what beard I had was ragged and patchy. I looked a bit like Denver Pyle on the old Grizzly Adams TV show—the eccentric mountain man, but without the folksy wisdom and the mule. No, scratch that—I didn't look that romantic.

I had told myself that, although I was alone on a remote mountaintop, I was in no danger of turning into a hermit. What hermit had a plasma television? What hermit had a computer? What hermit had a fancy single-serving coffee maker? But if I was a hermit on the outside, perhaps I was becoming one on the inside as well.

The rain had slacked off a little more, but I wasn't ready to go to Ellijay for a while yet. I drove a couple of blocks until I found an old-style barbershop, where I got a close-cropped trim and a shave. I've kept up the same look ever since. And I kept coming in to the library, once a week, to check out Lee Child thrillers and grilling cookbooks. When I started my World War I research project, I asked Sharon for help, and she got me started on places where I could find sources in English libraries. I don't have anyone I can call a friend, not anymore, but Sharon Walsh has been something close to that.

For this trip—on a Wednesday instead of my usual Thursday, as the library was closed on New Year's Eve—I had my game plan all set up. I wasn't going to push things, wasn't going to do anything foolish such as ask Sharon to go to New Jersey with me the first rattle out of the box. No. That wouldn't do. It was too far off, anyway—both in terms of time and geography. There would have to be at least one intervening date—in February, perhaps the week after Valentine's Day. That's how I figured it, anyway. It couldn't be on Valentine's Day, because that would send the message that this was a romantic proposition. I liked Sharon and respected her, but I didn't have strong romantic feelings for her, and I couldn't imagine that she had any romantic feelings for me.

Bringing a date wasn't about romance, anyway. It was a way to build my confidence and to guarantee that I had somebody there to talk to—perhaps even dance with, although I wasn't ready to commit to any such thing. If Danielle showed up with a date, then we'd both have one, and that would be fine. But if she had a date and I didn't, that would make things more awkward than they had any business being.

So all I would do this first trip would be to plant the seed by telling Sharon that my daughter was getting married at the end of April, up in New Jersey. I could bring it up again the next week, maybe say something charming and self-deprecating about needing a date. If I played my cards right, she might suggest going herself for the chance of catching a Broadway play, for instance. It could take a couple of months, but I had time, and it wasn't as though I had a reasonable alternative. *Be cool*, I told myself on the drive down. *Be cool.*

Sharon wasn't behind the circulation desk when I walked in, and I didn't see her anywhere else. It was Wednesday, after all. For all I knew, it was her day off, or she'd taken some vacation time over the holidays. The only person I could see working was the young woman who insisted on pestering me every time I went near a computer. I hated asking her for help, not least because it would make her day.

"Excuse me, but is Ms. Walsh in today?"

"Yes, she is, but she's in a budget meeting."

"Oh." I knew that libraries had budgets, and a payroll to meet, but I had never been confronted with the specific reality of such things.

"Is there something I can help you with?"

"Well, no. I'll wait."

"You have some books there; would you like me to check them in for you?"

"I need to give them to Ms. Walsh. She got them for me through interlibrary loan, and I need to give them to her in person."

"What library?"

"Newcastle University. The one in England, not the one in Australia."

"Why did you have to get them from all that way?"

"It's complicated. Look, I'll grab a magazine and wait."

"You sure I can't help you look up something? We have lots of nice books here. Maybe something with large print?"

"I'm good, thanks."

Sharon came out of her office as I was halfway through an interesting article in *National Geographic*. What it was about, I don't remember, because they're all the same now anyway. When I was a kid growing up in Alabama, *National Geographic* meant tribes of naked savages in the outback of nowhere—emphasis on the naked, of course. Now it's about mining and deforestation and whatever the trendy environmentalist topic happens to be that month. I think they had it right the first time, but then, your average boy these days doesn't need *National Geographic* to see someone's boobs.

I got up out of my chair, not without some difficulty, and met her over by the circulation desk.

"Are you done with those books? I need to send them back to England if you are."

"Well, sure."

Sharon looked tired—either that, or frustrated, I couldn't tell. My guess was she was having a rough holiday. The sweater she was wearing—dark blue with extra-large white reindeer—looked like something she hadn't had the time or the courage to return.

"What are you doing here, anyway? It's Wednesday. I didn't expect to see you for another week."

"You're closed tomorrow; I thought I'd stop by and return these. How was your holiday?"

"It was…it's not important, believe me. Do you have any other interlibrary books out?"

"Just these. Is there a problem?"

"I need a cigarette, that's the problem. Can you meet me outside?"

Sharon smoked Winstons, which I assumed still tasted good like a cigarette should. It had been my brand before Danielle made me promise to stop, after Francesca was born.

"End-of-year budget meeting." Sharon spun out the words like a dirge, which it may well have been. "We got the figures on our state aid a couple of weeks ago. Fifteen percent budget cut. No raises, no bonuses for anyone. No new acquisitions, no improvements to the building."

"That's harsh."

"I tried to explain all of this to our county auditor; that's who I was meeting with. She thinks she's a steel magnolia. You know why they call them steel magnolias?"

"There was a movie. With Dolly Parton." I liked Dolly Parton.

"They call them steel magnolias because 'cast-iron bitches' was already taken. I can't believe she has me smoking one of these already. I promised myself I'd quit."

"They're good for stress," I said.

"All I need is a few thousand dollars out of the county general fund, just to replace the cut in state aid. I could give my staff 2 percent raises and have enough gas to keep the bookmobile running this summer. But instead, no raises, and cuts to essential library services. Like interlibrary loan."

"Oh."

"You're the only one who uses it much anymore. I couldn't justify spending the money when we could use it elsewhere."

"I feel terrible. Is there some way I can make it up to you?"

She dropped her cigarette and crushed it into the pavement of the parking lot. "I'm sorry. I don't mean to be dumping all of this on you. It's not your fault. Is there something you wanted to ask me?"

It was the perfect opening, but all that came out of my mouth was the tiniest little sound, somewhere between an *urp* and an *uhngk*.

"I'm sorry, what was that?" she asked.

"I'm a little bit nervous about this. Sorry."

"Why would you be nervous? It's not like you're asking me out or something."

"Well, no," I said. "Not asking you out in an asking-you-out kind of way. Not like a date."

"What would be like a date and not like a date?"

"I am putting this very awkwardly," I said.

"Oh, wait. Now I get it. New Year's Eve is tomorrow. You want somebody to kiss when the ball drops."

"No. I wasn't…I didn't…I was going to tell you one thing and that was it."

"So tell me."

For the first time in years, I wished I had a cigarette. Not because I wanted to smoke but because I very much needed something to do with my hands, some way to stall this conversation before I said something stupid and irredeemable. If I didn't handle it the right way, I would wreck what little chance I had.

"This is the thing. My daughter is getting married in the spring, up in New Jersey. She wants me to come up for the wedding. I live alone on the top of a mountain, and I don't talk to that many people anymore. You're the closest thing I have to a friend these days, and I don't know anyone else who I could ask to be my date. It's not a romantic thing; I was thinking, maybe, if you weren't doing anything, that you might be interested."

She took out her lighter and shook another Winston out of a soft pack. "Look. You're a nice guy. Not unattractive for your age. If I wasn't already seeing somebody, you know, I might have been a little interested. But not now."

"I didn't know."

"It's not any of your business. And I'd appreciate you not mentioning it to anybody. It's kind of an unconventional relationship."

"Oh."

"Stop looking at me that way. It's nothing bad. And I'm not a lesbian, if that's what you're thinking. That's what you're thinking, isn't it?"

"None of my business."

"He's a man. He's a very nice man. But not very emotionally mature. He would not react in a very appropriate way if I went with you, let's put it that way."

"I understand," I said.

"It's a big world out there. I'm sure you can find somebody. There's a ton of places out there to find a date online; shouldn't be that difficult for you. I can put together a list if you like."

"It's OK," I said. "I should go."

10

I sat in my truck in the library parking lot for a long while, running the engine so the heater would stay on. I did my relaxation techniques, flexing my feet and ankles, stretching out the big muscles in my legs. The exercises are helpful, and one little side benefit is that it keeps you from driving. It's bad to drive when you're overstressed— you're that much more likely to get distracted and run off the road.

I kept my truck in park and kept my legs moving, but I could tell it wasn't doing much good.

What bothered me was not so much losing my chance with Sharon—not that I had ever had one—but my own stupidity. I hadn't seen past the stereotype of the spinster librarian. It had been unreasonable for me to expect that she'd drop whatever life she had going for her and fly up to New Jersey with me for a weekend for a wedding at which she wouldn't know anyone. I was foolish not to have thought of that sooner, foolish to think that I could have talked her into such a thing without taking her point of view into account.

I stopped flexing my feet when I realized I was hungry. I decided to make the short drive back to the highway and the restaurant in the Ingles parking lot. I didn't have my shopping list with me, but I could write down a few things while I waited for lunch. Friday would be New Year's Day, the biggest day on the college football calendar, and I needed to stock up on snacks.

I got the sarcastic waitress. I was hoping that Wednesday was her day off, but no such luck. She was short and a bit stout and had the pinched face you get only after a lifetime of negative thinking and bad character. She had never taken an order correctly in all of the years I'd been eating at the restaurant, except a few times by accident.

"You don't look so good," she said.

"I'm fine."

"You need to look at the menu? It ain't like it's changed none."

"Do you have the tomato soup today?"

"Chicken noodle. It's Wednesday, they make the chicken noodle."

"OK. That, I guess, and a cheeseburger. Do you have a pen I can borrow?"

"Do I look like a stationery store to you?"

I thought about it and concluded that she did indeed look like a stationery store, but I didn't say so. Not that there were such things as stationery stores anymore, but if there were, they would be squat and thick and slow-moving, if not immobile, as she was. But I kept my mouth shut.

"Here you go," she sighed, and she handed me a pen. It was my favorite cheap pen, a BIC Stic. It was bright purple and bore the legend "Mountain Home Realty." I took the opposite place mat, flipped it over, folded it in half, and started writing my shopping list. Pretzels, I figured, would be healthier than potato chips.

She came over with the soup when I was about halfway through my list. "It ain't really chicken noodle," she said. "It's turkey. They had a lot of turkey left over after Thanksgiving."

"It's fine."

"You sure you're OK? Looks like maybe your girlfriend dumped you."

"I don't have a girlfriend." I decided to think about finding another restaurant.

"You sure about that?" She hooked a thumb in the direction of Margie, who was taking an order from a group of the antique-store dealers in the far corner.

"You're kidding."

"She's kind of sweet on you."

"You *are* kidding."

"Suit yourself. Enjoy the soup."

I took a spoonful of the soup. It was disgusting. I didn't doubt for a second that it had been made from month-old turkey—a turkey, mind you, that had died of a broken heart. The noodles were slimy with age. I knew there was a reason I didn't come here on Wednesdays.

I picked up the pen again and drew a little doodle in the corner to stimulate my mind long enough so I could think about what else I needed at the grocery store. Was Margie interested in me? I couldn't imagine it. But then I hadn't imagined that Sharon was interested in me, and perhaps she might have been, once. All I knew about Margie was that she had a daughter. That implied a relationship, but that didn't have to be the case, not anymore.

I put it out of my mind. I went back to my list. *Popcorn,* I wrote. *Steak sauce.* I was trying to decide between the reduced-fat Oreos and the regular kind when Margie walked over with a sandwich.

"Connie's on break; she asked me to bring this over."

"Thanks." It wasn't a cheeseburger. It looked like it might have started its life as French dip sandwich, and then fallen on hard times. Typical. I guessed I was lucky not to get turkey chow mein.

"Were you telling me that your daughter was coming down from up North?"

"Yeah. She and her fiancée."

"Oh, how nice," she said. She slipped into the other side of the booth. "I'm glad for you."

"It was a surprise. I didn't know she was seeing anyone."

"I love weddings. Do you know when they're having it? And where?"

"End of April. Someplace in New Jersey called the Palace."

Her mouth opened a fraction, as though she were a gawping teenager. "Oh my God. Are you serious?"

"I may not have the name right. I know it's the Palace something."

"The Palace at Somerset Park? The one that looks like the White House?"

"I don't know what it looks like," I said, but a little chill went up my spine. It would be typical of Danielle to want Alicia to get married at the White House or the nearest local equivalent.

"Oh my God. I saw that place. On TV. It was this reality show, about these big elaborate weddings. It was like a fairy tale or something, this place. It looked just like the White House, like you were the president's daughter getting married. And it was *so* expensive."

"They said that they were able to get some kind of deal because of a cancellation." I felt a little guilty about not offering to pay for at least part of the wedding, but I had no doubt that Danielle's father wouldn't give a second thought to footing the bill.

"You're going. Tell me you're going. Oh, this is so exciting!"

"I haven't decided."

"It's your daughter's wedding! You have to go."

I had no intention of getting turned down twice in one day, but I wouldn't have a better chance. Margie might not have been interested in me, but she couldn't have been more interested in the chance of going to a fairy-tale wedding—and any wedding Danielle was involved in would be as fairy tale as you could get. And the sarcastic waitress had said that Margie was sweet on me.

"Well, I don't have a date. That's the thing."

"Oh. Well, that shouldn't be that hard. You could…Oh…My…God."

I held my breath, thinking that this might be easier than I had imagined.

"My Aunt Jenny watches that show. I bet she would love to go."

"Your Aunt Jenny." I sent a little brief burst of prayer upstairs, asking God to protect me and keep me safe from Aunt Jenny, whoever she might be.

"Well, great-aunt, really. She lives in Marietta. She loves weddings. She would be…oh, wait. She's having a hip replacement in March. Only one hip, mind you. The other leg is prosthetic. She's going to be laid up for a while."

"I'm sorry to hear that," I said, taking quiet joy in my deliverance.

"It's probably just as well. Unless…Wait—you're not asking *me* to go, are you?"

"Oh. Well. I hadn't thought about it, but if you were interested…"

"I mean, I would love to go, but it's so far, and I hate to leave Kaylee for that long. My daughter, I mean; that's her name, Kaylee."

"I wouldn't have brought it up, except you looked so excited." I was feeling good about my chances as long as I kept playing it cool. Part of playing it cool was trying not to imagine how Margie might look in a nice dress with her hair fixed up, and how Danielle's eyes might bug out if she saw her that way.

"It would be a dream come true. I mean, when I got married, it wasn't romantic or anything. It was in this little poky church in North Alabama, where Jimmy's family was from. I would love to be a part of a great big wedding like that, even if I wasn't the bride."

"There's nothing wrong with a small wedding," I said, hoping as I said it that Jimmy was out of the picture. "My ex-wife's family likes to show off how much money they have, is all. But you can have a lot of fun at a big wedding."

"But I wouldn't know anyone. It would be like I was intruding."

"I feel the same way, if you want to know the truth."

"But she's your daughter. You're giving her away. You're supposed to be there. And I would be out of place. It would be like pretending, like Cinderella going off to the castle for one night."

"It worked out OK for Cinderella in the end."

"But that's a fairy tale. They don't tell you what Prince Charming is really like. They don't tell you that maybe he can't get a good job with health benefits. They don't tell you that he spends all his money on his pickup truck instead of on life insurance. They don't tell you that he gets leukemia and dies right after your little girl is born. They don't tell you none of that when you get married, not a bit of it. They

59

make it real pretty, with flowers and candles and ribbons, but it ain't true. It ain't real. It's something for folks like me to watch on TV and tell ourselves that maybe it could work out for us, but it never does. Maybe it ain't supposed to."

Margie didn't have to explain her grief to me, or the suddenness of its appearance. I understood, and I knew better than to talk her out of it. "Margie, I am so sorry. I didn't mean to make you sad."

She grabbed the rolled-up paper napkin next to her, shook out the knife and fork, and wiped away her tears. "No, I'm sorry. It's nothing you did. You didn't know, the same as I didn't know when I asked about your family."

"It's hard, sometimes."

Margie didn't answer. She wriggled out of the booth and went back into the kitchen, and I didn't see her again. My French dip was cold, and the roast beef was rubbery, but I ate it anyway. I was rattling the last of the ice cubes in my plastic cup when the sarcastic waitress came over.

"Whatever you said to her, it sure set her off."

"We were talking. I didn't mean to make her unhappy."

"I'd hate to see what she'd look like if you had meant to. You want anything else?"

"Just the check."

"You sure you don't want the pie? I could bring the cook out; you could talk to him about how it ain't any good—make him cry a little."

"Just the check, please."

"Just don't go leaving a big tip or nothing. I might get the wrong idea and start crying myself."

I decided not to get any groceries after lunch. I got in my truck and drove around the block for a few minutes until I found myself behind the Conoco.

I got out of my truck. I looked around in the bed to see if I had anything throwable. There was an old, white bag from a fast food restaurant that had been in there for a month or so. I threw it in the dumpster, and then went scouting around for other things to throw. I found an old Budweiser bottle and chucked it in as hard as I could, and was rewarded with the sound of cracking glass. I thought about going into the Conoco and buying a six-pack of the cheapest beer they had, just so I could throw the bottles into the dumpster and hear them break, but that seemed a little too destructive, and anyway I was getting too old for such nonsense. Not to mention I'd never be able to explain to the cops that I was upset because I couldn't get a date with a waitress. I got in the car, slammed the door as hard as I could, turned the radio up as loud as I dared, and headed up the Appalachian Highway toward home.

When I got to my turn-off, though, I made a U-turn and headed back toward Blue Ridge. I went to the Conoco and bought a big bag of tortilla chips, some salsa, and two six-packs of Coors.

11

Hey, Daddy.

Hey, baby.

Long time since we talked.

Too long.

You hardly ever talk to me unless you've been drinking.

I'm only a little drunk. I'm half-asleep watching the Alamo Bowl, which is why I'm hallucinating that you're talking to me right now.

At least you talk to me. You don't ever talk to Trixie.

She's dead.

I'm dead too.

I know that, Francie.

Five and a half years now.

I remember. I never forget.

That's a problem for you.

I don't want to forget. Not anything. I want to remember. That's all I'm talking to anyway—not a ghost, but a memory. Something my brain thinks up to torment me.

I'm not here to torment you. I'm here to help you.

I know, baby.

And you need help right now.

I'm fine. I'm just tired and sad and old. There's nothing you can do to help that.

If you could talk to Trixie, it might help. You could move past this.

I can't. I never could. She doesn't want to talk to me either. All she ever does is shout at me, and when I shout back, that only makes it worse. You're the one she listened to. She loved you.

She loved you.

I know, baby. I loved her. But you were special to her. You were special to me.

Don't cry, Daddy.

I will cry if I want to.

I hate to see you cry.

I don't do it as much. Not every day. Not all the time the way I used to. I'm better now. But I miss you, baby. I miss Trixie. I miss Junior.

I wish I could be there for you. I wish I could help you. But I can't. You have to help yourself. You have to move on. You don't need to be sitting here by yourself watching football and eating junk food for the rest of your life.

I don't have anything else to do. I don't have a job anymore. I don't have friends. I can't go back to Atlanta without breaking down.

It's not right that you're here all alone.

Francie, it's how it has to be.

No. It doesn't have to be. You can get help. Lots of psychiatrists out there.

There's nothing wrong with me. I don't need a psychiatrist to tell me I have issues with grief and loss. I know that. All a psychiatrist can do is give me drugs.

You know I am here for you.

I know, baby.

You know I love you, and care about you, and want you to get better.

Yes.

You know Alicia loves you. You're her daddy. She's not dead, and she needs you.

Alicia has never needed anybody.

It's not true. She loves you. You need to remember that. If you love somebody, you want them to be happy, and you're not happy.

I'm happy she found someone. I'm happy she's getting married. I'm happy about the baby.

Then why are you going out of your way to make yourself miserable?

I don't know. Maybe that's what I'm good at.

Maybe you should try doing something else.

I know, baby. I know. I need to do better. I'll try.

Don't just try.

I don't know what to do other than to try.

Hope. Believe. Love.

I don't know how to do those things anymore.

You do. You haven't forgotten. There's still time.

I love you, baby.

That's a good place to start. But you have to do more.

OK.

I love you, Daddy. Go to sleep.

12

"Don't tell me," I said. "You made the left turn when you should have made the right."

"At least I did it on purpose this time," Dot said.

It was the first Saturday of the new year. I had been sitting at my kitchen table, eating a peanut butter sandwich and trying to work up the resolve to go into town and get provisions for the next week, including snacks for the NFL playoff games. I had managed to drink everything in the cabin that was alcoholic and drinkable, except for a medium-size bottle of hard cider I had found when I was rooting around the bottom shelves. I had poured the cider down the sink, partly with the idea that doing so would be the first step of a New Year's resolution not to let myself get that depressed again, and partly because it smelled like it had gone rotten. I had managed to clean myself up to the point I was looking presentable to go out in public again, but I didn't know if it was worth the effort. I was trying to talk myself into staying home and subsisting on the eggs and cheese left in my refrigerator and the remains of my pantry—bread, macadamia nuts, and a tin of stale Danish butter cookies—when Dot Crawford knocked at the door.

"If you're looking for directions," I said, "you'll have to tell me where you're going."

"If you don't stop teasing me, I'm headed back to Mercier Orchards to take all this back." She produced a white, plastic bag from under her parka.

"You have captured my attention," I said.

"I picked up a couple of things that I thought you might be interested in," she said. "As a thank-you, for putting me on the right road the last time I was up here. If you're not interested, though, I can be on my merry way."

"I am very interested."

"If you were interested, you might invite me to come inside so I can get out of the cold."

I got out of her way and held open the door. She came inside and placed the bag on the table, and then took off her parka and went over by the fireplace to get warm. I checked inside the bag, and there was a jar each of blackberry preserves, peach salsa, and toasted pecan syrup. I put the containers in the pantry and cleared away the crumbs of peanut butter sandwich that were still on the table.

"Can I get you something to drink?" I asked.

"A Coke, if you have one."

"You sure you don't want coffee?"

"I do want coffee," she said. "That was my sly commentary on your kitchen decor."

"At least it all matches. Any particular kind of coffee?"

"You have one of those little K-cup machines?"

"It just so happens."

"I thought so. I mean, it stands to reason. I have one. I live alone, you live alone."

"You figured that out the last time," I said. "I forgot to ask you how you knew that."

"Well, no offense, but it's not a very feminine environment."

She didn't look all that feminine herself, although I wouldn't have said that to her. She was wearing a black sweater with red-and-white paisleys. Her fingernails were square and un-manicured. She wasn't wearing any jewelry except for earrings, which were hammered silver with a turquoise stone inset.

"I do live alone. I'm not a huge coffee drinker, though. I have the Green Mountain pumpkin spice if you're interested."

"That would be lovely. I hate to intrude, though."

"Southern hospitality, you know," I said.

"I thought that died out with the rotary telephone and the hand-written letter."

"It did, most places, but you can still get a free cup of coffee around these parts."

"Cream and sugar?"

"All right."

"And pie?" she asked.

"I have some stale Danish butter cookies. Otherwise you're out of luck."

"I'll pass, thanks." She took her coffee and sat down at the kitchen table, just as though she had been by to visit a hundred times before. "So is your real name Billy Ray?"

"Oh. You saw the sculpture." I had put the little football Alicia had made for me up on the mantelpiece. "My daughter made that. Using that name must have been her idea of a joke."

"You kind of look like a Billy Ray."

"You'll have to tell my ex-wife that." I had been known as Billy Ray Morse all the way through high school and college, but when I started dating Danielle, she insisted on introducing me to her family as "Will." "She didn't think much of the name."

"Well, Will is a little shorter and easier to remember. Maybe she had a point."

"Let's not talk about my ex-wife."

"Fair enough," she said. "Your daughter came down to see you, though. That must have been nice."

"It was quite the experience." I didn't want to share that much more than I had already. I felt as though she knew everything about me, and I didn't know anything about her other than her name. "Of course, now she thinks that you and I have some kind of relationship."

69

"Oh, dear."

"She referred to you as the mystery woman."

"Oh, goodness," she said. "I did not mean to embarrass you like that, honestly I didn't."

"Don't worry about it. If she didn't tease me about you, it would have been something else."

"I feel bad, though. Let me make it up to you."

"Unless you have some apple butter from Mercier out in your car, you don't need to bother," I said.

"As you may have guessed, I didn't just happen to be in the neighborhood delivering quality jams and syrups. My friend Beth is throwing a party at her lake cabin, and she invited me to stop by and bring someone. Her exact words."

"I appreciate the offer, but I don't need the company."

"Hear me out. It's a small party. Beth and her husband, and three other couples. We go there and eat a quick lunch, something light. You go and watch the football games in the den with the other men, and the women and I sit in the kitchen and gossip. It won't be all that different than watching the game here, but you get a free meal and a nice spread of snacks."

"Honestly, I'd rather stay here. Nothing personal. I'd rather watch the games here in my own chair."

"There's dinner afterward too. They cook up some rib eyes. Inch thick. And scotch."

"You can't tempt me with steak. I have a freezer full of it."

"It's not just steak. Beth and Ben always put out a huge spread. They used to have a restaurant in Sandy Springs. Cheese dip. Warm pretzels. Smoked salmon."

The best smoked salmon I ever had was in this Asian fusion place in Midtown. It had an orange glaze, but to keep it from being too sweet, they served it with a green horseradish sauce that was burning hot but enhanced the flavor. Anyway, it was the one thing on the buffet that I recognized, and I ate a bunch of it. I hadn't eaten there before and never ate there again—I'm not sure it's even still open—but it was delicious, and I still think about it sometimes.

Francie picked out the place. It was her party, and it was some-place that she knew and liked, and I stood up to Danielle when she wanted to move it to the country club. We might have had better food, but Francie wouldn't have been as happy, and she deserved to be happy for once.

We asked Francie to move back home when she was twenty-six. She'd been out of Cornell for four years by then. She had a good job working as an industrial chemist for BASF in upstate New York. She came home for Easter, right after Trixie got out of the hospital for the first time. When Francie started packing to go back to New York, Trixie retreated to her room and sobbed like a lost thing. I drove Francie to the Atlanta airport, and she cried all the way there.

So we made a deal. Francie quit her job and moved back in to her old room and helped take care of Trixie. I called the people I knew at work who had an in at the chemical engineering program at Georgia Tech, and we were able to get her enrolled for the summer semester. I would pay for Francie to get her master's degree, and Francie would help Trixie keep things together.

The party wasn't just Francie's graduation party; it was a big thank-you for Francie's help with Trixie. But it was also a going-away party in more ways than one. Francie had met somebody in grad school—Paul, his name was. He was studying poultry management, and when he graduated, he planned to move back to his dad's chicken farm north of St. Louis to help run things. Francie was going with him. She got a job developing agricultural chemicals with Monsanto. All of her stuff was on a moving van. She was planning to live on her own in St. Louis until she and Paul decided if they were going to get married. Trixie wasn't excited about her sister moving away, but Francie was as happy as I had ever seen her.

Francie and Paul set their wedding date for September of Trixie's junior year at the University of Georgia. About a month before the wedding, they drove up from St. Louis to Chicago for the week-end to catch a Cardinals-Cubs game. On the way back, they were crossing the Mississippi River when a truck jackknifed in front of them on the bridge, sending their car and three others over the railing and into the water. They were both killed instantly. At least that's what the coroner said, and I want very badly to believe him.

It wasn't the memory of the smoked salmon that changed my mind about going with Dot to her party. It was Francie's voice.

"Hope. Believe. Love," she had said, and even if it was just a hallucination, she had a point. If I just stayed here on my mountain and never interacted with anyone again, it wouldn't be that much different than being dead. I was nervous about leaving, nervous about spending time in a social setting. But I probably wouldn't have to talk to anyone else very much, and I could always drive home if I felt uncomfortable. Besides, it wasn't as though tall blondes were lining up outside my door to bring me Mercier Orchards salsa.

"OK," I said. "You talked me into it. Give me a minute to change my clothes."

"You look fine," Dot said.

"You promised me thick, juicy steak. I don't want to get meat drippings all over this shirt. I have to do all my own laundry up here."

"If you insist."

13

The party turned out to be about what Dot had said it would be, although the food wasn't as good as she'd promised. The salmon was dry. The side dishes were too salty. They didn't have Coke, or even beer. The women drank cheap California white wine, and the men downed something called a "John Daly" cocktail, which was an "Arnold Palmer" (iced tea and lemonade) laced with vodka. Somebody claimed that if you put amaretto in it, you'd have a "Tiger Woods," but that seemed more of a cheap racial joke than anything anyone reasonable would ever drink.

The women stayed in the kitchen, as Dot had predicted they would. I headed out with the men into the TV room, which was a windowless bunker in the center of the house. What they'd done was knock out a wall between a coat closet and the walk-in closet in a bedroom on the other side, and turned it into a screening room. It could fit five people, if they had showered in the last few hours. The TV signal ran into a projector, mounted in the ceiling, and what you ended up with was close to an eighty-inch display. I was a bit envious, but the picture wasn't that much better than my plasma set at home, and I'd rather look out the glass doors and see the country-side during commercials anyway.

The one thing the room had going for it was that it was dark, and that meant that nobody could see me or talk to me, and I was fine with that. The other four guys were, or so I gathered, fraternity pals from Mississippi State who had all relocated to Atlanta; they'd married coeds and had a tight little social circle. I gathered that Dot's ex-husband had been part of that group, but he was gone—why, I could not tell. I was thereby admitted ex officio to their group as "Dot's new boyfriend," emphasis on the *new*.

They would have left me alone the whole time if I hadn't opened my mouth. It was the third quarter of the first game. I forgot what the score was, but the offense was driving and took a sack on second down, setting up third and long. One of the other fellows made some sarcastic crack about the offensive line not earning their salaries.

"Not their fault," I said.

"How do you mean?" one of them asked.

"Coach's fault. They've been running sweeps and screens all day, and the line is worn out, and they're losing focus. They need to put some fresh legs out there."

"They're all overpaid now," someone else said. "Makes them lazy and not want to do what they need to do to be conditioned."

"You ever play ball?" I asked.

"In high school. Cornerback and safety."

"What did you weigh then?"

"Not what I weigh now."

"Fair enough. But these guys are up there, over 350. Have to be in order to block a big NFL lineman. They're paid to train to build their strength and technique, not for sprinting, and the coach has them sprinting on every play. And they're not skinny high school boys who can run all day. They get paid to be road graders. They don't have the stamina for all these screen passes and sprint-outs, not at the end of the season. They're exhausted, so that's why you get pass-protection breakdowns and false-start penalties."

Fortunately, the quarterback got the third-down pass off, and the receiver took it all the way to the five, so I was spared having to lecture further on the finer points of football. This was just as well, as

74

I had no plans to tell these very nice, very hospitable, but half-drunk people who I was and how I knew so much about offensive line play in the NFL. I kept my mouth shut from then on, and that was good enough for all of us.

I went to check on Dot during halftime of the second game. She was pouring the dregs of a bottle of wine into her glass with a practiced hand. There were a couple of empty bottles on the table that hadn't been there before. I hoped that nobody had to drive back to Atlanta tonight.

One of the women was telling a funny story about an interior decorator who had set fire to some monumentally ugly curtains in someone's house. I had heard the same story from Danielle, years ago, about the same guy—he'd tried to blame the arson on a wandering Siamese cat that had supposedly knocked over a space heater. Everyone was giggling at the story, the way you do when you're drunk and everything anyone says sounds hilarious. I edged around the kitchen and found the warm pretzels and cheese Dot had promised. The pretzels were cold, and a thick skin of fat floated on top of the cheese. I fixed up a plate anyway, to give myself an excuse to be in there.

"Hey," one of them said. "How's Tom Brady doing?" The Patriots were playing in the night game.

"Oh, pretty fair. But the game's not over yet."

"But he's still awesome, right?"

"I guess. He's a good quarterback. I don't enjoy watching him play, though; it's like watching a cat teasing a mouse."

"But he's incredible, isn't he?" She drew out the middle syllable of "incredible" far past what you'd expect from a drunk Mississippi State sorority girl.

"Yeah, he's fabulous," another one bleated. "Fa-a-bulous." The others dissolved in giggles.

"Excuse me," I said, and took my plate and headed back toward the man cave.

"You stop that," Dot said, "all of you. Poor Will here doesn't know what you're talking about."

"Tom Bra-a-dy," one of them said. "Tom Bra-a-dy. He's your boyfriend."

"Good Lord," Dot said. "Now y'all are acting like third graders. For God's sake, Iris, you don't even know who you're talking to."

This had no effect on Iris, who kept giggling at her own wit until it choked off her wind and she started coughing.

"You will have to forgive my friends here," Dot said. "The wine has set back their sense of humor about forty years. Also, they are confusing you with my last boyfriend."

"Oh."

"He went to Michigan, and he was a bit…well, shall we say *overenthusiastic* about Tom Brady last time we were up here." Dot's mention of the former Michigan Wolverines quarterback sent the rest of the table into a coughing fit.

"I'll go watch the rest of the game," I said.

"Say hi to Tom for us," Iris said.

I was disappointed in the rib eyes; they hadn't bothered to marinate them. But whoever had cooked them had cooked up an ungodly lot of them, enough that I didn't feel bad about liberating a couple in a plastic storage bag, which I hid under my jacket. I'd had a good time and was set as far as sandwiches for the rest of the week, which made it probably the most successful social outing of my entire life. I said goodnight to our hosts, once I figured out which ones they were, and followed Dot outside.

"I had a good time," she said. "Thank you for coming. It would have been awkward if I was here by myself."

"I had a good time too." I said. The food wasn't up to par, and the company was a bit tiresome, but the football games were both close and it was nice to be around other people again. Plus, I was sober enough to drive home, which is more than I could have said about Dot. In her high heels, she was swaying like a loose gutter in a brisk wind.

"So how are we doing this, anyway?" she asked.

I was going to ask her what she meant by "this" and then realized what she had implied. There was no way she was going to drive back to Atlanta that night; it was late enough and she was drunk enough that it was unreasonable. There were a couple of chain hotels in town, but I didn't feel right dropping her off at a Comfort Inn without her car. I wasn't sure whether she had a change of clothes or not.

"Can they put you up here?" I asked. "I could pick you up in the morning, and get you to your car."

"No way," she said. "Not enough beds."

"OK," I said. "I have a spare bedroom. Well, it's my daughter's room, but you're welcome to it for the night."

It was a big decision, but I didn't have another choice that made any sense. I hadn't had anybody spend the night under my roof since the divorce. I hadn't been upstairs to so much as dust for three years, maybe more. I doubted that she'd notice, though, not as much as she'd had to drink.

Dot looked at me and slurred something that I didn't quite catch. We both got in the truck. I turned the key and shifted it into reverse. She shut her eyes and wriggled into the corner of the cab, trying to get comfortable. She snorted a little, and then repeated what she'd said earlier—but this time I caught it. She'd said, "Tom Brady."

I dreamed of Dot that night. I dreamed that she came downstairs in an old robe and climbed into bed, pressing her warm body to mine. I dreamed she was wearing a short, sheer slip and was in the kitchen, making toast and coffee and smiling in a happy, satisfied way. I dreamed that I surprised her in the hot tub, and she emerged from it naked, with glistening drops of water resting lightly on her skin. And in these dreams, all she would say was that she had been dreaming of me too.

14

Dot woke up a little after eleven. I waited until I heard the sound of running water upstairs before I started on breakfast. I hadn't cooked breakfast for anyone else for years, but I had confidence in my long-dormant abilities. I scrambled four eggs, because although Dot had a nice figure, she was not thin to the point where I figured she wouldn't touch egg yolk. I put a pod of the hazelnut coffee—I had run out of the pumpkin spice—into the K-cup machine. I made French toast too, just so I could use the pecan syrup she had brought. Considering that I didn't have any bacon or sausage or pancake mix in the cabin, I thought it was a substantial enough breakfast to chase away the lingering effects of a bottle and a half of Napa Valley white. If she didn't like it, she was free to drive into town and have an Egg McMuffin or whatever.

She came down in the same clothes that she'd had on the night before, looking a little rumpled. She was carrying the absurd boots she'd worn and was wearing an old pair of bunny slippers that had been Alicia's.

"Do you want breakfast?" I asked.

"Coffee. Dear God, I need coffee like I need my next breath of oxygen."

"Cream and sugar?"

"Don't ask stupid questions about irrelevant subjects. Give me the coffee and I promise not to throw these boots at your head."

I handed her the coffee and put another pod in to brew.

"Is that one for me too?" she asked.

"Yes, if it'll keep you from throwing things at me."

"Keep 'em coming. Do I smell eggs?"

"Yeah. Give me a minute to fix up your plate."

She took a long gulp of coffee, pouring it down like she was using it to put out a fire. "I am far too old to be drinking that much wine."

"They say age brings wisdom, but it isn't true. All you ever get is a better sense of your own limitations."

"Is that the voice of experience?"

"You could say that."

"I am not in the mood for the voice of experience this early."

"What are you in the mood for?"

"Tabasco sauce. For the eggs, I mean."

"Don't have any. Would peach salsa work?"

"Even better."

I got the salsa out of the cabinet and handed it to her. "What they never tell you is that once you find out what your limitations are, they start moving around."

"Is that second cup of coffee ready? I might manage to feel human with its assistance."

"Here you go." I put in a pod for myself.

"This is good," she said. "The salsa brings it all together. I hope you'll give me a chance to repay this extravagant hospitality."

"It's not extravagant. If I had bacon, it might be."

"I would fix you lunch if I could," she said. "But I have to go back to work. I teach writing at Georgia State. Classes start tomorrow, and I'm not ready at all."

"OK." I didn't want her to go, not then, but I knew that it would happen. I knew there had to be some job, some relationship that would pull her back into its orbit and away from me.

"I need to get back so I can go over my lecture notes. I'm guessing that you have a football game or two to watch anyway."

"It wouldn't kill me to miss a game," I said. I could always record them.

"What I was thinking is that I could come up here next Saturday. We could go out to dinner. There's supposed to be a place on the river that's good."

"I'd like that," I said. "But I would rather eat here. We could have tilapia on the grill or something."

"Wouldn't hear of it. My treat. You know of someplace nicer, we can go there. Or we could go someplace in Atlanta. We could hit Fat Matt's, say, or someplace fancier if you want that sort of thing."

"Not really." I suppressed a shudder. I liked the barbecue at Fat Matt's, don't get me wrong, but it wouldn't be worth it to drive all the way into Atlanta. *Maybe I could talk her into bringing up some ribs next time*, I thought.

"We could meet halfway. Go to the Big Chicken in Marietta."

"Is it still there?"

"Last I saw." The Big Chicken was a KFC with a huge neon sign— it's a landmark in Marietta, and that says a lot about Marietta.

"The place on the Toccoa sounds fine. That's about my limit in terms of travel these days."

"Then it's set. I'll meet you here on Saturday, and we'll drive out there, because Lord knows I am not finding it by myself."

"I'd like that."

"Until then, goodbye, anonymous hermit."

"Goodbye, mysterious stranger."

She got up from the table and we both stood there for a long moment, unsure of what to do. "This would be a lot more elegant of an exit," she said, "if I weren't still wearing these bunny slippers."

"It does seem that way."

"I'm going to go over to the couch and try to put on my boots. Promise not to laugh."

"And miss a free meal? Wouldn't dream of it."

15

It was Monday morning, and I realized that I had to go upstairs. I was trying to figure out my schedule for the rest of the week—something that usually never took long because it didn't change all that much. Tuesday was laundry day, because I hate laundry and I hate Tuesdays, and I figured that they deserved each other. It wasn't all that time-consuming in a normal week, but I thought that I would wash the sheets on my bed, which meant another load. I realized that I had to do something about the sheets on Alicia's bed. For all I knew they were covered in dust half an inch thick. Even if they were fine, I would have to go up and make the bed. Dot didn't seem like the sort of person who made her bed every morning—but I wasn't judging; I'm not that sort of person either.

Like it or not, I had to go upstairs—and I didn't like it. The stairs are steep, and my knees wobble. There's no real reason for me to go up there and several reasons not to. But I figured that if Dot was going to stay here Saturday night—as much as she drank at the party, it was a real possibility—she'd at least want the bed made ahead of time. Of course, there was the other possibility—that she would want to spend the night in my bed—but that didn't seem realistic. Not that I would kick her out, but the odds didn't seem worth calculating.

I got halfway up the stairs before I started faltering. I was breathing hard, and my right knee was pounding the way it used to after an hour hiking on the Stanley Gap trail. I thought about turning around and scooting up the stairs on my butt, but that seemed childish. I caught my breath and leaned a little harder on the handrail. *One step at a time*, I told myself, not caring how cliché it sounded.

Two steps from the top, my left knee started complaining too, but I knew I had it made. I almost pitched forward on the top step but kept my balance. Going downstairs would be harder, so I would have to rest a bit before attempting it.

The hallway at the top of the stairs was narrow, with three doors. The door ahead of me was to the bathroom, and I decided to go in there and drink a little bit of water, which I cupped in my hand and slurped up. I checked and made sure there was plenty of shampoo and soap and toilet paper—I hadn't thought about the bathroom at all when I was downstairs, and I didn't relish the thought of coming back to replenish the supplies there. I flushed the toilet to make sure it was working and went back into the hall.

Alicia's old room was on the right, on the side of the house that faced west. When we bought the cabin, Danielle had opened her own design business. She got the idea that the best way to promote herself was to get a write-up about our house in Buckhead in *Architectural Digest*. She worked for weeks with a freelance reporter and a photographer to make it happen—which meant that you couldn't eat anything or put so much as a page of the newspaper on the floor without risking Danielle going into Warpath Mode. To make a long story short, *Architectural Digest* said no, but *Southern Living* said yes, which I thought was just as good but which mortified Danielle to no end.

So the cabin became her new design laboratory, and one of the ideas she had was to turn Alicia's room into the "Sunset Suite," and Trixie's room, which she shared with Francie when Francie was home from school, into the "Sunrise Suite." It was a good idea, and it did help get the cabin into *Better Homes and Gardens*. It was, of course, not *Architectural Digest,* but it seemed to make Danielle happy, which was a nice thing.

What Danielle had done in both rooms was to take the steep angles of the ceilings and smooth them into barrel vaults. In the other room, the ceiling was painted the rosy pink of dawn, softened with patchy clouds. Trixie complained about this for a solid week and then forgot about it. Alicia, though, had taken the corresponding dark-blue design and made it her own, adding a thin crescent moon and a small galaxy of stars arranged in unlikely constellations.

I hadn't done much to the design since I had moved in. All I did was to take out the kids' books that had accumulated there and donate the bulk of them to the library. That left me plenty of shelf space to display the various bowls and other objects I had gotten from Alicia over the years. Alicia is one of those people who believe that you should make gifts for people rather than buy something, and for years, on Father's Day and Christmas and my birthday, I got little ceramic bowls or paper-clip holders or what have you. At first they tended to be awkward and misshapen, and I had to work very hard to pretend to be proud. Danielle was the one who told me to hold on to them, because Alicia had real talent and with the right encouragement might become a great artist. And sure enough, by the time she was in high school, she was turning out elegant hand-painted bowls and vases.

I had unpacked them and arranged them, with pride of place going to a bright red vase with a thin neck that happened to be shaped like a Coke bottle. I picked it up off the shelf, noted that it had gotten a little dusty, and promised myself that I would come back up here and clean at some point. Then I put it back and stripped off the sheets and put on some new ones and made up the bed. It would do for now. If Dot did become a regular visitor, I would have to air out the room a little—maybe call up the property management people who used to rent it out for us and see if they could spare one of their housekeepers for a day. But there was no point in doing that until I had a better idea of where things were going.

My knees were still bothering me a little, so I wadded up the dirty sheets and tossed them down the stairwell to the floor below. I decided to sacrifice my dignity and scoot down the stairs on my butt rather than risk falling. I knew I would look ridiculous, but I didn't care. Besides, the national college football title game was that night, and I had no intention of missing it because I had fallen down the goddamn stairs. I sat down on the landing and grabbed hold of the railing and got ready to take the first scoot.

I took a quick glance down the hallway in the other direction. The door to Trixie's bedroom was locked. The key was downstairs; I hadn't wanted to tempt myself by putting it in my pocket. I knew what was in there—a messy bed, a closet full of clothes, and five cardboard boxes that I hadn't touched since I'd carried them up there five years earlier.

The biggest of the boxes held the trophy Trixie took home for winning the NCAA singles tennis tournament her sophomore year at the University of Georgia.

The smallest box held a hospital bracelet, a blood-flecked pillow-case, a copy of the *Atlanta Journal–Constitution* for December 4, 2005, and a KA-BAR combat knife with a seven-inch chromium steel blade.

16

"Is that a new shirt?" Dot asked.

"Is it that obvious?"

We sat together at a small table by the window, overlooking the Toccoa River. She was picking at her salad. I was trying to keep my tomato soup from staining my new shirt, which I guessed is what had tipped her off.

"Well, no. It looks a little stiff. A little formal for a casual dinner, is all. It's perfectly nice on you."

It didn't seem that formal when I'd ordered it—it was a plain twill shirt in a rich burgundy color, what you'd wear to go someplace that served red wine and you didn't want to get a stain on if you spilled something. I'd gone through my entire wardrobe and hadn't found anything I wanted to wear. After years of wearing whatever Danielle bought me, all I had left now were comfortable clothes—baggy T-shirts, a couple of polo shirts for cooler days, warm flannels, and comfy cotton sweaters.

Eddie Bauer shipped the shirt to me on Friday, so I had washed it once. It was itchy in places, and stiff, as Dot had noticed. I decided not to worry about it—she was making conversation. And that was a good thing. After five years alone on the mountain, I was not what you would call a gushing fountain of small talk.

"How did your classes go?" I asked. People always want to talk about their work. I know I did, even when it got to the point that I didn't understand everything that I was doing. When I was married, I listened to Danielle talk about her work, which involved people I didn't want to be associated with picking out colors I'd never heard of for rooms in houses that I didn't care much about. But I had learned the difference between a valance and a jabot, so it wasn't a complete waste of time.

"These students today. I mean, good Lord God above. They don't write, these students—kids, I mean, although you're not supposed to call them that. You know what their problem is?"

"I think there's a long list."

"They text. All they do, all day long, *text text text*. Which in a way is fine—at least they're using language. But they don't learn to spell that way, or use grammar, and when they try to write, those bad habits carry forward."

"I guess having those phones makes their lives easier, though. More convenient than payphones, and you don't have to lug quarters around."

"They don't need their lives made any easier. Everything's already too easy. None of them has had to struggle, so they complain about everything. I assigned them an essay, and three of them wrote an essay complaining about how hard it was to write an essay all by themselves. A couple more recycled their college entrance essays; at least, that's what I'm thinking they did."

"I guess they're too busy drinking and trying to get laid."

"Was that how you spent your college years?"

"Well, that, and playing football. But yeah, sure. Of course, that was the sixties, you understand."

"Wasn't that much different in the seventies. But we had better music."

I didn't argue with her. She was wrong, but I didn't argue with her. You don't get anywhere questioning people's taste in music or movies. I did wonder how my future son-in-law would evaluate her musical background and then realized that I hadn't thought about him in weeks. That reminded me about the wedding, which caused the soles of my feet to get cold. Whatever I did, I was not going to talk about kids, or weddings, or do anything that might reveal my need for female companionship for Alicia's wedding—or in general. I was going to try again to play it cool, and this time I would succeed. Or that's what I told myself.

"You went to school at Mississippi State?" I asked.

"What? No. Emory. I grew up in Jacksonville, but I never liked it much. Atlanta's been home for years now."

"I figured, because your friends went there."

"Hal—that's my ex-husband's name—he went to Starkville with Beth and Iris and them. They're really his friends, but they stuck with me afterward."

"How's your salad?" I asked, just to break up the uncomfortable silence.

"It's fine. Look, I don't want to talk about my ex, OK? I bet you have one you don't want to talk about either."

"You can say that again."

"Well then, let us enjoy our dinner, if it ever gets here."

She got the trout. I got the prime rib. Halfway through our respective entrees, she tried to strike up a conversation again.

"So, I've been meaning to ask you, and I can't think of a nice way to do it, so here goes. What do you do all day?"

"Pardon me?"

"No offense. I mean, you're all alone all day in an isolated cabin. You eat, you sleep, and maybe you watch some football."

"Maybe." Auburn had won its bowl game, but Alabama had won the BCS championship. I wasn't in the mood to talk about it, and I didn't peg Dot for a fan. Besides, she taught at Georgia State, which wasn't even in Division I.

"So what else is there?"

"I cook. That's how I get things to eat. I cook them, and then I eat them."

"What else?"

"I clean up after myself. I read a little bit."

"Well, look at it from my perspective. I have a commute. I have a job. I write, and then I have something of a social schedule. And I have no time. I mean, zero. I don't get a chance to read or watch TV. And you have all the time in the world, and you can't tell me what you do with all of it."

"I don't have all the time in the world. And if I do, I've earned it. I've earned my retirement—and my solitude, if that's what I want."

"That's not what I'm saying. You can be as retired as you want to be. I would hope that if it was me, I'd be doing more with my retirement, is all."

"You can do whatever you want when you retire. That's the point. This is what I want to do right now."

"It sounds dull to me. Don't you have a hobby or something?"

"I have a research project I'm working on. I spend a little time on it now and then. Other than that, no, unless you count watching football and baseball when they're on." And college basketball, and golf, and NASCAR every once in a while, but I didn't feel the need to explicate all that.

"Interesting. Tell me about it."

"It's hard to explain. It has to do with the First World War, specifically one officer in the British Expeditionary Force. You could call it genealogy if you wanted to."

"Skip it, then. Nothing's more boring than other people's ancestors. How's the steak?"

"Not bad. Prime rib isn't that tasty, but the sauce is pretty good. How's yours?"

"A little dry, but it's fine. Are you getting dessert?"

"If you are."

"That sounds like something my ex would say. Exact same intonation, exact same lack of interest in my answer, as though the question of whether to get dessert wasn't a matter of extreme importance."

I thought that Dot over-pronounced the "ex" sound at the start of words, but I decided not to point it out. "I have a gallon of Blue Bell pistachio almond back in the cabin," I said. "You can have some if you'd rather not pay restaurant prices for dessert."

"Oh, for God's sake. We barely know each other, and here we are talking like an old married couple."

"I used to be an old married couple. Part of one, anyway."

"Me too. You miss it?"

"I don't miss my wife. Or I don't miss what she was at the end of the marriage. I miss being married sometimes; depends on the day. I miss the comfortableness of it, the togetherness. Those aren't actual words, but you know what I mean."

"I know what you mean."

"Until I moved up here," I said, "I hadn't ever lived alone. I had my family or a roommate or the guys in my fraternity. It took a long time to adjust to being by myself all the time, but I managed."

"Do you enjoy it? Being alone?"

"It's not something that you *enjoy*. There are compensations, but it's not enjoyable. That's the wrong word."

"What's the right word?" she asked.

"Tolerable, I guess. Better than the alternative."

"Have you thought about the alternative? Finding somebody? Reconnecting with the world?"

"I don't think that will happen. It's hard for me to talk about why. When I'm around other people..."

"What? What happens?"

I had to be honest with her. If she stuck around me for any length of time, something would happen. I couldn't say what, but it was inevitable. We could be sitting in the cabin watching TV, and someone in a shampoo commercial or sitting behind the baseline at a basketball game would remind me of Trixie, and I would dissolve into a puddle of emotion. She could be sitting beside me as I drove somewhere in my truck, and a song would come on the radio that Francie liked, and I'd have to pull over because I couldn't control the wheel anymore because my hands shook from frustration and loss. She could be sitting on the back porch, watching the setting sun light up the colors of the forest, and turn to see me with tears running down my face like icicles on a sunny day for no good reason at all. If she saw that, it would spark a reaction—fear, perhaps, or concern, or pity. Whatever that would be, she would try to talk away the pain, and that would make things far worse. Better to be honest.

"I don't always handle my emotions very well," I said. "When I'm alone, it's...I don't know what the word is."

"Tolerable."

"Let's say I'm not always good company."

"You did fine at the party."

"Nobody was paying much attention to me, except for your friend who thought I was in love with Tom Brady. That was so absurd that I could tell it wasn't directed toward me. And there was a football game on." That helped more than I could explain. Football is all about channeling emotions; that's why it's played by young men with testosterone to burn. But the mechanism still works, whether you're out on the field putting your inner rage into a clean block on a blitzing linebacker, or whether you're sitting in an easy chair griping about a bad call or a dumb coaching decision.

"So what would have happened if people had been paying attention to you? Are we talking full-scale emotional breakdown here? Something else?"

"It's not just attention. People ask questions I don't want to answer. Being around people can make me nervous, and when I'm nervous, that makes it harder to keep control."

"I see."

"It's not something that happens all that often. And I do try to control it, and I think I'm getting better at it. But when I can't, it's better if I'm by myself."

"I'm glad you told me. It can't be an easy thing to admit."

"I'm a grown man. I ought to be able to handle my emotions. Not being able to—well, where I grew up, that was a weakness, and you never show weakness."

"Since you're being so honest with me," she said, "I have to be honest with you."

"That's fine. If we're acting like an old married couple, we should be honest."

"Old married couples aren't this honest; that's the problem. They have too much invested in the relationship to be honest with each other."

"Well then, go ahead." There was no point, I figured, in encouraging people to lie to you. And she had a point. I wasn't about to be honest with her about everything.

"When I came up here last week, I had an ulterior motive. Not directed at you, I mean. Directed at Beth."

"OK."

"I am in a writer's group with a few other women. Once a quarter we go somewhere, somewhere quiet, and have a retreat to talk about story ideas and bitch about the nuances of the publishing industry. It is my turn to host, and I happen to be flat broke at the moment, with Christmas bills and all. I asked Beth, before we all got too drunk, if I could borrow her house for the retreat. And she said no."

"The nerve," I said, and then realized where this was going. "On the other hand, it's her property, and her right to use it as she sees fit. Maybe she had a good reason not to let you invite all these other people over."

"It's a favor for a friend. A close, personal friend. You do favors for friends, don't you?"

"Well, there are favors and there are *favors*. You have a date set?"

"March, sometime. Look, I realize this is an imposition. I would not ask if I were not so desperate. The last woman to host it had it at this B&B on one of the squares in Savannah. I can't top that. If I can't borrow your cabin for a few hours, I am going to have to have this thing in a tent out on the Chickamauga battlefield or some other ridiculous location."

"Maybe we can talk about it later," I said. "If you can't work anything else out, that is."

"We'll leave it at that, then. What did you decide about dessert?"

"I'm getting the pecan pie. I could not fail to have an opinion about something that important."

"You are making a mistake. It is not going to stop me from having a bite of yours, but it is a mistake nonetheless."

The moon was nearly full and hung low over the canopy of trees as we made our way back to the cabin.

"I think I am going to drive back to Atlanta tonight," she said. "It's not that late, and I have a ton of papers to grade tomorrow."

I was a little disappointed, but I was too invested in playing it cool to let it show. "Sounds reasonable. You want to sleep in your own bed—anybody would."

"Maybe I can come back next weekend, though, and stay over. Hit the antique stores on Sunday while you watch the ball games."

"That would be nice," I said.

Alicia had called Dot a "mystery woman," and she wasn't wrong. I still had no idea whether Dot was attracted to me, and if she was, I didn't know why. I didn't know exactly where this relationship was going, or if it was going to move into something physical or not.

All I knew for sure was that I was sorry to see her go, and that I was looking forward to her coming back. That was quite a bit better than what I had before. I was content to accept the mystery for the time being.

17

A cold front blew through that night. I got out of bed in the morning and turned on the Weather Channel. The local forecast showed a mass of air moving down from Canada. That was bad enough, but there was also a warm front moving up from the Caribbean. I didn't need the Weather Channel to tell me that that could mean ice storms or worse.

I went into the kitchen and got a box of Cream of Wheat out of the pantry. I was going to go outside and chop wood, and you can't do hard work on an English muffin and a cup of coffee.

I had enough wood already chopped and split to get through a smallish ice storm, but I decided to stock up. One of the first things I did when I took up permanent residence in the cabin was to make sure it could withstand severe weather. The furnace and the stove ran off gas, so my biggest expense was a gasoline generator in case the electricity went out. I could have cranked up the furnace, but it was cheaper to have the fireplace burning, and besides, it was a good workout to chop and haul all that wood.

I liked having the cabin warm. Visitors might think it was stuffy, but I didn't have enough of those to care. Like many old people, and most Southerners, I can't stand the cold. My first winter in

Philadelphia, I thought the world was getting ready to come to a snowy and abrupt end. Winter in the mountains isn't anywhere near as cold as it is in the Northeast, but you get more ice and snow than you do living in Atlanta.

Danielle liked her winters, which is one reason why we bought a cabin in the Blue Ridge—summer vacations in the cool mountain air for me, cold winter nights by the fire with hot chocolate for Danielle. If she hadn't liked her winters, I might be living in Port Charlotte or Marathon Key now, not needing to chop any wood or do much of anything other than watch the sun rise and set.

I ate my Cream of Wheat, but I was still a little hungry, so I put some raisin bread in the toaster oven. I went back in my closet to get the soft knee brace I kept there. I had to wear it after the last surgery—the last ditch before total knee replacement, which loomed in my future like something from the horror movies of my youth. I didn't need the brace most days, but it helped with my stability when I chopped wood. I found my black parka. The work gloves were in the pocket. When the bell on the oven dinged, I got the toast out and gobbled it before it could get too cold. I was ready.

I got halfway off the front porch before I realized I had forgotten my keys. I kept the axes and the wedges in a locked cupboard that I had built years ago on the side of the house. I had a combination lock on it at first, but it turned out that you can't turn a combination lock very well wearing gloves, so I switched to a padlock.

In a way, it was ridiculous to still keep them locked up. I could have taken the padlock off the door. But at the time I locked up the axes, it made the hardest kind of sense. There are four of them in there now. One is a maul—half axe, half sledgehammer—which is what I use most often to drive the steel wedges into the soft wood. One is a hatchet, which I use to knock off stray twigs and splinters. One is a great big heavy axe that I can still heft, but I don't use it often, and the day will come that I have to retire it altogether.

The fourth one is slimmer and a bit shorter, but it has a heavy blade that is wickedly sharp. I never use it. I don't like to touch it.

It still reads TRIXIE on the side, the letters marked deep into the handle with my old wood-burning kit.

Trixie started chopping wood during winter break of her freshman year in high school. She had never expressed any interest in it before, never asked me if she could take a hand in chopping, never even wondered how the wood got into the fireplace as far as I knew. One morning, I woke up at six and heard a grunt, followed by a *thunk. Grunt… thunk. Grunt… thunk.*

I went outside to investigate and found Trixie, flailing away at a good-size piece of wood. She dealt it a glancing blow with the heaviest axe, and it spun off the block. She replaced it, and *grunt… thunked* it a couple more times until it started showing signs of splitting. Her form wasn't that great, but there was substantial confidence in her swing, and I knew she'd get the hang of it before too long.

Trixie turned around and saw me standing there.

"I just felt like it," she said.

"Want some breakfast?" I asked.

"Pancakes?"

"I was thinking Waffle House. I'll leave your mother a note so she knows where we are in case she wakes up."

"Can I get some coffee?"

"If you like. It would be a good idea to get a peppermint for the ride back, so your mother won't smell it on your breath and get upset with me."

"I guess. Can I finish up here?"

I put the tip of my tongue to my teeth to say no, but you didn't say that to Trixie, not unless you wanted to hear a twenty-minute exegesis on the rightness of her position and the unfairness of the world. You could resort to what I called the preemptive counteroffer, or what Danielle called bribery—an ugly name for a necessary tactic.

"I was thinking maybe we'd stop at Walmart on the way back and get you a lighter axe and some decent work boots. You can chop wood all you want, but it takes one slip of the axe and you've cut off half your toes. And a lighter axe is going to be easier to control."

"You're OK with me chopping the wood for you?"

"As long as you're careful and take sensible precautions, sure."

"I thought it might help me. You know, for tennis. My serve is still a little slow, and this ought to help build up my wrist muscles, give me a little strength in case I need to power the ball past someone. Since I can't practice up here."

"Sounds reasonable. You want to get in the car?"

"Can I drive?"

"You need a learner's permit."

"It's not fair," she said, and she kept saying it, with variations, all the way to the Waffle House and all the way back from the Walmart.

Trixie chopped wood through the afternoon and got up early the next morning and chopped some more. She didn't stop until she had reduced the cord of wood I had bought for the winter to kindling and splinters. I turned off the gas furnace, and we ran the cabin on wood the rest of winter break. After I caught her trying to chop down a fair-size pine tree, I had another cord of firewood hauled up, and she tore through it like a beaver with a construction permit and the promise of a bonus for quick completion.

The axe and the work boots came back with us to Atlanta, and Trixie spent the next week figuring out which of her classmates had wood fireplaces and excess firewood sitting around. She made two hundred bucks chopping wood that January and would have made more if I had taken time out of my schedule to drive her up to Marietta to recruit new clients.

The tennis coach at Trixie's school named her to the varsity team in February, and that put an end to the wood chopping. Her serve was a bit stronger, but what made the difference was that it was more accurate—the hours of chopping wood hadn't bulked up her wrists that much, but she had better control over what her hands did. By the time regional play-offs rolled around in May, she was the top singles player at her school, and she took them all the way to the state semifinals. They lost to a Catholic school from North Atlanta.

It wasn't Trixie's fault—she squashed her opponent—but they had a deeper team and dominated in the doubles matches.

Trixie never said what had motivated her to chop all that wood, other than the explanation about improving her tennis game. Danielle thought she was obsessive-compulsive, that it didn't matter what it was—it could have been an interest in jogging or pop music or making the perfect biscuit. I thought she was stubborn but in a good way—she had a goal to reach and was driven to sacrifice to achieve that goal, which is what you want your children to do. If she was a bit obsessive or a bit compulsive, lots of people were, the same way Danielle was a bit manic and the way I was a bit depressive. Maybe more than a bit, now.

We didn't know the real motivation and wouldn't find out for a couple of months. We didn't know that Trixie wasn't attracted to the wood, or the hard work, or preparing herself for tennis season, or working hard to achieve a goal, or even the twin furies of obsession and compulsion. For Trixie, it was the blade, the sharpness of it, the way that the light caught it, the sound that it made as it whistled through the wind, the wound that it made in the soft, yielding wood. It was the blade, again and again, relentless, separating softness from softness, cutting through the sinews of the wood to reveal the heart of what used to be a tree. That is what drew her, and we didn't know.

We found out.

It wasn't too long after we found out that I built the cabinet to hold all the axes and bought the padlock and put another lock on the knife drawer.

It wasn't enough.

I don't think there was anything we could have done other than what we had done. Or that's what I tell myself. It helps me sleep some nights. Other nights it doesn't.

18

You would have to say that we were dating now. Dot spent the next weekend in Blue Ridge, reconnoitering the antique stores in preparation for a future assault. I cooked her some tilapia and listened to her complain about her students and the cold weather and the lack of decent Chinese food in Midtown. She stayed in Atlanta the weekend of the Super Bowl, and I surprised myself by missing her company more than I thought I would. The only real argument we had was over my refusal to make the drive down to Atlanta to see her. I wasn't ready for that, and I didn't want to explain why, and I think that vexed her more than she cared to say. I stayed up on my mountain, and as long as she was still willing to make the drive up the Appalachian Highway to see me, things were going about as well as you could expect.

I hadn't talked to Dot about the wedding. I knew I would have to ask her eventually, and I thought she would say yes, but I didn't want to make my move until I was sure that she would. It would be asking a lot, and she hadn't asked me to do very much. To the extent that I thought about it, I had planned to ask her the next time that she asked me about using my cabin for her writers' group. It was the logical way to approach it, but I didn't want Dot to come to the wedding out of guilt or some quid pro quo. I wanted her to come because I wanted to go, and I hoped that she would want to go with me.

Outside of that, I couldn't say honestly that I had an emotional attachment to Dot at that point. Emotional attachments, for me anyway, usually followed close on the heels of physical relationships, and I hadn't gotten any further in that department than a chaste peck or two on the cheek. Both of those things would come in time, I reasoned, and there wasn't any need to be anxious about where the relationship was going.

It was early on a Friday evening, and I was sitting at my desk, trying to put the piles of paper in some kind of order—copies of old World War I personnel records over here, unpaid bills over there—when the phone rang. I don't have an answering machine—I'm home most of the time, and anyone who calls when I'm gone can call back. It means I have to talk to the occasional phone solicitors, but I can always hang up on them. Sometimes I ask them if Jesus Christ is their Lord and personal Savior, and that always gets them to hang up on me.

I expected Dot to be on the other end of the line. She'd called a couple of times before to tell me she was running late or something. But it wasn't her.

"Hey, Daddy," Alicia said.

"Hey yourself, sweetie. How are you?"

"I'm…I'm…"

"What's wrong?"

There was a pause then, a pause you could drive a Buick through. It was not a pause that indicated a minor problem. This was a pause that would be followed by something very bad indeed.

"Sweetie," I said, "tell me what happened."

"I lost the baby," she said, in the smallest voice you could use and still be understandable over the telephone.

"Are you all right?" I asked. "Are you at the hospital?"

"I'm home," she said. "I'm OK, or the doctor said I was. I'm tired, mostly."

"That's terrible, sweetie. I know you must be feeling bad about this."

"I'm sorry, Daddy. I'm so sorry. I know you wanted a grandbaby."

"Don't worry about me," I said. "And don't blame yourself. It's not your fault. You didn't do anything wrong. It's one of those things that happen."

I heard a muted *thud* and then nothing for a long moment.

"Hello?" an unfamiliar voice said at last.

"Hello?"

"This is Will?"

"Yeah. Is this Toby?"

"Yeah. She had the miscarriage yesterday afternoon. They let her out of the hospital this morning. She's pretty upset about it, of course. She wanted to be the one to tell you about it, but maybe that wasn't such a good idea."

"What happened? Is she going to be OK? Did the doctor say anything?"

"Physically, she's fine," Toby said. "The doctor said there may be a little difficulty if we want to try again. I can tell you about it, but it's complicated, and I'd rather not go into it right this second."

"Two things. First of all, I'm coming up there soon as I can. Second, you get off this phone right now and go take care of my daughter."

"Yeah. Right away. Bye."

It was a bad thing, as bad as can be, but as long as Alicia was all right physically, and there was no reason to think she wasn't, I figured they would come through it all right. They had each other and they could have another baby. I knew Alicia would be sad and miserable about the whole thing, and knowing that allowed me to put my own emotions aside long enough to make the necessary plans.

I assumed that airfares would be extortionate, but I checked them out online and saw that I could fly up for a reasonable price, as long as I was willing to take a six-thirty flight the next morning. It was flying out of the terminal concourse at Hartsfield, which I liked because it meant that I could avoid the little airport tram. I booked a room at the Courtyard at the Virginia Avenue exit for cheap enough and a midsize car at the Newark airport. I figured I would wait until I got up there to see about booking a hotel—I didn't know the area around Alicia and Toby's house and couldn't figure out where the best option would be.

I was packing when Dot called. "Hi, there," she said.

"Hey."

"I thought I'd let you know I was for sure planning on coming up this weekend, tomorrow afternoon sometime."

"I hate to tell you this, but I won't be here. I have to go to New Jersey. My daughter just now called and told me she had a miscarriage, and I'm going up there to see her and try to help her out some."

"Oh, how sad. This must be terrible for her. Would this have been her first?" she asked.

"Yes. I hate to hang up on you, but I'm right in the middle of packing. I'm driving down tonight and staying at a hotel and flying out at first light."

"You don't have to do that. I have an extra room in my condo. You can stay here tonight and take MARTA down to the airport."

"I'd rather not, thank you," I said. I could only just handle making the drive to the airport. There wasn't any way I could stay in Atlanta. The burden of memory would be too much to handle right then, on top of everything else.

"I can at least pick you up at your hotel and drive you to the airport," she said. If she was annoyed with me, she disguised it well.

"Thank you, but no. It's a six-thirty flight. I can catch the shuttle from the hotel, so it's no hardship."

"What can I do to help?"

"Nothing. There's nothing anyone can do. I have to go, and I have everything all planned."

"At least tell me what hotel you're staying at."

"The Courtyard, over by the north entrance."

"Well, that's a start. Do you have my cell number?"

"No."

She rattled off the digits. "Call me as soon as you check in," she said.

I pride myself on my self-reliance—of course, living the way I do, it's not that I have a lot of choice. I didn't need Dot's help, and I would never want it, but I would rather take it than hurt her feelings.

"I'll call," I promised.

"Good. I will meet you in the lobby."

I went back to packing. I tossed a pair of balled-up socks into the suitcase. They hit with an unsatisfying, muted *thunk*. I picked up my other pair of shoes and threw them in, one by one, as hard as I could. The impact knocked the suitcase halfway off the bed. I climbed on the bed and punched it off, scattering clothes everywhere. I started hitting the mattress, first with my fists, then with my feet, like an overgrown toddler throwing a tantrum. The headboard banged against the cabin wall. The frame shook enough that I had to stop myself from doing any more damage than I already had.

I knew better this time. I knew not to ask why. There was nobody to ask, no guiding intelligence, no master plan, no guardian angel that was asleep on watch. I knew not to ask why it had to be me—misfortune and tragedy are no respecter of persons. I knew not to pray. And I knew that knowing all of this would not help anything.

So I did the one thing I could do, the only thing that was left to me, the only thing I knew would work: I cried. I cried for Alicia. I cried for Toby. I cried for the little baby alone in the dark who was gone, who died without knowing sunshine or air or kindness. I cried for Francie, who was crushed by the pressure of tons of river water flowing through her car, pulling her down into darkness. I cried for Trixie, who screamed her life out in the emergency room on that blood-soaked gurney. I cried for Danielle and her grief. I cried for myself, although I did not do that for very long.

Some uncountable time later, I got up and took a shower, running the water as hot as I could stand. I got dressed and repacked the suitcase.

On my way out, I grabbed the return envelope for the RSVP to the wedding—it was the only thing I had with Alicia's address. I had no real idea how to find New Brunswick from Newark, but I figured somebody at the rental car place could give me a map and suggest a good route. I threw my bag in the truck and made my way down the mountain.

I called Dot as soon as I parked my car at the Marriott. "Give me fifteen minutes," she said. "I'm on the Connector; shouldn't take me any longer than that if the traffic stays clear. You go check in, and I'll meet you in the lobby."

"That's fine."

I checked in, got my little card key, and found a quiet place in the lobby to sit. The couch was a bit lower than I thought it was going to be, and I worried that I wouldn't be able to get out of it by myself. I closed my eyes and did my relaxation techniques and waited for Dot to show up.

When she did, she was carrying a big plastic bag and a couple of Styrofoam cups with her. The bag had a familiar logo.

"You went to The Varsity," I said.

She smiled a big, happy smile. "Are you surprised? I thought you might need something to eat, and I figured you didn't want to go to a restaurant this late."

"I am not only surprised but deeply impressed. What do you have in those cups there?"

"Didn't know what you wanted. One's a Coke, and one's an F.O."

"The F.O. What's in the bags?"

"Two hot dogs, two burgers."

"Chili?" I asked

"Chili on the burgers, slaw on the hot dogs."

"Fries or rings?"

"Both. What do I look like, an amateur?"

I took a big, cold sip of the Frosted Orange—orange soda mixed with soft-serve vanilla ice cream, a Varsity specialty—and attacked a chili burger. I hadn't eaten at The Varsity in five years—I'd eaten there about once a week, every week, until Danielle made me stop when I turned fifty. It's right across the Connector—the merger between I-75 and I-85 that cuts through downtown—from the Coke headquarters and the adjacent Georgia Tech campus. The food is almost too greasy to eat, but not quite, and that's what's great about it.

"Thank you so much," I said. "This is just what I needed."

"Seemed like your kind of place," she said.

"It used to be, when I was young and indestructible."

"Are you OK? Are you going to be able to make it up there all right?"

"I should be fine," I said. "I used to travel a lot when I was younger, and it never bothered me any. You get used to it."

"This must be so terrible for your daughter."

"It must be. She and her fiancée are getting married in April, so at least she'll have plenty to do so she can take her mind off of it for a while. And they can try again on the honeymoon."

Dot put down her slaw dog. "Your daughter's getting married! When did you find that out?"

"Back in December, when they came down here. It's going to be in New Jersey."

"And you didn't tell me." Dot looked a little hurt, and disappointed, and I guessed she had a point.

"I didn't want to put any pressure on you about going."

"Are you going?" she asked. "Please don't tell me you're thinking about not going."

I took a bite of onion ring. "She wants me to go," I said. "I want to go. But there's a lot of other stuff that's involved. I guess I'll have a better idea once I get up there and talk to her."

"It shouldn't be a complicated decision. You're her father, she's your daughter. You should go. If it were my kid, you couldn't keep me away."

"Do you have kids?" I'd never asked. Dot didn't seem to be the maternal type.

"Well, no. So, yeah, it's easy for me to say. If you're in a complicated situation, then I guess I can appreciate that."

"If you have a couple of hours free sometime, I guess I can try to explain it."

"I'd like that. While we're on the subject, I happen to have a nephew who is getting married in August down in Jacksonville."

"Is that a fact?"

"It is."

"Well then, maybe we can work something out."

"Maybe we can. We don't have to decide now."

"Is there ketchup in that bag?" I asked.

"Of course. I wouldn't let you down."

We finished our dinner in silence, if you don't count the sounds I made slurping down my F.O. "Thank you for coming," I said. "It means a lot. Not just the dinner, I mean. I'm glad you were here for me. I haven't had anything like that in a while."

"Don't mention it. Make sure to get some sleep tonight. You've got a hard day ahead of you. Go take care of your daughter."

I managed to get up out of my chair without too much embarrassment. Dot put up her arms to give me a hug, and we held each other for a long time.

"I can stay," she said. "If you need me."

"I need you," I said. "But like you said, I need to get some sleep, and I have to get up early. Maybe this isn't the best time."

She handed me a pink Post-It note with a phone number written on it. "When you come back," she said, "give me a call. Let me know how it went. We can go from there."

"Good night."

"Good night. Give your daughter a hug for me."

I picked up my bag and went down the hallway to find my room. I thought for a little while about Dot, and Atlanta, and the Frosted Orange, but not for too long. I needed to sleep, and at length I did.

19

It turned out that the GPS gadgets that do such a bad job of directing delivery people and tradesmen to my cabin do a much better job of locating people in major urban areas. Without the GPS in my rental car, I would still be on the New Jersey Turnpike looking for the New Brunswick exit. With it, I found Alicia and Toby's house—an older two-story structure, mock Victorian, with a rickety front porch and peeling paint here and there—with a minimum of fuss.

Toby answered the door. "You weren't kidding," he said. He was wearing a tattered pair of sweatpants and a black T-shirt that read "NIИ", whatever that meant. He hadn't shaved in days, and his hair had the greasy sheen you see in bad cop movies.

"I never kid," I said. "You look like hell."

"I need a shave, a shower, and a three-day nap," he said.

"Where's Alicia? Is she OK?"

"She's asleep. That's a good thing right now. I'd run the shower, but I don't want to risk waking her up, and I don't want to go anywhere in case she does wake up."

"If she's asleep, you should be too."

"Can't sleep. Anyway, we have to clean this place up before Alicia's mom gets here. She's supposed to be coming today."

"Is she in the habit of calling before she comes?"

"Why? Do you want to make yourself scarce?"

"It might be for the best. Until that happens, I can help clean. You can at least lie down if you can't get some sleep."

I couldn't believe that Danielle would be all that critical under the circumstances, but the mess inside Alicia's kitchen would not make her happy at all. I started clearing out the fast-food wrappers and then got started on the dishes. It wasn't hard work and it kept me occupied.

I fished out a can of cleanser from under the sink and was trying to remove a couple of layers of grease off the backsplash when Danielle walked in.

"Oh, it's you," she said. "I was wondering whose car that was."

"Hello to you too."

She looked as she had always looked, trim and elegant, a little fragile. She had on a long coat and a pastel silk scarf that resembled the modern paintings they were selling thirty years ago. Her hair was longer but still Clairol blonde. Age and sadness had made her faded and distant, like some science-fiction hologram projected from a doomed planet.

"What are you doing?" she asked.

"I'm cleaning up. Helping out. Trying to make myself useful." I wasn't surprised that Danielle was being this nasty and disagreeable with me, but I wasn't going to put up with it. "What are you doing here?"

"Don't be ridiculous," she said. "I'm here to check on my daughter. Have you talked to her?"

"I got here maybe fifteen minutes ago. She was asleep upstairs when I got here. I told Toby to go up there and take a nap, and I hope he's asleep too."

"If she doesn't know you're here," Danielle said, "it won't make any difference if you leave now. You can come back after I'm gone. Or you can go back to Atlanta, which would be my personal preference."

"I'm not leaving without seeing Alicia," I said.

"I don't want you here. There's no reason for you to upset her. You're not going to help, and you just might make things worse."

"If you want to upset her," I said, "you can keep arguing with me. That would do it. I'm not leaving. If you want to go, you know where the door is."

"You've been cleaning?"

"Something to do," I said.

"If you're going to be here, at least you can make yourself useful. I went to the deli and got a few things for lunch. There should be enough for everyone. If you feel you have to stay and help, you can start by getting everything out of the car."

Danielle was driving a pearl-colored BMW convertible these days. It looked to be about four years old. I guessed the interior design business hadn't done so well in the recession. She had six bags of groceries in the car, which I supposed was something of a tribute to Toby's eating habits.

When I got back into the kitchen, Danielle had taken off her coat and rolled up the sleeves of a red flannel shirt. That meant I was going to be dragooned into doing something other than what I wanted to do. Danielle was a bit strident about concepts such as obedience and hard work and pulling your weight. Something bad was happening, and I didn't know what it was other than that it was going to involve a hell of a lot of cleaning.

"Fridge," she said.

"What about it?"

"Everything in those bags goes in there. Everything that's in there now gets thrown out unless there's some reason to keep it. Organize it the best way you can, and I'll look at it when I'm done with the laundry room. What did Alicia tell you about the baby?"

"All she said was she lost the baby, but that she was going to be OK physically. Toby said that there was something that could be a problem, but he didn't tell me what it was."

"And you believed her?"

111

I looked up from loading the refrigerator. Danielle's jaw was set, the look she gave when she was trying to interrogate you. "Yes. Of course. Why wouldn't I?"

"I want to make sure I understand your side of this before we go on."

"I don't know what you're talking about. I don't have a side. Alicia called me. She told me what happened. I came up here to see her and make sure she was OK. That's it."

"When she came down to see you in Georgia, did she tell you she was pregnant?"

"Yes, she did," I said.

"Was she happy about it? Sad? Upset?"

"She was kind of emotional about it. Anyone would be. She looked happy enough."

"What did you tell her?"

"I told her I was happy for her. What do you think I said?"

"Did you tell her anything that would make her want to end the pregnancy?"

"What are you talking about?" I asked. "She didn't end the pregnancy. She had a miscarriage."

"She did not. If she told you that, she's not telling you the whole truth."

"Danielle, for God's sake, why would Alicia lie to us about having a miscarriage? She wouldn't do a thing like that."

"How could you know that?" Danielle asked. "You've seen her once in the last five years."

And that's your fault, I thought.

"I know my daughter. I talked to her on the phone. There's no way she was lying to me. She was upset and crying. She sounded miserable. You can't fake something like that. Danielle, I know you're upset about her losing the baby, but it doesn't make any sense to blame Alicia."

"You are not doing this to me again. I am not going to stand here and have you not tell me what I want to know. Not this time. If you know anything about this, you need to tell me, now."

"Anything about what? There's nothing to tell you. She lost the baby, and it's a terrible thing, but there's no way she did anything intentional to make that happen."

She gave me a look, a look that I had seen before. It was a look that told me that she thought I was an idiot and a fool in the bargain. She went into the laundry room and started throwing clothes in the washer. I made space to put deli meats and olives in the refrigerator.

I had no clue why Danielle had the idea that Alicia was lying to us about having a miscarriage. But I knew Danielle. She wasn't crazy, and she wasn't delusional. She had a reason for her suspicions, whatever that might be. I hoped like hell that Danielle wasn't right, that there was some kind of misunderstanding or other reason that she was acting this way. But I couldn't come up with what that might be.

Danielle finished in the laundry room and repaired to the living room, where she started rearranging furniture. When she turned on the vacuum cleaner, I made the strategic decision to fix myself a sandwich. I had noticed a container of tuna salad and wanted to get to it before Toby scarfed it down.

I went out to the backyard so I wouldn't get any crumbs on the floor. A square of concrete out back served as a rudimentary porch. The lawn was patchy and brown with winter, and a white mound of snow sat in the far corner, resisting the afternoon sun. Along one of the fences was a small wilderness of bamboo. I ate my sandwich and thought about what I would do if it were my lawn—fertilizing to start with, and then seeding in the spring, and maybe planting some roses by the other fence. I was trying to figure out whether I'd put down some topsoil when I saw some orange sparks in the corner of the yard. I went over and saw Alicia, hiding behind a garden shed, smoking a cigarette.

"Hey, sweetie," I said.

"Hey. You made it. Toby said you would be here, but I wasn't sure when you would arrive."

She looked awful: pale skin and dirty hair. She was wearing a purple hooded sweatshirt that had spent serious time wadded up in the back of somebody's closet. It might have said "NORTHWESTERN" across the front at one time, but the letters had mostly peeled off.

"How are you?" I asked.

"I get to smoke again. That's the upside, I guess. Other than that, I'm still a little sore, and I can't go twenty minutes without crying or wanting to eat something disgusting. Or both at the same time."

"If you're hungry, you should eat. Your mother's here; she brought lots of food."

"I saw her car pull up. When she started vacuuming, I snuck down the back staircase."

"She was moving furniture around before that."

"Oh, that's not good," she said. "Warpath Mode, Level Four. At least she isn't painting; that's something."

"I guess." I would not have stuck around very long if Danielle had been brandishing paint cans.

"Did you do something to cheese her off? Please, tell me you said something awful to her to make her act that way."

"I have not done one thing that I'm aware of to antagonize your mother, other than coming up here in the first place. She's not mad at me." *At least not yet,* I thought. "But she seems to be a bit confused about what happened to the baby."

"Confused? Confused in what way? What did she say?"

"She has it in her head that you didn't have a miscarriage."

Alicia dropped her cigarette. "Damn damn *damn,*" she said and fished another Marlboro Light out of a soft pack.

"It's not true, is it?"

"I need to talk to her," she said. "Goddamn it to hell."

"You need to shower first," I said. "Calm down a little bit, maybe. Put on some fresh clothes so your mother doesn't smell the smoke." I knew the smell of cigarette smoke would set off Danielle if nothing else did.

"Yeah. That makes sense. You might want to go, Daddy. You don't need to be caught in the middle of this."

"In the middle of what? Sweetie, I don't even understand what she's talking about."

"I do."

"This is great, Mrs. M." Toby was plowing through a gross-looking plastic tub of potato salad. "Hits the spot."

"Glad to hear it, dear," Danielle said. "Did Alicia tell you how much longer she'd be? She needs to eat something."

I had a small pile of potato chips in front of me, but I wasn't eating them. I didn't know what was going on, but I wanted to protect Alicia if I could. She came downstairs a few minutes later, barefoot and her hair still wet.

"Hey, guys," she said. She looked the way she did when she was fifteen years old, sad and defeated, like she'd gotten a D in algebra and was sorry about it.

"Do you want something to eat?" Danielle asked. "We've got sandwiches, or I can fix you some pasta or something."

"I'm not hungry," Alicia said.

"You need to eat something."

"I'll fix some cereal. Is there any coffee?"

"I'll make a pot," Toby said.

"Thanks, babe. I have a horrible headache. Caffeine will help."

We sat around for a long time, watching Alicia plow through a bowl of Froot Loops. "Are you sure you don't want a sandwich?" Danielle asked. "You need some protein."

"I'm fine," Alicia said. "I'll feel better tomorrow. Maybe we can go over the centerpiece options."

"Before we do that," Danielle said, "I would appreciate it if you can tell me what happened to the baby."

"I lost the baby. I'm sorry. I didn't mean to. I stopped smoking, I stopped drinking, I tried so hard to keep it, but it didn't happen. I don't know what else you want to hear."

"Just the truth," Danielle said.

"That *is* the truth," Toby said.

"Young man," Danielle said, "this is between me and my daughter. I know you're trying to be supportive, but you're not helping."

"Mother, please," Alicia said. "Toby's right. That is the truth. If you want more truth than that, I can't help you."

"There's no need for you to be unhappy with Alicia," I said. "Let's just finish our lunch and get out of here."

"This is not about me being unhappy," Danielle said. "Alicia, I am not unhappy with you because you had an abortion. That's not what this is about. I would like to know why, however, and I want you to tell me."

"I am a grown woman," Alicia said. "If I had an abortion, it was my choice and my decision. I don't owe you an explanation. I don't owe you a reason. If you don't believe me, I can't do anything about that. If you're going to be upset with me, though, I'd rather you go home and do it."

"Danielle, she's right," I said. "There's no point in this. I don't know what you think happened, or why, but you need to back off."

There was a pause then, another one of those pauses that I knew would be followed by something very bad indeed.

"You will tell me," Danielle said. "You will tell me why. You will tell me why you killed that baby, a baby you wanted, a baby you loved. You will tell me why you would do such a thing to my only grandchild."

"Or?"

"Or you will regret it," Danielle said, splitting every word off like she was breaking glass.

There was another pause, a little longer this time. "I did it," Alicia said. "I had an abortion. Are you happy now?"

"No. I want to know why you chose to have an abortion, and why you lied to your father and me about it."

"I did it for you, for you and Daddy."

"Why?" I got it out a second before Danielle did.

"Because of Junior," Alicia said.

"Junior?" I asked. Junior had died thirty years ago. I couldn't imagine how his death had impacted Alicia's decision after all this time.

116

"You were three years old when Junior died," Danielle said. "How could you remember that?"

"Because of Junior," she repeated, and then she went outside. She stood out on the back porch for a long moment. I could see her shoulders shaking.

"You need to go out there," I told Toby.

"No," he said. "Not right now."

"Then I'll go."

"No. You stay here, both of you. Give her a little peace. If you like, I can explain what happened."

"I don't know that it's necessary," I said.

"It's complicated," Toby said, "and I am only going to go through this once. If you want to hear me explain everything, sit down."

"I would rather hear this from Alicia," Danielle said.

"No. You've already done enough," Toby said. "You were willing to torture her for this information, so the least you can do is sit still and listen to it."

20

"It's called 'X-linked severe combined immunodeficiency,' " Toby said.

I looked at Danielle, and she looked at me, and we both looked at Toby. "Break that down for us, please," I said.

"Something to do with the immune system?" Danielle asked.

"Right," Toby said. "'Immunodeficiency' means you don't have an adequate immune system, and when that's severe, it means you don't have any kind of immune system at all. You know the story of the boy in the bubble?"

"There was a TV movie about that. John Travolta was in it," she said.

"Right. He was in the bubble because he didn't have an immune system. If he left the bubble, he would catch an infection and die."

"That's what the baby had? The X-linked thingy?"

"That's what the baby had. Here's the thing. When we got back from Georgia last month, Alicia got an e-mail from her cousin, Mona."

"Beverly's youngest. She lives out in California; I haven't seen her in years."

"She heard Alicia was pregnant. She sent an e-mail with a link to this *Wikipedia* article about the illness. So Alicia e-mailed her back, asking her why."

"What did she say?"

"Mona had a baby two years ago who died. They diagnosed him with the disease. It's genetic. That's the 'X-linked' part of the disease. The mother passes the X chromosome on to her children. If the mother is a carrier, she has a 50-50 chance of passing the defective X chromosome on to her children."

"So Alicia has this disease?" I asked.

"Alicia doesn't have the disease," Toby explained. "If a girl is born with the defective X chromosome, that doesn't make her sick. It just makes her a carrier. Mona is a carrier. Her mother Beverly is a carrier, and she passed it on to Mona. And Beverly's mother—your mother—she was a carrier too. It runs in the family."

"But what does that have to do with Junior?" I asked.

"That's the other part of it," Toby said. "When you're a carrier, and you have a little girl, there's a 50-50 chance that the little girl grows up to be a carrier. When you have a little boy, there's the same 50-50 chance that the boy inherits the defective X chromosome. But a little boy has XY chromosomes—if a little boy gets the wrong chromosome, then he gets the disease and doesn't develop an immune system."

"What are you trying to tell me?" Danielle said.

"Your mother was a carrier," Toby said. "We know that. You had a brother who died before you were born, and we think that he had the disease. And we know Alicia is a carrier. She tested positive. That means you're a carrier too."

"That's not possible," Danielle said.

"I'm afraid it is. You had a 50 percent chance of passing the gene for the disease on to any boy baby, and we think you passed it to Junior."

"You have no idea what you are talking about," Danielle said. "I can't imagine why you are trying to take the tragedy of my son's death and use it to justify yourself."

"It's what happened," Toby said, "whether you like it or not."

"Junior didn't die of a genetic disease," I said. "He died of meningitis."

"Yeah, exactly. He caught meningitis because his immune system was compromised. He had eczema, didn't he?"

"How did you know that?" Danielle asked.

"Because it's a symptom," he said. "It's one of the things you get. You don't have an immune system, you catch things."

"Nobody told us that at the time," I said. "They never said anything like that."

"They didn't know," he said. "I mean, they knew about the disease, but it's rare, and they didn't know about the genetic side of it thirty years ago. A baby gets an infection, they treat the infection. It's how they're trained. If they had done an autopsy, they might have figured it out, but they didn't. And there's not anything they could have done to treat it."

"Is it treatable?" I asked. "I mean, now?"

"We asked the doctors that," Toby said. "I mean, you have to believe, once we got the test results back, and confirmed the diagnosis, we analyzed this every way we could do it. There were three options. First was a bone marrow transplant. We would have had to have found a match. The best match is a sibling, but obviously that was out. Next best is an aunt or uncle. I don't have any brothers or sisters, and… well, you know. You can go through the genetic registry, get some stranger to donate the marrow. We might have found a match in time, but we might not have. Then there was gene therapy. They tried that in France, about four years ago. Worked great, but then half of the kids in the study got leukemia. So that was out. Last option was to put the baby in the bubble, keep him isolated from everything, and that didn't seem… that wasn't what we wanted for him. Nobody would want that for a child. Every day you'd be worried sick that he'd catch something and die."

"So you gave up," Danielle said.

"We decided not to go through with it," Toby said. "We decided to try again. Maybe the next one will be a girl, or we can adopt. We didn't want to put ourselves and our families through what you went through with Junior. It didn't seem fair."

"Life's not fair," I said.

"No shit," Toby said. "Look, that's what happened. You wanted to know, and now you do, and I am tired and going to go upstairs and try to get a nap."

"Thank you," I said. "I know this was difficult for you."

"This was the hardest thing I've ever done in my life," he said. "I mean, I know both of you have lost children, but you didn't have to sit here at the kitchen table and decide whether your children would live or die."

"I am so sorry," Danielle said. "For both of you. It was a cruel thing that happened."

"No, it wasn't," Toby said. "It was genetics. Genetics aren't kind or cruel, they just are. What's cruel is you coming in here and treating your own daughter like a perpetrator on a TV show. You had no right to treat her that way."

Danielle shot him that familiar, hateful look of hers. "You should get some sleep," she said. "I'll see myself out. Give Alicia my love, and tell her I will talk to her tomorrow about the centerpieces if she's up to it."

I walked Danielle out to her car. "I can't believe Toby talked back to me like that," she said. "It's unlike him."

"He was right," I said. "That was a cruel thing to do."

"Don't you dare use that word to me. I'm willing to forgive Toby; he's tired and emotional. You don't have the right to call me cruel."

"You didn't need to know all that. Not that badly. Not that way."

"Anything I know about cruelty I learned from you. And it was necessary. Painful, but many necessary things are painful."

"How did you even know she had an abortion?" I asked.

"I went to the wrong hospital. She called me and told me she'd had a miscarriage, and she was at the hospital. I thought she'd gone to St. Peter's. That's where she was going to have the baby, that's where her

OB-GYN is. But she wasn't there; she was at Robert Wood Johnson. St. Peter's is a Catholic hospital. They don't do abortions."

"It was an emergency situation; they would have taken her to the closest hospital."

"But it wasn't, and they didn't."

"You couldn't have been sure about that. You just had a theory. You could just as easily have kept your mouth shut."

"Will, for God's sake. She's my daughter. I can tell when she's lying to me, even if you can't."

"There's no way you knew that for sure. You accused her based on a guess. That's cruel, and there wasn't a reason for you to be that cruel."

"She lied to us," Danielle said.

"It wasn't a lie that would ever hurt anyone. If anything, she was trying to protect us. She's our daughter, and there was no reason to treat her like that."

"Our only daughter."

"She's not our only daughter."

"She is now," and again there was that sound of breaking glass in her voice.

"All the more reason for you not to mistreat her. Not to mention that she lets you get away with it. If you'd tried treating Trixie like that, she'd still be screaming at you."

"But Trixie's dead."

"I know. I was there. If you still want to blame me, that's fine. I can live with it. But don't push Alicia away because of what happened with Trixie."

The hateful look Danielle had on her face shifted and became contorted with something deeper, and more painful, like I had slapped her.

"Everything I have loved in my life has been taken away from me, piece by piece, bit by bit. And do you know the worst part of it? I don't know why. I don't know why the North Vietnamese shot down my brother Leo's plane. I don't know why Junior had to get that disease Toby said he had. I don't know why that truck driver rammed Francesca's car off the bridge. And I don't know why Trixie had to die. I don't know anything about that night."

"I am not having this conversation with you," I said. "Not here, not now."

"You've never told me. You've never said anything. What was I supposed to think? Did she just pull that knife out of thin air?"

"You should go."

"I haven't forgotten. Don't think that because I am standing here, talking to you, that I don't remember what happened, what has been done to me."

"I haven't forgotten either." And I hadn't, not any of it. We had hurt each other badly, although not as badly as Trixie had hurt both of us, and herself.

Danielle clicked her key ring and opened her car door. The rage on her face had faded, and she looked tired and defeated again. "I'm going home," she said. "Go talk to Alicia; she always listens to you."

As soon as Danielle's BMW had turned the corner, I went back inside the house to see if I could be any comfort to my daughter. I knew she needed it, but I knew that it wouldn't be that much help.

21

Alicia was still outside. She had fetched a long and sharp instrument from the shed, and was using it to hack at a growth of bamboo over by the back fence.

"Is she gone?" Alicia asked.

"Yeah."

"That's good. I let her off easy, you know. I should have yelled at her or something. She deserved it."

"Toby let her have it when he was done explaining."

"He did? Good for him. He hasn't had that much experience dealing with Mother; I was worried that she was going to steamroll him. You know how she can be."

"I know. Or I should have remembered. I'm sorry, sweetie. I should have stepped in and said something to stop her from going after you. I told myself I was going to try to protect you, and I let it happen anyway."

"You're out of practice on the whole parental thing," she said.

"I know."

"Don't worry about it. It was bound to happen. She kicks into Warpath Mode, and all you can do is watch out. It happened last week, when we had this big fight over bridesmaid dresses. I wanted white dresses. She wanted dark purple. So now they're going to be wearing white dresses with purple satin sashes. They're going to look like crossing guards."

"She had no right to treat you that way," I said.

"Maybe she did."

"Don't say that."

She clipped off another chunk of bamboo. "See what I did? I killed a living thing."

"Alicia…"

"It's true. It's my job, keeping the bamboo cut back. I have to kill part of it every so often to keep it from taking over the whole backyard. And I thought it would be that way. You kill a living thing so that it doesn't take over your life. To have a baby with a severe medical problem would have been a disaster. It was supposed to be an easy decision. Toby said so, the doctor said so."

"But it wasn't."

"I loved that baby. I didn't know how much. I didn't know how much I would miss being pregnant. I didn't know *anything*. I thought it would make things better, but it didn't, not at all."

"I'm so sorry, sweetie. But it wasn't your fault."

"*Yes it was.* I was that baby's mother. I was all that he had in this world. That baby boy was alone in the dark and counting on me for everything, and I let him down, because he was sick and was going to die. It was my responsibility to keep him alive. And it's my fault that he's dead. I never should have—never, not ever. I loved him, and now he's gone, and it's my fault."

She dropped the pruning tool she was using, and I moved in to give her a hug, and that's when she started crying.

"I loved him," she said, over and over again, like it could change something, although we knew it couldn't.

"We need to go inside," I said after a long moment. "You have to eat something."

"That's what Toby kept saying. You have to eat something. Keep up your strength. The whole time I was pregnant, when I was throwing up and couldn't eat a damned thing."

"It's still true. Come on. I bet your mother got you some of those green olives you like."

"I need to tell you something," she said.

"What is it?"

"One of my professors at VCU is now the department chair for visual arts at the University of Colorado. He made me a job offer. I can start in the fall, if I decide I want it. And it's tenure track."

"That sounds good," I said. "If that's what you want."

"It's so hard finding something that's tenure track these days in the arts. I'm just a scholar-in-residence, and Toby's really just an adjunct. But I turned it down."

"Why?"

"Because of Toby. There's not a slot open in the music department. He'd be unemployed, basically. I think he'd be OK with that—he's talented, he'll find something eventually. But he didn't want to leave. And I wanted to stay close to Philadelphia, so Mother could help with the baby. So I had to turn it down. Now I'm not so sure that was a great idea."

"Please tell me you're not planning on ditching Toby."

"I could. I don't know that I would. I might. It's tempting."

"He loves you."

"I know. And I love him. I do. I told you that I love him with all my heart, and nothing will change that. But that doesn't mean I have to stay here, or even that I want to stay here."

"Oh, sweetie." I don't know why I was surprised, because I shouldn't have been. Alicia had done this kind of thing all her life.

"Last night I looked it up on Google Maps. I can take 287 up to 78, to Allentown. You hit I-70 somewhere in Pennsylvania, and then it's a straight shot all the way to Colorado. It would take me twenty minutes to pack, and I could be out of here and headed west before anybody could say anything."

"But you don't have to do that today. You can wait. Figure out what you want and then decide. No reason to make any irrevocable decisions now."

"I don't know when I'll know. I don't know anything anymore."

"It will feel like this for a while," I said, thinking back to how it was after Junior died. "Everywhere you look something will remind you. You'll see some other woman with some other baby and you'll start crying and you won't understand why at first. You might cry for half an hour because of a diaper commercial. You'll see yourself in the mirror and maybe you want to cry or maybe you want to throw something. You'll blame each other for every little thing if it gets that bad. But one day, you'll wake up and get some breakfast, and there'll be a happy song playing on the radio, and you'll sing along with it, and that will make things a little better. It takes time and patience and love, but you can get through it."

"Don't be offended, Daddy, but you're not the best advertisement for time healing all wounds."

"Some wounds are worse than others."

"Maybe we should go back inside. Do you know if Toby ate all the green olives?"

"I think there are some left, but you're out of luck if you want any potato salad."

"I love you, Daddy. I'm glad you came. I'm sorry for unloading all this on you."

"I love you too, sweetie."

22

I wanted a boy. We had two daughters, and I wanted a boy. I didn't think it was that much to ask, but apparently it was. If we'd known about the genetics at the time, I guess I would have wanted another girl, but we didn't.

We had the name picked out even before he was conceived. He was named Leonard Charles, after Danielle's brother Leo and my brother Charlie. Leo went to the Air Force Academy and learned to fly the F-4. He got shot down over North Vietnam in 1965. He was trying to take out an antiaircraft missile battery, but the Russians manning the battery found him first, and he never got to pull his parachute. Charlie was a sergeant in the Marine Corps, and he went MIA in Laos when his helicopter went down. It took the State Department until 1989 to get the bodies back.

Leonard Charles Morse was a good baby, as babies go. He slept when he was supposed to and ate when he was supposed to. He was a big, fat, happy baby, and when Danielle put him in those OshKosh overalls, he looked just like Junior Samples from the old *Hee Haw* show, so that's what we called him. The only times he was cranky was when he had an ear infection or something like that. He got those every once in a while, that and the eczema, but we didn't have any idea that he was sicker than any other baby until he got the fever that killed him.

For months after Junior died, Danielle would wake up in the middle of the night and think she had heard a baby cry. Most of the time she'd realize it was a dream, and I'd wake up and hear her crying. But sometimes she'd elbow me and tell me to go look after the baby, and I'd have to explain, and that would start us both crying. Part of the reason we decided to have another baby was so we could hear that baby crying again and know it was real—so hearing the sounds of any baby would become bearable again.

When you lose a baby, a big part of what you lose is the potential of what that baby can become—you lose birthday parties and high school graduations and seeing that baby grow to be brave and strong and noble. All that exists as potentiality and not memory—you grieve for your child as a baby, cuddly, sweet, sensitive, inquisitive, all those things. I never saw Alicia's little boy. I never got to hold him in my arms or burp him or have him spit up all over me. But I grieved just the same.

I woke up the next morning to find that an Arctic cold front had dumped half an inch of what the Weather Channel calls "wintry mix" on New Jersey. After a good bit of cursing, I managed to clean all the snow off my rental car. I found a Dunkin' Donuts not too far from my hotel and grabbed a coffee. I hadn't been too impressed with the Dunkin' Donuts coffee you get in the K-cup, but it tasted a lot better on a freezing morning in the Northeast. I got a dozen crullers and a big jug of hot coffee to take to Alicia's.

I let the little GPS widget guide me through the side streets to Alicia's house. Her car was gone. Toby's was parked on the street; someone had cleared the snow off of it. I didn't know if that meant she was still around or not. I hoped so.

Toby came around from the back of the house as I pulled into the driveway. He was wearing a huge gray parka with a fur hood that enveloped his thin frame and made him look like a refugee from a failed mission to the South Pole.

"Thought I heard someone pull up," he said. "What's in the bag?"

"Crullers and coffee," I said. "Where's Alicia?"

"Work. She decided to go in to the studio today; they're casting bronze, and it's warmer there than it is in the house. Let me take that inside for you; I'll be a second—keep the car running, if you don't mind."

"OK. Why?"

"Oh. Alicia sent you a text. Did you get it?"

"I guess not." I'd left my cell phone in the glove compartment of my truck, which was still sitting in the hotel parking lot in Atlanta, but I didn't think that Toby needed to know that.

"OK. Let me get this inside and I'll print the instructions."

I couldn't guess what she had written to me, but if she was letting Toby print it, it couldn't be anything too bad. Toby emerged from the house, dusting cruller sugar off his nylon gloves, and got in the passenger seat.

"You ready to go?" he asked, waving a small sheaf of paper. "Big day ahead."

"You say so. Um, some of that coffee was for me."

"Don't worry about it. We're going to get a real breakfast. You like bacon?"

"I like bacon. I don't eat breakfast out a lot, but I like bacon."

"Then we're set. You know how to get back on 287?"

"Yeah."

"Good. Let's go. I'm starving."

We went to a place called Harold's, which was a few exits east of New Brunswick—someplace called Raritan Center, although it didn't look like the center of anything except ugly. A big FedEx depot sat across the street. It was how I expected New Jersey to look, which is to say a hundred and eighty degrees different than where I grew up in Alabama.

"What kind of food do they have here?" I asked.

"Deli sandwiches. I mean, it's not a real Manhattan deli. It's not kosher either—you can get bacon. And you want the bacon. I mean, I'll get the bacon, and you can have some if you want."

"What's the attraction? There's got to be closer places in better neighborhoods."

"Food's good."

We got a table, and I took a look at the menu. "You've got to be kidding me," I said.

"What?"

"Pancakes. Look at this. They want seventeen ninety-five for pancakes. I know stuff is more expensive in the Northeast, but that's insane."

"That's what I'm getting, the Danish pancake. Wait until you see it. It's huge. It's the size of a spare tire."

"Why would you want a pancake the size of a spare tire?"

"All the food here is huge," he explained. "The sandwiches here are huge. It's expensive, yeah, but the portions are big enough to share. If you're not all that hungry, you can have some of my pancake, and we can split the bacon. My treat, anyway. You might want to take a look at Alicia's list."

I ordered some coffee and pulled out the list—which wasn't long by itself, but Alicia had printed out Google Maps directions for every place we were supposed to go. "It's my day off," Toby said, "so I get to drive around with you, get you set for the wedding. I don't know how it was when you got married, but there's stuff you have to do I never thought about. Never even imagined."

"Men's Wearhouse?" I asked.

"Tuxedo rental. First stop. Both of us need to get measured."

"I wasn't planning on wearing a tux," I said. It did make at least a little sense, though—I wouldn't have to leave Blue Ridge to buy a suit, so that was convenient in its way.

"I got news for you. Tux. With a currant cummerbund. Try saying that five times fast."

"What's current about the cummerbund?"

"Not current as in current *affairs*. Currant as in currant *jelly*. It's a dark purple, and it's the secondary wedding color. You get a currant tie so you match the red cabbage in the salad."

"So I match what again?"

"Hand to God. We went to the Palace for an event last month—some continuing-education event for nurses. I mean, that's not why we were there—they brought us in and put us in a back room so we could sample some of the things on the menu. Set up the table the way that the tables for our wedding would be set up, complete with these purple napkins."

"Please tell me you didn't invite my ex-wife to this."

"She was the one who set it up, so of course she was there. And they brought out the salad, which was this incredible thing, ham and pasta and chopped olives on a bed of red cabbage. And Mrs. M throws a fit because the red cabbage clashed with the purple napkins. I thought we were going to have to move the wedding someplace else the way she was going on about the napkins."

"I'm not surprised."

"Well, they can't change the color of the cabbage, so they brought out these different napkins—nicer ones, I guess. They were a darker purple—currant is what Mrs. M called it—and that became the secondary wedding color. Didn't cost us anything extra, which I expect is why she did it."

"Again, not surprised. She's an interior designer. Pitching fits about color schemes is part of the job description. So is getting expensive stuff on the cheap."

"Danielle's dad is picking up the tab, so I'm not complaining about it. Not one bit."

Toby's pancake came, and it was as large as advertised. I cut off a wedge for my breakfast—far more than anyone normal would ever need—and he went to work on the rest of it.

"So we get the tuxedos rented," he said between bites. "Then we run over to the Macy's in the Bridgewater mall—we have to pick out groomsman gifts. You get one too, so whatever you're good with, that's what we're going to get. Then it's over to the florist to pick

133

out boutonnieres. Last stop is the printer's to pick up the thank-you cards. If you'd like, we can drive by the Palace so you'll know where it is when you come back up here."

"I wouldn't mind seeing Alicia at her studio," I said. "I want to get a look at that big football."

"She'll be wearing a welding hood the whole time and won't acknowledge your existence. Not while they're casting, she won't. It's a busy day, and it's a big project. I'm just glad she didn't take that job in Boulder, or she never would have got it finished. She told you about that, right? She said she'd mentioned it."

"Oh. I didn't know she'd told you about that."

"We had a long talk last night. I don't know what you told her, but I appreciate it."

"All I did was ask her not to make any decisions she couldn't take back. To be honest, I wouldn't have been surprised if she was halfway to Colorado already." Toby looked up, startled, and I instantly knew I'd made a mistake.

"What do you mean, 'halfway to Colorado'? Did she tell you she was planning on leaving without me?" He sounded injured.

"Well, no. I mean, yes. She said she wasn't sure what she wanted to do."

Toby put his knife and fork down and took a thoughtful sip of his coffee. "She told you she was thinking about canceling the wedding?"

"Is that what she told you?"

"No. She's unhappy, yeah. It's understandable. I'm not happy about it either. But we love each other. She wouldn't leave me."

"I guess not," I said. I could have told him about all the boys she'd unceremoniously dumped in high school. I could have told him about Sean, the boyfriend she'd left behind in Berkeley who showed up at our door looking for her. I could have told him about Eric, the philosophy professor she'd gotten engaged to in New York—that engagement didn't last three weeks, and Alicia was halfway to New Mexico before he noticed she was gone. I figured Toby either knew about all of this or else he didn't, and if not, it wasn't my place to tell him.

134

"I know what she's like," he said. "If she wants to go to Boulder, she will. But I don't think she wants tenure—she'd rather move around. But if she wants to go, I'll go with her, even if I have to work in a warehouse or something. I love your daughter, Will, and I'm not going to let her walk out on me if I can help it."

"Well, I wish you all the luck in the world," I said, not telling him that I thought he'd need it. "Why are we going to Macy's again?"

"Groomsman gifts."

"Like a beer stein?"

"No. Can't do that. My best man just got his five-year sobriety chip."

"Oh. Well, screw it. We can go to Home Depot, get power drills."

"That sounds a little phallic. No offense."

"Well, you pick something then."

"We'll figure something out. Hey, did I tell you I saw Auburn playing in one of the bowl games? I thought they looked very sharp."

I took a piece of bacon off the mound next to the giant pancake. It was every bit as good as Toby had said. Maybe there was hope for him after all.

"I mean, compared to the other team. Those were the worst uniforms I've ever seen anyone wear. In terms of aesthetics, Auburn was loads better."

I tried not to roll my eyes. "Well, it was a good game. I wish Cam Newton had stayed another year."

"Who's Cam Newton?"

"Finish your pancake, son."

23

"So how did you guys do on your big day out?" Alicia asked.

She'd picked up sushi for them and chicken teriyaki for me. I have nothing against sushi. I just think it would be better dipped in cornmeal batter and deep-fried in peanut oil. But that's my opinion. I'm not what you would call adventurous in terms of food. I didn't eat very much anyway, as I was worried about what the teriyaki sauce would do to my system, not to mention the fact that my slice of breakfast pancake had settled way down in my gut.

"We got the tuxes, no problem," Toby said. "The flowers and cards, no problem. We did a little detour on the groomsman gifts, though."

"Should I be worried?" Alicia asked. "Please tell me you didn't talk each other into getting something stupid or dangerous."

"We got binoculars," I said. "They're very nice."

"The fireworks stand was closed," Toby said. "It's too bad. Nothing says 'thank you for coming to our wedding' like a twin pack of cherry bombs."

"That would be so much funnier if I didn't think that your cousins wouldn't sneak out the back door and fire Roman candles into the woods."

"No fireworks, babe. Promise. Not emotional ones either."

"Let's hope not. Did you drive by the Palace and show Daddy?"

"He did indeed," I said. The Palace at Somerset Hills did look something like the White House—by which I mean it looked something like what you'd get if you took the White House, built an exact replica on the back side of it, and built a Greek temple in the middle. It was a mile or so down the street from my hotel, screened off from the nearby convention center and office parks by a thick stand of pines.

"Isn't it gorgeous?" Alicia said. "I never would have picked it out myself, but we got lucky. Aunt Linda's daughter Susan was going to get married there, but her fiancée turned out to be bisexual, so she called off the wedding. Granddaddy had already put down the deposit, so he told us that we could use it."

"How did the casting go?" I asked around a mouthful of rice.

"Lovely," she said. "Couldn't have gone better. Last time we tried it, one of the forms cracked, but this time it worked out great. We have to let it cool some more and we'll be able to try welding on the struts tomorrow."

"This is for the big football?" I asked.

"Yes. The football is divided into four sections, like a real football is. Each section is then divided into sixteen different slices, each slice with a slightly different shape and surface pattern—sixty-four pieces total. When each slice is done, we bolt it onto a stainless steel structure that holds the entire sculpture together—finished that over the summer. These were slices eighteen and nineteen, so we're over a quarter of the way finished."

"Can I come by and see it tomorrow?"

"Sure, if you don't mind a little noise. But you have to tell me one thing first."

"Shoot."

"Who exactly is Dot Crawford, and why did she send me a bouquet of cut-up pineapple and melons at work?"

"Pineapple?" For some reason, the second part of her question surprised me more than the first part.

"We have pineapple?" Toby asked.

"In the fridge. Try to save me some of the chocolate-covered ones if you don't mind."

"She sent you a *pineapple*?" I asked.

"It's this new thing. Instead of flowers, you send cut-up fruit that looks like flowers. Now quit stalling, Daddy. Spill."

"It's complicated," I said.

"Oh, my God," Alicia said. "She's the mystery woman. The one in the blue Honda that pulled out when I drove up there. You've been holding out on me."

"That's her," I said. "I mean, kind of. That day you were there was the first time that I ever saw her, but she came by a few days later, and one thing kind of led to another. I'm sorry. I haven't had a chance to tell you about this."

"That explains how she knew who I was. Did you tell her about the baby?"

"I'd mentioned your name and where you lived. And I told her why I was coming up here before I left."

"Oh, my God. This sounds like a serious relationship," Alicia said. "I'm impressed, Daddy. I didn't think you had it in you."

"Hey, we could have a double wedding," Toby said.

"I did not come all the way up here to be teased about my relationship," I said.

"If she's coming to the wedding," Toby said, "it'll foul up the seating arrangement."

"It's not a big deal," Alicia said. "We can work around it. So how serious is this, anyway?"

"I don't know, not yet," I said.

"She must like you if she went out of her way to send me pineapple," she said. "Do you know for sure whether she's coming or not?"

"I mentioned it before I left. I think so. I'll let you know."

"Right now," Toby explained, "we have you sitting with my mother."

"You have a mother," I said. "That's too bad. For a moment I was wondering if you were the last survivor of a doomed alien race."

"You two stop it. Daddy, trust us. We have it all set up. You'll be in one corner with Toby's mom, and Mom is in the opposite corner at the same table with Toby's dad and stepmother. So everybody's happy, and nobody is going to spend the evening sniping at each other. Will you let me know if Ms. Crawford decides to come with you?"

"Of course."

After Toby finished plowing through a huge bowl of ice cream and chocolate-covered pineapple, he started on the dishes, and Alicia went outside for a cigarette. I went out with her.

"So what do you think of him? Now that you've had the chance to see him in his native environment?"

"I envy his metabolism," I said.

"I don't know where he puts it all. He's a bad influence on me. I'm going to have trouble squeezing into my wedding dress."

"So you're sticking around. What changed your mind?" I asked.

"Casting the bronze today. I told you that the last time we did it, the form cracked, right?"

"Yeah."

"Ruined a week's worth of work. I was so upset. I'd worked hard on making sure everything was perfect, and it wasn't. Not because of anything I did wrong; it just cracked. When we talked to the doctor about having the abortion, I remember thinking about how the baby was just broken like that, that he couldn't be fixed. And then, I kept thinking that maybe other things in my life were broken like that, too broken to fix, the way that you and Mom were after Trixie died."

I couldn't think of something to say that wouldn't make things worse, so I didn't say anything.

"I could have melted the whole thing down. I felt that way about it, the same way I felt about taking off and going to Colorado. But when I woke up this morning, I went into the studio, and I made another form. This time it was stronger. It was the same bronze, the same heat, but this time I knew better, and I made something beautiful, and it was OK. I liked that. I liked that feeling. I liked having a second chance to fix things."

"That's all most people want, is that second chance. Did you tell Toby?"

"No. But I need to. I will. I couldn't stand knowing that I would break his heart if I left. I couldn't just turn my back on him. And I can't turn my back on my baby, even after what I did. I loved him too, and if I left, it would mean that the love I felt for him didn't mean anything. I couldn't do that."

"I know what you mean."

"I know you do," she said, and we stood there a long time, listening to Toby wash the dishes. "I'm glad you came, Daddy. It meant a lot."

"I'll stop by tomorrow morning. I'm looking forward to seeing your giant football."

"Don't be too disappointed. It doesn't look much like a football yet, but it will. You have to give it a little time, that's all."

It didn't look much like a football, but you could tell that it was going to be impressive. Alicia gave me the cook's tour of her workshop, and then I drove to the airport, turned in the rental car, and got a seat on the four o'clock flight to Atlanta. I cashed in some of my frequent-flyer points for an upgrade to first class. That turned out to be a very good idea. The only problem with it—as it turned out—was that I hadn't thought to bring a book with me, and I didn't think to get one at the airport. So after the shot of whiskey they served me, a nap seemed to be in order.

That turned out not to be such a good idea.

24

So Alicia had an abortion.

Is that you, Trix?

Who else would it be? Perfect Alicia. Pretty Alicia. Everyone's favorite daughter.

Don't talk that way, Trixie. You know that's not true.

Sucked that baby right down the sink. Mommy must have been furious. If I ever pulled a stunt like that she'd kick me right out of the family, but I bet she forgave her darling, sweet Alicia right away.

It's not right to judge her. She was in a bad place. Anyone might have done the same thing.

That's right, Daddy. You go right ahead and make excuses. That's what you're good at. She kills your grandson, and you make excuses. Some half-literate dimwit truck driver crashes into Francie's car, and you make excuses for that too.

We've been over this, Trixie. It was a terrible thing that happened. But it wasn't anyone's fault. It was an accident. If they had left ten minutes earlier or later, they wouldn't have died.

But they did. Now they're dead. Now I'm dead. Now your baby grandson is dead. Dead dead dead dead dead. How do you like that?

I don't, not at all. And I hate talking to you when you're acting this way.

HOW AM I SUPPOSED TO ACT?

You're not real. You're a hallucination caused by stress.

IF I'M NOT REAL IT'S BECAUSE YOU KILLED ME.

I did not. You know what happened. You did it to yourself.

IT WAS YOU. YOU AND MOMMY. YOU MADE ME DO IT. YOU KILLED ME; DON'T LIE AND SAY YOU'RE NOT FUCKING RESPONSIBLE.

Stop it, please, Trixie. Stop screaming at me. You don't know what you're saying.

I KNOW EXACTLY WHAT I'M SAYING. I'M DEAD NOW. YOU CAN'T DO ANYTHING WORSE TO ME THAN WHAT YOU'VE ALREADY DONE. YOU CAN'T TELL ME WHAT TO DO ANYMORE. I HOPE YOU ROT. YOU AND YOUR PRECIOUS, PERFECT ALICIA. I HOPE YOU ALL FUCKING ROT IN HELL HELL **HELL HELL HELL**.

Stop it. Stop it. Make it stop. Make it stop.

25

"Make it stop. *Make it stop.*"

"Sir? Sir? Are you OK? Mr. Morse?"

"Make it—wait, wait, wait. Where am I?"

"You're on an airplane headed for Atlanta. Are you all right?" the flight attendant asked. "You seemed upset."

"I'm all right," I said. "I could use some cold water."

"You don't look so good," she said, and she was right. I was breathing hard and my hands were shaking more than they usually do. I could barely hold on to the water once she brought it, but I was able to drink it and only spill a drop or two.

I spent the rest of the flight being thankful I had gotten the upgrade to first class. If I had stayed in coach, chances were that I would have been corralled by an air marshal and frog-marched off the plane once we landed. But I was in first class, where you get a little more leeway.

The plane landed in Atlanta, as they say, without incident, and a wheelchair waited for me at the end of the Jetway to take me to the little clinic they have at the airport. At the clinic, a nurse took my temperature and blood pressure, and asked me for a urine sample.

"How come?" I asked.

"We want to make sure you're not diabetic," the nurse said. "You could have had low blood sugar and not been aware of it."

I figured that this was a white lie; they were probably checking for alcohol or drugs, but I wasn't worried either way.

"It was a bad dream," I said.

"Well, it could be something more serious," she said. "Do you have any trauma in your recent past?"

"Yes," I said.

"Do you want to talk about it?"

"No."

I remember all of it. I remember Trixie's naked white body streaked with red gore. I remember driving her to the hospital. I remember hearing her scream for death in the backseat. I remember leaving her to die in the emergency room. I remember waiting in an antiseptic, sterile examining room—not too different than the one I was in—and knowing that it was her blood clotting on my clothes. I remember how I didn't sleep for weeks after she died, not until my lawyers arranged for me to get pills so I could appear before the grand jury and sound reasonably coherent in doing so. The threat of prison didn't scare me as much as what was waiting for me when I fell asleep.

The doctors said the dreams would recede, and, for once, they were right about that. I don't see Trixie's death in my dreams unless I do something foolish, like watching a horror flick or a graphic documentary—or unless I see someone get hurt on a news show. But she does show up in my dreams from time to time, and they always end with her screaming at me, and when I wake up, it's because I'm screaming back at her.

"It's better if you talk about it," the nurse said. She was older, late thirties, with dark red hair like the embers of a dying campfire, streaked here and there with ash.

"My oldest daughter and my youngest daughter died five years ago, about four months apart, and it was very traumatic," I told her. "But it doesn't have anything to do with what happened today."

"What makes you say that?"

"My middle daughter had a miscarriage. I went up to New Jersey to check on her. While I was there, I ran into my ex-wife, and she threw a fit. It wasn't pleasant. And then my daughter almost broke up with her fiancée. It was a stressful trip, that's all. I had a drink on the plane, and that means I let my guard down. I'm sorry if I caused any problems."

"It's the prior trauma that I'm concerned about. Anyone can have a stressful day. But if there's an underlying reason behind it, then it can be an indication of a more severe problem."

"I had a bad dream, that's all. It could happen to anyone."

"I think you're OK to go home. But I would feel better if someone was able to drive you back to Blue Ridge. Is there anyone who can pick you up and take you home? If there is, I can call them, explain the situation, and you're free to go."

"If not?"

"I can call you an ambulance and send you to Grady and have them keep you overnight for observation."

"Her name is Dot Crawford. The number's in my wallet."

26

"I'm sorry I'm late," Dot said. "I had a class, and I didn't get the message until after it was over. I came as soon as I could."

"Don't worry about it," I said. "I'm just glad you could come."

We sat in a booth at the IHOP off I-75, north of the airport. I needed coffee, and Dot wanted to go someplace nicer than the Waffle House.

"How is your daughter?" Dot asked.

"She's fine," I said. I had decided to spare Dot all of the details about the abortion. "I mean, it was a little rocky, and a little emotional, especially with my ex-wife being there. But I think she'll be OK."

"I felt terrible for her, losing her baby all of a sudden like that."

"You must have," I said, "because you sent her that pineapple bouquet."

"'Pineapple,' he says. That was a forty-dollar floral fruit arrangement. It looked very nice on the website."

"I understand. It was a nice thing to do. I couldn't figure out how you were able to send it to her at work."

"Well, it was easier that way," she explained. "I knew her name, and you said you were going to New Jersey. I found her faculty page on the Rutgers website. I checked out her bio, and it said she'd gone to high school in Atlanta, so I was sure it was her and not somebody else."

"The wonders of modern technology," I said.

"Speaking of the wonders of modern technology, if you wanted to ask me out again, there are more direct ways than asking Delta Airlines to arrange it for you. I mean, it was very sweet, but maybe a little awkward."

I took a big bite of my French toast. "I'm sorry that I put you on the spot like that. All that happened was that I had a bad dream. I was on the plane, and I had a bad dream, maybe the worst dream I've ever had. I've had a very stressful few days, and it caught up with me. Anyway, I woke up and I was screaming, and they were worried about me and wanted me to get checked out."

"Was the dream about Trixie?"

"It was. I didn't know you knew about her. I guess they told you."

"I knew already. I recognized your name on that little football on the mantel. Besides, if I didn't, I would have found out when I Googled you."

"You knew all this time?" I asked.

"I remember when it happened, and how terrible it was. I don't hold what happened against you. Nobody should, including you, but I have a feeling that you do anyway. If that makes sense."

"Is that what you want to talk about?"

"No," she said. "I want to talk about whether or not I am going to have to do this again anytime soon."

"I can't think why. This was an unusual occurrence."

"You're an unusual man."

"Be that as it may, I don't want to put myself through this again any more than you want to come down here and bail me out."

"I talked to the nurse," Dot said. "She thought you had PTSD, and I think that makes sense. Have you gotten any treatment for it? Talked to anyone?"

"More than once. It hasn't been helpful. They gave me medication for a while, and I took it, but it didn't help."

"Maybe if you talked about it," she said.

"There's no treatment for grief and sorrow. That's what I have. Can't be fixed by doctors; can't be washed away with drugs or drinking."

Dot waved over a waitress and got a coffee refill. She poured in a little sugar and a little cream, trying to get the balance right. She took a sip and then put the cup down.

"I like you," she said. "You're smart and honest. I could see this relationship turning into something, down the road. But I'm worried about you. I don't want to be with someone who's as emotionally damaged as I think you are. I'm concerned, not because I want anything from you, but because I care about you."

"I'm flattered."

"You believe that, right?"

"Of course," I said, although I wasn't that sure. I did want to believe that Dot cared about me, but part of me still thought that I might be fooling myself. "I don't think the conversation ends there, though."

She sat back in the booth, her platinum hair framed in the cheap brown leather. "This is what we're going to do. You're coming back home with me. I told the nurse I wouldn't let you drive home tonight. We'll get some pizza or something, unless you want to eat here."

"Pizza is fine." I don't believe in eating breakfast for dinner.

"I have a spare bedroom, and you're welcome to it. I can make you breakfast if you want."

"With you so far."

"In the morning, I go to work. You can walk from my condo to the North Avenue MARTA station and take the train to the airport to pick up your truck. If you want to have lunch, you can pick me up at Georgia State, and we'll go somewhere."

"I think I need to head home," I said.

"Suit yourself."

"And what happens then?"

"I think we both need a little time off. I am driving down to Columbus this weekend for a project I'm working on. But the next weekend, though, if the weather cooperates, I can drive up Friday evening and stay over maybe through Saturday night. If you're ready, we can talk a little. You can tell me about your daughter, as much or as little as you want to tell me."

"Why do you want to know?" I asked.

"For heaven's sake. I would think such a thing would be obvious to the dullest imagination."

"Indulge me." I drank the dregs of my coffee and put the cup off to the side; the waitress loped over and refilled it. It was a slow night, I guessed.

"I won't deny that I am curious, and if I can satisfy my morbid curiosity, so much the better. But if we're going to be together, however we can manage to be together, I need to know about you. If you wake up in the middle of the night screaming, I want to know why, and the only way I can do that is if you tell me."

"I don't know that I'm ready for that," I said.

"Maybe we can start off small. Tell you what, you tell me one thing about you—something I don't know or couldn't guess—and I'll tell you something about me."

"Why do I have to go first?"

"Because I bailed you out of airport jail," Dot explained.

"OK. But if I tell you, you're going to think I'm crazy."

"Sounds promising. Spill."

I took a sip of coffee, more for the dramatic pause than because I needed it. "You know that World War I genealogy stuff I was telling you about?"

"Sure," she said.

"I don't have any way to prove it, you understand, but I think I may be the rightful heir to the Duchy of Newcastle-on-Tyne."

She coughed a little bit, the way you do when you're covering up a laugh.

"I told you," I said.

"Well, in for a penny, in for a pound. Explain, please."

My grandfather fought in the First World War. He was serving as a private in the British Expeditionary Force under the name of

Harry Cavendish. He got hit with gas in 1915, somewhere around Ypres, and got sent back to England to recover. He met my grandmother, who was a nurse at one of the big military hospitals, and they got married. They sent him back to the front lines, and he died in October 1917, during the First Battle of Passchendaele. As best I can determine, a German shell fell on top of him and ground him into paste. My mother was born three months later.

My mother grew up in England and became a nurse, as her mother had been before her. She met my dad in a military hospital in 1944. He was one of the original Yanks in the R.A.F., although—being from Alabama and all—he hated being called that. He was a tail gunner on a Lancaster bomber; it crashed on takeoff on what would have been his seventh bombing mission over Germany. He made it out of the wreckage with a broken ankle. The pilot and two others weren't so lucky.

They got married in 1945, the same day they dropped the bomb on Nagasaki. She came over with him, and he opened up a dental practice in Dothan, Alabama, where my brother Charlie and I were born. My mother never went back to England. She worked hard to lose her accent and become an American.

All my mother ever told us about my grandfather was that her mother's impression was that he was well educated, and that he might have been an aristocrat, a "gentleman private" serving under an assumed name.

"That's where I started looking," I said. "I wanted to find out his real name and why he was hiding it."

"And you think he was a duke."

"I still don't know for sure, not enough to convince anyone. I think Cavendish was an alias. But it turns out the first Duke of Newcastle was a Cavendish."

"So it's a family name."

"The family name was Clinton—there were several names, but that's one of the main ones. There was a Henry Clinton—he was a nephew of the duke—who was a lieutenant with one of the first regular army divisions sent to Belgium. He was court-martialed when he refused an order to send his company into machine-gun fire."

"Sounds unfair," she said.

"Well, the point is that Henry Clinton disappeared after he was court-martialed, and Harry Cavendish enlisted in a territorial regiment not too long after that. I don't have any way to prove that they were the same person, but if they were, that puts me in line to inherit the title. It's vacant; the last duke died years ago."

"And what would you do with it once you had it?"

"I hadn't given that much thought," I said. "I don't want the seat in the House of Lords, and the family castle belongs to the National Trust. I know it would make my mother happy, but she's been dead a long time. I'm not sure why I care, but it's been interesting finding out, and the research has been keeping me busy. Does all this sound crazy yet?"

"Yes. But you seem to be thinking coherently and are oriented in reality, and I don't think you're going to start foaming at the mouth anytime soon."

"That's a relief. You mind if I pick up the tab?" I asked.

"Thank you, Your Worship."

"It's 'Your Grace.' I looked it up."

"A thousand apologies, my lord."

"That's 'my lord Duke,' " I explained. "If you're going to make fun of me, you should do it right."

"Of course."

"So now it's your turn to tell me something."

"On our twentieth wedding anniversary, my ex-husband told me he was gay. He moved out a week later. The last time I checked, he was working in a Mexican restaurant in San Diego and shacking up with two illegal-immigrant busboys."

"That's quite a story."

"Unlike yours, it has the advantage of being concise. You finished with your coffee?"

"Yeah," I said. "Let's go."

154

27

Dot lived in a condo a little north of downtown, between the Gordon Biersch microbrewery and the Vortex hamburger joint. She ordered in from Domino's, pepperoni and black olives for me, pineapple for her. We watched an episode of something called *Hoarders*, which I enjoyed because it was about people who are more screwed up than I am.

I decided to stay up and watch some more TV after Dot went to bed. She had a forty-five-inch plasma screen, which was adequate for my purposes. Better yet, it had the feature that turns on the closed-captioning when you hit the mute button—not something I need in the cabin when I'm the only one there, but it's more considerate that way, and I didn't want to fumble with the TV controls if I didn't have to.

Around three in the morning I found a Charlie Rose interview with some academic or other. It was boring, but quiet, and I found myself yawning deeply about ten minutes in. I knew I was going to fall asleep any minute, and I was worried that I would fall asleep and have another bad dream and give Dot more cause for alarm. But it was too late and I was too tired. I switched off the TV and fell asleep on the couch.

When I talk to Trixie in my dreams, she's always fourteen. That was the worst year of her childhood, the year we had to hold her out of school, the year we had to put her in the hospital. That was the year when her sullen teenage angst metastasized into a deep need to cause emotional—and sometimes physical—harm to everyone around her.

That's the Trixie I don't want to see, the Trixie who screams, the Trixie who curses, the Trixie who takes gleeful pleasure in the suffering of others, the Trixie who says horrible things as loud as she can because causing you pain is the only way to relieve her own.

I fought for years to help her keep that part of her personality under control, and I thought I knew how, but I was wrong. In the end, it took over and destroyed not only Trixie, but the hopes and dreams of everyone who loved her, who wanted her to be happy and succeed and find some peace in her life.

I wish I could talk to the adult Trixie, the young woman she was becoming, to let her know that I love her and miss her. But that part of her is gone. All that's left is what wakes me up in the middle of the night.

When I woke up, it was a little after ten. Dot had left for work, but she had set out a couple of bagels with cream cheese and a nice note with a MARTA token taped to the top of it. I got my stuff together and walked out in the cool January air, taking my time on the way down to the station.

I had avoided Atlanta for so long that I had almost forgotten why. Even now, in the late morning when the streets were a little quieter, it was intimidating and impersonal and gray. I didn't recognize that many landmarks until I made the turn onto North Avenue to get to the MARTA station. The Coca-Cola skyscraper loomed bone-white in the distance.

Coca-Cola was the only place I ever worked after I got cut by the Falcons. I had worked my way up to a big office on one of the upper floors. I had friends there, and at my church, and throughout the

Auburn and NFL alumni networks. All of them turned their backs on me after Trixie died.

If the police had listened to me, if they had ruled her death was a suicide from the outset, it might have been very different. But that's not what happened. I was taken to the police station straight from the emergency room, still wearing the surgical scrubs a kind nurse had given me when the cops took my blood-soaked shirt away. The next morning, I was arraigned and charged with murdering my daughter. The judge denied me bail, and I stayed in jail for three months. They let me out to go to the funeral, which drew hundreds of people, not one of whom would talk to me or look me in the eye.

It was hard to blame them. The police said I was a murderer. The district attorney went on the local news and did interviews and called me a monster. Trixie's death was the lead story on the Nancy Grace show for a week.

The murder charges were absurd, but it took my lawyer a long time to convince anybody of that. The district attorney was determined to nail me for something, though, and I suspect Danielle was behind that particular effort. So I went before the grand jury, charged with reckless endangerment. They declined to indict once they heard all the details about Trixie's fascination with knives and her history of harming herself.

Danielle still blamed me. She didn't so much as visit me in jail, and she served me divorce papers the day after I was released for good. Her friends and her family sided with her, of course, but even people who knew me and not Danielle thought I must have been at fault.

I went back to Coca-Cola after I was freed. I was met in the lobby by a brace of security guards. I thought they were going to fire me right then and there, but they didn't. They tried very hard to get me to take early retirement. I was all in favor of that, but I worked it out so I could stay an extra couple of months to allow my stock options to vest.

Those last couple of months, I mostly wore out a circuit between my sterile Midtown condo and my office. But every once in a while,

I'd go out to The Varsity or the Nuevo Laredo, places I used to hang out, and people would point their fingers at me and talk about me behind my back. One of Trixie's friends from high school screamed at me in the middle of Lenox Mall, calling me a murderer and all sorts of vile names. I could have called the police on her, but I'd had my fill of dealing with them. I'd had my fill of Atlanta, too.

I bought my ticket at the MARTA station. To keep myself from getting vertigo, I gripped the handrail of the escalator all the way down to the platform. I had to wait only a minute or two for the train. I got off at the Hartsfield station, at the end of the line. I took the shuttle over to the hotel, where I picked up my truck. I stopped to gas up and get some coffee, and then pulled onto I-75, north toward home.

Somewhere around the far side of Marietta I decided I needed to get good and drunk. I stopped at a liquor store in East Ellijay and picked up the essentials—two big bottles of Smirnoff vanilla vodka and two plastic bottles of Coke Zero, because they were both on sale. I knew I needed milk, so I got a gallon at the Conoco in Blue Ridge and decided to pick up a couple of cans of honey-roasted cashews— they were a bit overpriced, but they would help the drinking process along.

If you want to get drunk in a hurry, vodka is a good way to go. It's cheaper—as long as you stay away from the overpriced stuff, which is not too hard to do—and it doesn't have as much of the chemicals that cause hangovers. I don't intentionally decide to get plastered all that often anymore, but when I do, I want it to be as effective and pain-free as I can manage.

The Coke Zero is part of that. I don't enjoy it much, but it's a tolerable drink when you mix in the flavored vodka. I could have gone with real Coke and plain vodka, but drinking as much Coke as I'd need to get as drunk as I wanted to get doesn't make sense for me anymore. The sugar makes me tense when I want to be relaxed, and it activates my mind when all I want to do is shut it down for a little while. And I can't drink Diet Coke at all. I never liked the stuff. I understood why the company had to put it out, to get back its market share, but I never figured out why it had to taste like the inside of a chemical vat instead of, well, Coca-Cola. I felt the same way about New Coke when that came out, but it's still a sore subject, and I see no reason to rehash it. Coke Zero isn't a great drink, but it's an improvement.

Part of it was about being able to sleep for a few hours without being disturbed by anything other than the threat of a hangover. Part of it was a hope that the alcohol would wash away the stress of a trying week. Part of it was not having that much else to do for the rest of the week other than be alone with my thoughts.

I put the milk in the fridge and spread the rest of the supplies on the coffee table. I got out of my sweaty traveling clothes, took a shower, and put on a soft thermal shirt and sweatpants. I was going to wake up in those clothes, and it was a good bet that I was going to throw up in them, and there's no reason not to be comfortable. I switched on the TV and turned it to the bluegrass music channel and poured my first drink. It didn't take long to finish, or to pour the second, or the third.

28

Hey, Daddy.

Hey, Francie.

You're drinking again.

Don't you start with me, young lady. I've had it up to here with you hallucinations. All you ever do is cause me problems.

You've been talking to Trixie. Only Trixie gets you this worked up.

I don't want to deal with your sister right now. I spend too much time thinking about her as it is.

She's upset, that's all. You know she's always been jealous of Alicia.

She could have had whatever she wanted in life, and she chose death. She doesn't get to be jealous.

She still has those feelings, though. Death doesn't change that. Death just changes your perspective on things a little. Trixie wasn't ever that great at the whole perspective thing. It is all or nothing with her. You know that.

I am not inclined to cut your sister any slack. I know she is angry and bitter and jealous, but she does not get to take that out on me.

She doesn't have anyone else.

I know.

It's not just about her being angry. She has to watch Alicia getting married, and that means she gets all the attention. Trixie doesn't have any of that, and it makes her act out.

I had a long trip, and I had to deal with Alicia losing her baby. Not to mention hanging out with and her space cadet of a fiancée. Not to mention your mother shifting into Warpath Mode. I don't need Trixie making my life any more difficult than it is.

I was so sorry to hear about Alicia losing the baby. She must have felt terrible.

It was a hard thing that she did. I wish that the baby would have been all right, but he wasn't.

He's all right.

I wish I could be sure.

He is. This is a good place for babies. His uncle Junior is showing him the ropes.

I miss Junior. I miss Trixie, even though she yells at me. I miss you.

I know you do, Daddy. I miss you too. You know that.

I don't know anything anymore, Francie. I just don't. I wanted to be there for Alicia, but I couldn't protect her when she needed me. I want to be part of her life, but I don't want to bring her any more pain. I want to go to the wedding, but I don't want to ruin it for her.

You want to be with your lady friend, but you don't want to risk getting hurt.

Oh, for God's sake. That's not what I'm unhappy about.

Is it more that you're unhappy with her, or is it more that you don't want to talk about her with me?

It's not any of your business.

You're sensitive about this. She must be something else.

I don't want to talk about this with you right now. OK, look. I am seeing somebody. I like her, and I think she is starting to care about me, at least a little. Everything is fine as far as that goes.

Not buying it, Daddy. You didn't get drunk after Trixie talked to you. You didn't get drunk until after you talked to your friend. Until after she said she wanted to help you. That tells me your big problem is her, not anything else.

She wants me to talk to her about Trixie. You and Trixie, I mean, but mostly Trixie. She thinks if I talk about my emotions, she'll be better able to understand me and to help me.

That sounds like a good idea, Daddy.

I don't want to do it. She doesn't need to know. It's not any of her business.

It's important that you tell her. You need to tell her how you feel. You need to tell her what you went through. That way she can understand you, and maybe you can understand yourself.

Talking about what happened can't change anything.

You can't change what happened. Don't you think I would change things if I could? I didn't want to die. I didn't want that truck to smash into us. I didn't want Trixie to get depressed and upset about me being gone. But these things all happened, and you can't change them. All you can do is try to get better, and live your life, and if you have someone who wants to help you, you shouldn't push her away. You should let her help you.

I know. You're right.

Hope. Believe. Love.

You said that last time.

It's still true.

I love you, Francie.

I love you too, Daddy. Try to get some sleep.

29

On Friday evening, Dot brought chicken salad and organic potato chips from the Whole Foods on Ponce as well as a plastic bag full of miscellaneous K-cup pods.

"I thought I should repay you for all of the coffee I have been drinking," she said, picking up one of the pods. "Crud. These are the wrong ones. I thought I bought the French roast."

"What is it?"

"French *toast*. You want to try it?" she asked.

"Maybe after dinner," I said. It sounded disgusting.

"It should go nicely with dessert," she said.

"You brought dessert?" I asked.

"Blackberry cobbler. If I put it in the oven right now, it ought to be warm in time for dessert."

"I love blackberry cobbler," I said. "Most people like peach better, but I think blackberry is the best. How did you know?"

"I have sources," she said.

"You've been talking to my daughter," I said.

"That's a very interesting conclusion to make with so little data."

"Am I wrong?"

"You're not wrong, but I'd like to know how you came up with that."

"You either found out about the blackberry cobbler thing from my daughter or my ex-wife. If you'd talked to my ex-wife about me, there would still be steam coming out your ears. Process of elimination."

"Your daughter is very nice," Dot said. "We had a long talk the other day. She found me on Google, the same way I found her. She sounded like she was doing OK. Busy, but OK."

I wasn't sure how I felt about Dot talking to Alicia. If Dot was going to be part of my life—and especially if she was coming with me to the wedding—then obviously they'd have to interact at some point. That was kind of inevitable. It was better that they got along and liked each other than the alternative. But I didn't want them ganging up on me, either.

Dot found the paper plates in the cabinet and dished out the chicken salad. "Did you want to spend some time over dinner talking, like we said we were going to, or do you want to wait awhile?"

"How did that thing you were doing last weekend in Columbus go?" I asked.

"That would be a no, then."

"I'm actually curious."

"Things did not go as planned," she said. "I thought I had everything nailed down, but something unexpected happened. I would be more specific about it if I could, but it's kind of an ongoing project and I promised some people I would keep my mouth shut about it."

"That's too bad," I said. "Sounds frustrating."

"Just a little bit."

"These chips are pretty good," I said. "Did you get these at Whole Foods?"

"I completely understand if you don't want to do this for a while. That's fine. Up to you. I've got all weekend. I won't even pester you about it."

"No, let's go. I guess now is as good a time as any," I said. *The best way was to get this over with quick,* I thought. "It's just that it's kind of hard to know where to start. I don't know what to tell you and what not to tell you. I don't know what you know and don't know. If you know a lot of things that aren't true, that impacts how you react to the story."

"I only know what I've read—what I read in the papers at the time. There was a five-year anniversary piece in the Athens paper not too long ago."

"There was?" I would have seen it if it had been on the website for the *Atlanta Journal–Constitution*, but I didn't read the Athens paper. "Oh. Wait a second. I had somebody call about this last month—he said he was a journalism student and wanted to interview me about Trixie. I told him I didn't want to talk about it. Nothing against him, he seemed to be a nice enough person."

"It was a very nice article. It wasn't about anything negative. It focused on your daughter—what she achieved, what she accomplished, how she won the tennis championship. I can print it out for you if you like."

"I'd like that," I said. It would be nice to see something positive about Trixie after all this time.

"When I read the article," Dot said, "the problem I had—the problem I guess most people have—was wrapping my mind around why somebody that young and athletic would kill herself. It didn't make sense. I mean, it never makes sense, but when somebody is young and has her whole life ahead of her, it makes less sense."

"Whenever Richard Cory went down town / We people on the pavement looked at him / He was a gentleman from sole to crown / Clean favored, and imperially slim," I quoted.

Dot capped the verse: "And Richard Cory, one calm summer night / Went home and put a bullet through his head."

"Correct. Understand why Richard Cory killed himself, and you'll understand the whole human condition."

"But your daughter wasn't Richard Cory."

"No. You have to understand that Trixie had significant mental-health issues. We had to hospitalize her when she was fourteen because she'd been harming herself. She was manic-depressive, and she had a morbid fascination with knives and blood. She was stable when she took her medication, but every day was still a trial for her. But if you met her on the street or watched her play tennis, you'd never know."

"Mental illness doesn't always equal suicide, though," she said.

"Of course not. And by the time she got into college, I thought she'd turned the corner. She seemed to have a handle on things. She was enjoying her studies. She had learned to relax a little bit, which I never thought would happen."

"And then she killed herself."

"No. Not then. A couple of things happened first."

The last time we were all together as a family was in New York, the summer before Francie and Trixie died. Trixie was a junior at the University of Georgia, and she had won the NCAA singles tournament that May. Shortly after that, she got a "wild-card" invitation to play in the US Open.

We were all surprised by this, as well we might have been. Only those in the top tier of the top tier of professional tennis players get invited to the US Open. Trixie wasn't in that class—hardly any of the good college players ever are, because the elite players don't waste time in college.

I played in the NFL, which is the top tier in that sport. If you follow the game at all, you can probably name a hundred different players in the league right now without thinking hard about it. Ninety players—forty-five from each side—get to play each year in the Super Bowl, and half of them will win rings. But in tennis, only maybe six or seven people in a given year have a chance of playing in the finals of one of the major tournaments, the only ones casual sports fans care about. For Trixie to play in the US Open and do well was like expecting a sophomore college quarterback to lead a Super Bowl team on a touchdown drive.

Playing in the US Open was an incredible opportunity for Trixie, but the wild cards and the other qualifiers are, more or less, first-round cannon fodder for the top seeds. The draw put Trixie up against a young Russian woman, about nineteen or so, who was ranked twelfth in the world at the time.

Trixie was not going to win the US Open. Everyone knew that. She kept reassuring us that she knew she couldn't win, that she was going for the experience, the fun of playing at least one match against one of the world's best.

So we were determined to make the most of the time we had. Alicia came down from Boston—I think she was still teaching at Northeastern at the time—and, of course, Francie put her wedding planning aside for a week and flew in from St. Louis. Danielle was over the moon about the whole thing and put us up in the Plaza and cut a wide swath through the various shopping locations of the great city. I took everyone out to the fanciest steak place I could find; it was amazingly expensive, although nobody drank wine since Trixie was in training and couldn't have any.

We tried to keep the whole thing relaxed and fun for Trixie's sake, but it wasn't easy. She was a competitor's competitor, which was one of the things I loved about her, but it was always a challenge for her to use her competitive streak and not let it get used against her. When she got behind, it ate her up, and when she lost, it devoured her.

I knew Trixie was in trouble from the start. The strongest part of her game was the serve. She had worked hard for years on the technique—the toss, the wrist snap, the follow-through—and she could unleash the ball with speed and accuracy. She didn't have the pinpoint control over it that she would have needed to make a career playing tennis at the world-touring pro level, but it was a serve that could devastate any lesser opponent.

The first time Trixie got a chance to use her serve against the Russian, she hit the ball with power and authority. It was a beautiful serve, all the more so because I knew she was putting everything she had into it.

And the Russian flicked at it. Just a slight, quick motion of the wrist, and the ball rebounded off her racket, cleared the net, and dribbled harmlessly on the artificial surface. Love-fifteen. Trixie took out another ball, tossed it in the air, and smacked it again, a little bit harder. The Russian flicked at it again, with the same result. Love-thirty.

The Russian won the first three games until Trixie figured out that she couldn't power a serve past her. Trixie eked out a couple of points but lost the first set, 6–0.

In the second set, she had a better handle on what to do, and the Russian never managed to break her serve. Trixie got off a lucky cross-court shot to force a tiebreaker.

"She's got a chance," Francie told me. "If she can keep playing this way, she's at least got a chance."

"There's a long way to go," I said.

"She's got a chance."

But she didn't. Trixie was worn-out, dripping with sweat. The Russian looked annoyed but not worried, and she didn't have any reason to be. Watching her in the tiebreaker was like watching a stock-car driver shift gears—she found a speed most other people didn't have. As the sportswriters say, it was over before it started, and Trixie was out of the tournament, 6–0, 7–6.

"Well, OK, so what?" Dot asked.

"So what?"

"She got a chance to play at the US Open. Not everybody gets to do that. And she lost. So what? That's not a reason to kill yourself."

"You don't understand," I said. "We didn't find this out until later, but Trixie had convinced herself she was going to win."

"Well, of course she did."

"No. She had convinced herself she was going to win the tournament. She had it all planned out. She had her heart set on playing Venus Williams in the final."

"I thought you said she knew she wasn't going to win?" Dot asked.

"That's what she told us. It wasn't what she told herself. You see, she had stopped taking her medications."

"That doesn't sound good."

"It wasn't good. She thought her medications took something away from her game, and not taking them would give her an edge. Maybe they did. But when it was all over, she couldn't handle the emotional trauma of losing. She did manage to get to the locker room before she broke down, but when she did, well…"

"It was ugly."

"Worse than that. I mean, I didn't see it myself. They wouldn't let me inside. But Danielle said Trixie just turned into a puddle. She just lay on the floor and rolled around and wouldn't let anybody touch her or talk to her. Alicia tried to comfort her, Danielle tried, her coach tried. None of them could get through to her. Trixie made herself so miserable that she couldn't do anything else but lie there and cry."

"So what happened?" she asked.

"Francie was there. Francie was always there for her, had been ever since Trixie was born. Francie got down on the floor with her, put her head in her lap, stroked her hair the way she did when Trixie was three and throwing a temper tantrum. She sang to her. And thank God she did, because I was this close to calling an ambulance."

"They must have been very close."

"It was more than that. It always had been. When Junior died, Francie was eight. She was crushed. I mean, we all were, but I think Francie blamed herself. When Trixie was born, Francie latched on to her and never let go. They were inseparable, at least until Francie went to college. And when Trixie started having her problems, we got Francie to come home and help take care of her."

"It was more than your normal sibling relationship, then."

"When Trixie was in that locker room, she didn't come to me. She didn't go to Danielle. She went to Francie. She wanted Francie to hold her, Francie to tell her that it was going to be OK, Francie to help her get dressed and out the door and back to the hotel. She wouldn't talk to anyone else when she was that upset. She needed Francie then more than I've ever seen anyone need someone else."

"And then Francie went and got herself killed in a car wreck," she said.

"And then Francie went and got herself killed in a car wreck."

30

We took a little break; long enough to eat some of the blackberry cobbler Dot had made me for dessert. She said it was a Paula Deen recipe, and it was certainly sweet enough.

"You don't like it," she said.

"It's good. It maybe needs ice cream. All I have is pistachio almond, which wouldn't really go with blackberry cobbler."

"You can't have everything," Dot said. "So how did you find out about Francie?"

"I was in my office in Atlanta. I actually got an e-mail about it—there was a CNN breaking news alert, but all it said was that seven people had been swept into the river in a bad car wreck in St. Louis. I didn't think anything about it. I didn't even know Francie and Paul—that was her fiancée's name—were traveling anywhere that day. Then I got a call from Paul's father. He'd just gotten off the phone with the Missouri state troopers. They identified their car from the traffic cameras."

"That doesn't mean she was dead, though."

"At that point, no, they hadn't found the bodies. But the troopers said it was just a matter of time. Even if they survived the crash, they couldn't have survived the fall into the river."

"What did you do then?"

I hightailed it. I don't know how I got out of the building so fast, but I did. I was halfway up the Connector before I knew where I was going. There's no good way to get from Atlanta to Athens, so I decided to take I-85 as fast and as far as it would take me in that general direction. I should have gotten at least three speeding tickets, but I guess the Georgia Highway Patrol was busy elsewhere. I made top speed crossing the Perimeter and stayed on the highway until I hit 129, then I made the turn south toward the University of Georgia campus.

I was on the phone the whole way. I couldn't get hold of Danielle, but I wasn't too surprised by that—she was shopping with a client in Charleston that day, and she usually turned off her phone when she was working. There wasn't any way she could get to Trixie any faster than I could. I was able to get hold of Alicia, up in Boston—she'd seen the story on CNN and was worried that she couldn't get hold of Francie. I asked her to keep calling Francie's number and to try to get hold of her mother and let her know I was driving to Athens.

That was my first priority. My second priority was figuring out a way to keep Trixie from finding out the news until I got there. If I called to say I was coming, she would want to know why. She wasn't what you would call paranoid, but she did tend to get a little defensive about her newfound independence and would get nervous if she knew I was coming without good reason.

I tried calling her roommate but didn't have any luck—she had a late class, as it turned out. I was twenty miles out of town before I thought to call Trixie's tennis coach. She was the one who had recruited Trixie to come to Georgia. We'd explained Trixie's psychological problems, and she agreed to work with Trixie to protect her and keep her grades up. She understood the situation and dropped everything and drove over to Trixie's apartment to keep her away from TV and the Internet until I got there.

When I got there, they were on the ratty little court behind the apartment complex, hitting the ball around. When Trixie was on the tennis court, she was focused and tough-minded and relentless, but not then. Then, she was relaxed and carefree, and I thought I heard her laugh when she whiffed on a volley. It was everything I ever wanted for her, and I was there to take it all away.

"Why did you do all that?" Dot asked.

"What do you mean?"

"Nearly breaking your neck driving halfway across the state to tell your daughter in person that her sister was dead. You didn't have to do that. You could have called her."

"Oh, no. I had to be there for her. Somebody responsible had to be around when she found out. Somebody who knew what she was like, somebody who could deal with her when she got emotional and upset. You couldn't slough that off on her roommate or something and expect them to deal with it."

"You called Alicia," she said. "You let her know what was going on."

"I didn't need to be there for Alicia. Not then. She could handle the shock of the news. She was unhappy and upset about it—anyone would have been. But Trixie was … *unpredictable* isn't a good enough word. I didn't have any idea how she'd handle it."

"You thought she might have tried to harm herself."

"I wasn't sure. I thought that she'd try."

"You put your own shock and grief aside to comfort your daughter."

"Well, of course," I said. "Anyone would have done that. It's not that I didn't feel all that, because I did. I still do. But I didn't know how Trixie would take it, and the fear I had for her trumped everything else."

"And how did she take it?"

"You're worrying about nothing," Trixie said.

"I wish that was true," I said. "The state troopers identified Paul's car as one of the cars that went into the river. They saw the license plate on the traffic camera."

"You don't know if Francie was in the car," she said. "She could have decided to stay an extra day in Chicago and fly home. Maybe she doesn't have her phone turned on for some reason. Everything is going to be fine."

She had a calm confidence I hadn't seen in her before, which in and of itself was a good thing, but her denial was going to make things worse.

"Maybe you're right," I said. "But you need to be prepared if you're wrong."

"I'm not wrong," Trixie said. "Give her a little time. She's supposed to call me at nine tonight when she gets back home. She always calls, and she's always on time."

"Always?"

"If she's going to be late, like she's at a movie or something, she'll send me an e-mail. But she'll call. She will."

"OK," I said. "You may very well be right, and if you are, I apologize in advance for worrying you. But I'll stick around." I checked my watch; it was a little after five. "Why don't you two keep playing? I have a couple of phone calls to make."

I got hold of Danielle a little bit later, and it turned out that her client had a private jet and was willing to fly her to the Athens airport. I drove over and waited for her on the tarmac. She got off the plane and ran over to me, and we held each other for a long time, crying. After we pulled ourselves together, I drove over to the Papa John's and picked up four pizzas. We'd need all of them. We needed dinner, of course, and so did Trixie, but we also had her Athens psychologist waiting for us at her apartment, and her coach and her roommate and a few of her friends from the tennis team. I didn't know if anyone was all that hungry, but having the pizza helped give everyone else something to do. And, of course, you didn't need knives to eat pizza. Danielle went through the kitchen and rounded up all the knives and skewers and other potential sources of injury.

Trixie kept up her sangfroid—if that's what you call the other-worldly calm of complete denial—the whole time. "I don't know why all of you have to be here," she said. "You'll see. Everything will be fine, and then all of you can go home and leave me alone." The last part came out a little shrill, and she didn't say anything much after that.

A few minutes before eight, I got a call from Paul's father. They'd found his body, washed up on the Illinois side. His father said he was bad about wearing his seatbelt; they said he'd been thrown from the wreck and hit the water hard, so there wasn't any water in his lungs. I knew Francie always wore her seatbelt, which meant she would have been trapped in the car. He told me he was sorry, and that he would get back to me about the memorial service.

Francesca didn't call Trixie at nine.

Trixie sat on the floor, her phone in her lap, rocking back and forth. It was gentle at first, gentle enough that we didn't notice what she was doing. Then her motion got so violent that Danielle placed a throw pillow on the floor in front of her so she wouldn't hit her head.

At nine-thirty, Trixie threw the phone across the room.

"Goddamn it!" she shouted. "Why won't she call?"

"Calm down, sweetie," Danielle said. "It's going to be OK."

"Why won't she talk to me?" Trixie pleaded. "What did I do? What did I do wrong? I don't understand."

Danielle and I went to her, but she forced us off and started wailing, a loud and inhuman sound. Whenever anyone tried to touch her or get her to calm down, she started swinging her fists. When we had all backed off, she started pounding on the floor with her fists, hard enough that I thought she was going to do serious damage to her hands.

The doctor tried to get her to take a sedative—he was there for that purpose—but she wouldn't let him get close enough. He decided to let her wear herself out first and then try to sedate her. It took nearly two hours for Trixie to collapse in on herself in rage and sorrow. The doctor moved in and gave her an injection and helped me move her down the hall to her room. Danielle got her undressed and lay down in bed with her.

Everyone had left except Trixie's roommate, who didn't have anywhere else to go. I thanked her and asked her to loan me a pillow. I would camp out on the couch for the night and see if things looked any brighter in the morning.

"And did they?" Dot asked.

"No, they didn't."

"Are you OK?"

My eyes stung with tears. "No, I'm not."

"I know this is emotional for you."

"No, you don't. You never had kids. You don't know. You can't know."

"It can't be that different from any other kind of tragedy," she said.

"It *is* different. You love your kids. You *need* your kids. You want them to be healthy and tall and eat all their vegetables and grow up to be good citizens of this rotten old planet. Junior never did that, never got the chance, and that's too bad. That's life."

"So it goes."

"But when they're grown up…when you have the chance to see what they are, get to know them, and you know that you had a hand in raising them, it's different. Francesca was *smart*. She was a research chemist. She was going to make the chemical fertilizer that would save family farms. She was *special*. And then, to have some truck come out of nowhere and plow her into the river…it's *not fair*." The last two words were supposed to be a bellow, but they came out as a bleat.

"Calm down, Will," she said. "It's going to be all right. You're doing so well."

"No, I am not," I said. "I am not going to be all right. I am never going to be all right."

"What do you do when you get this way?"

I stopped for a second. I noticed I was breathing hard. I tried to place myself out of my head for a moment and take an objective look at what I was doing.

"Sometimes I cry," I said. "Not like I'm crying now. Serious crying. I wrap myself up in that blanket over there and cry it out. Sometimes I go out and hike on one of the trails, but not this late in the year. Sometimes I go out on the back porch and yell and cuss and throw things into the forest. Sometimes I just take a shower and go to bed."

"What do you want to do now?"

"Drive my truck off the top of the mountain," I said.

"You don't mean that."

"I've thought about it enough times. Maybe nothing that dramatic. But I've thought about it. I'm not brave enough to do it. I don't know what to do."

"It's getting late. Why don't you try to take a shower and get some sleep? Things will be better in the morning."

"People say that all the time."

"Because it's true."

In the end, I did what she had suggested. I took a long, hot shower and put on my pajamas and felt almost human. Dot was waiting for me in bed. She was wearing a charcoal-gray sweatshirt with an Emory logo on it and fleece pajama bottoms.

"It gets cold up here," she said. "I overdress for it."

"It's OK. You'll sleep better upstairs, though."

"I thought about it. You might need me down here. That's the most prudent course of action. You think you can go to sleep?"

"I hope so."

"Then good night. Wake me if you need to talk."

31

"I still cannot believe that you wanted me to go outside with you this morning," Dot said.

"It's not that cold."

"It's below freezing."

"The hot tub would have been nice and warm," I said.

"You wanted me to go outside. On the back porch. Without so much as a swimsuit."

"Nobody would have seen anything."

"You would have seen something, probably something you didn't want to see."

"I'll be the judge of that," I said. I had planned to make a more elaborate breakfast than usual, thinking that we'd want something hot after getting out of the hot tub, but instead we were just eating toast with jelly and drinking coffee as fast as we could get it out of the K-cup machine.

"You don't understand. It's cold out there. I don't care how hot that hot tub is, it would have been cold, and it would have been colder when we got out. If that's your idea of a good time, you can count me out."

"Beats hanging around antique stores and not buying anything."

"Of course, look who I'm talking to. Your idea of a good time involves playing football outdoors in wretched places like Green Bay, Wisconsin."

"That's one place I've never been. We played Green Bay my last year with the Falcons, but that was in the old Fulton County Stadium."

"What was the coldest game you were ever in?" she asked.

"It was plenty cold when I was in Philadelphia, but I wasn't on the field all that often. The last game I started—I didn't start that many games—we played the Steelers in Pittsburgh. It was the first year they won the Super Bowl. Not only was it freezing, I had to block Mean Joe Greene for four quarters. It didn't go so well."

"The guy in the Coke commercial?"

"You remember that?" I asked. "That was a great commercial. I loved that one. It kills me that Pepsi has the exclusive NFL account now. I'm sure you don't care, though."

"Not one little bit. I do have one question, though."

"Shoot," I said.

"Do you remember me asking you about having my writer's retreat up here?"

"There was some conversation about such a thing at some point. I remember that distinctly."

"Do you remember whether you said yes or no?"

"I remember not making a decision at the time," I said. "I take it that this is a decision that can't be put off any longer."

"Let me ask you this. Are you opposed in principle to the idea of me having a writer's retreat in your cabin, or is there something specific that bothers you? Because if there's something specific, maybe I can address that."

"In the last four years, I have let five other people in this cabin. You, my daughter, her fiancée, the guy who installed the dishwasher, and the UPS guy. The UPS guy was in here last August for five minutes to drink a Coke, and that was because he was so dehydrated that he looked like he was about ready to pass out. I am not what you would call social."

"I know that," Dot said.

"I know you're annoyed with me." She was trying hard not to let it show, but there was a tension in her voice that she couldn't disguise.

"I am not annoyed with you," she said, in a way that made me think that she was more annoyed with me than I had thought. "I recognize that this is a very big imposition on your privacy and your solitude. What I would like to do, if you can give me a minute, is explain exactly what it is I have in mind."

"If you have figured out a way to do what you want, and it doesn't infringe on my privacy and my solitude, I'll be happy to consider it."

"That's all I'm asking," she said.

"So go ahead."

"The way these things usually go is two hours of deep literary discussion and two hours of soaking up wine and talking trash about men. And before you say anything, believe me, I understand if you don't want to be here for any part of that. If you want to clear out of here and go see a movie or something, I completely understand that. I support it. I'll buy you a ticket to see whatever you want."

"I have cable," I said. "I can see whatever movie I want right here, and I can make my own popcorn."

"Shopping?" Dot asked. "You can hang out in Home Depot or something."

"Anything I need I can get UPS to send me. I have zero interest in shopping."

"Maybe there's some project or something around here that you've been putting off."

There was a project that I'd been putting off, but I saw no reason not to keep putting it off.

"I'm not hearing anything so far that is going to make me one little bit interested in doing this," I said.

"The light dawns," Dot said. "You want to know what's in this for you."

"You said it was a big imposition. If you're going to make a big imposition on me, you need to explain what you have in mind that's going to encourage me to go along with it."

"That's quite the selfish attitude," she said.

"It is. And as long as I'm being selfish, I'm getting the next cup of coffee."

"That's not being selfish. That's being piggish."

"Now who's got the bad attitude?" I asked.

Dot got up to put another pod in the coffee machine. "Was that the last of the hazelnut coffee?"

"It may have been."

"Like I said. Piggish."

"There are still some of those French toast pods left," I said.

"Not just piggish, then. Heartless."

"Calling me names is a poor strategy to get what you want."

"Does that mean that you're open to a reasonable compromise?" she asked.

"A reasonable compromise, yes."

"It just feels like I am setting myself up for extortion. You're going to ask me to participate in whatever heartless, piggish plot you have in mind. Probably dragging me out there into that hot tub."

"My intentions are noble and pure," I said.

"In a way, that's almost more frightening."

"It might be. It depends on how you react to my wife's family."

"Will Morse, are you asking me to go with you to your daughter's wedding?"

"Yes," I said.

"For pity's sake," she said. "Of course I will go with you to your daughter's wedding."

"I'm glad."

"I don't know why you think I wouldn't have agreed to go," she said. "I know that I tease you a little, but that doesn't mean I don't like you, and care about you."

"I know," I said. "Thank you."

"Don't mention it."

"I mean, thanks for everything. For being here."

"I know. You're welcome. And thank you."

"For what?"

She gave me the tiniest little kiss, and then got her cup of coffee and sat back down. That was all the answer I got.

32

Dot came up with what I thought was a good plan for the next weekend. She ordered six bottles of California chardonnay and had it sent to the cabin; I put it all in the fridge. That was the extent of my preparation. Instead of making me cook anything, she and her friends had brunch at a café downtown, and did all of the literary talk there. I was hoping that the weather would be nice enough that everyone would decide to hang out on the back porch and let me watch college basketball, but an early March wind was blowing through the mountains. So they all decided to hang out in the living room, which meant that I could either barricade myself in my office or go upstairs. I thought long and hard about the office, but it was clear that going upstairs would be the quieter option.

I staggered my way upstairs and went into the other room, the room that Trixie and Francie had shared. I started going through all the boxes that I had salvaged five years ago and not touched since.

I started with the biggest box, which had most of Trixie's tennis trophies. The NCAA trophy was actually the most understated—it was a three-foot high piece of polished wood with an engraved piece of glass in the center. I cleared some knickknacks off the bookshelf and set the trophy on the top shelf. I put the knickknacks in the box.

I realized I was stirring Trixie's things instead of organizing them, and I told myself to pay attention to what I was doing.

The next box was full of books. A couple of them were textbooks, I guessed, and probably some of the others had been assigned to her in school. I riffled through the titles, trying to discern some common theme. *Darkness at Noon. The Bell Jar. A Confederacy of Dunces. Infinite Jest. Orlando: A Biography. For Whom the Bell Tolls.* If there was a pattern in what Trixie was reading, it didn't make any sense to me. I knew I could read every one of the books and not come any closer to understanding why my daughter had taken her own life. I decided to take the books downstairs and see if Sharon wanted them as donations for the library.

The other two boxes were just random bits of memorabilia—yearbooks, snow globes, tennis balls. As best I could, I arranged most of it on the bookshelf and on top of the desk. Everything that I didn't find a place for, I put back in the largest box, and I was able to wedge that onto the closet shelf. That left one box, and that was the box that I didn't want to deal with.

The knife was wrapped in an evidence bag, and it would stay there as long as I had anything to say about it. I didn't want to touch it. That knife had caused me more grief than any other single object in the world.

I'd left the knife in Trixie's bedroom that night. Once the police found it, they asked me how she'd gotten it about seventeen different ways, trying to get me to change my answer. Danielle asked me twice—once when I was in jail, and once over the conference table at her lawyer's the day the divorce was final. I didn't tell her; she was far too volatile and the truth was far too dangerous. The only person I'd ever wanted to tell was my lawyer, and he told me not to say anything.

Alicia asked me about the knife one time, right after the grand jury set me free.

I should have told her the truth.

I hadn't.

I knew Dot was going to ask me about the knife. It was the key fact in the case, the central mystery. If Trixie had found the knife or stolen it or got it in some other way, it would mean that I was telling the truth and that she had killed herself, and that there was nothing I could have done to save her. If I had given her the knife, it would mean that I had either been negligent in letting her near the thing, or that I had given it to her as part of a conspiracy to help her kill herself.

Dot would want to know, and would want me to tell her. I knew she was going to keep asking and that I was going to have to give her an answer. What worried me more than anything else was that I didn't know whether I could tell her the truth or not.

I put the box with the knife in it in the darkest corner of the closet. The room was as straightened up as it was going to get, so I decided to head downstairs. I put the box of books at the top of the stairs, with the intention of asking Dot to bring it down later. I didn't want to run the risk of carrying it myself. I gripped the handrail and gingerly lowered my feet down the steps.

Dot and her friends had moved into the kitchen. They were about halfway through the wine, so I guessed that they were probably sticking around for a while longer. I thought about sneaking through my bedroom and getting out on the back porch that way, but I wanted a Coke and didn't want to feel like an exile in my own house.

"I'm telling you, it's boring," Dot said. "Cut it."

"It's an important scene," the woman to Dot's left said. She had long, iron-gray hair and thick glasses. "It sets up the motive for the killer."

"Come on, Michelle. There's other ways to do that," one of the other writers said. "You don't have to interrupt the narrative to show a funeral. It just bogs everything down, and you have all this extraneous stuff about the body and the cremation and the bit about spreading the ashes in the community garden. You can just skip all that and do the exposition another way, like reading the will or something."

"Michelle writes murder mysteries about organic community gardening," Dot explained.

I got my Coke out of the fridge. "Do a lot of people get killed doing organic community gardening?" I asked. "That sounds like a relatively safe activity."

"Well, of course it is," Michelle said. "So reading murder mysteries set in that environment makes it seem more interesting."

"They're called cozies," Dot said. "It's a big genre. Cozy little mysteries with female protagonists doing female hobbies. There are knitting ones, cooking ones, and I think I saw one where the detective had fourteen cats."

I wanted to ask if they had books where the detective did wood carving or restored old cars, but I decided to keep my mouth shut.

"Maybe what we need here is the male perspective," Michelle said.

"I don't think I'd be very much help," I said. "Excuse me."

"You might have some special insight," the other writer said.

"My ex-wife used to tell me that," I said. "She's an interior decorator, and every once in a while, she would hand me a fabric swatch or a paint chip and ask me what I thought of it."

"What did she do then?" Michelle asked.

"She ignored me and did what she wanted to do," I said.

"Do you read mysteries, Will?" Michelle asked.

"Yeah."

"Would you stop reading a mystery novel just because it had a funeral scene?"

"Will is being extra special nice and letting us take over his beautiful mountain cabin for the day," Dot said. "Please, let's not give him a hard time."

"It's OK," I said. "You read murder mysteries for the mystery, right?"

"Sure," Michelle said.

"Funerals aren't mysterious. You go to the church, people say nice things, and then you go to the cemetery, and you put the box with the dead person in the ground, and then you go get something to eat. That's not mysterious."

"But you can have something mysterious happen at a funeral," Michelle said. "A mystery woman could show up. A long-lost family member can return. People's lives can change."

"But the dead person is still dead," I said. "Excuse me. I'll be out on the porch if any of you need to find anything."

Dot came out on the porch a few minutes later. "They're all gone," she said. "You have your house back."

I was sitting on one of the benches, idly tossing dead leaves over the rail into the forest below. "Did you have fun?" I asked.

"I enjoyed it. I know you didn't. I'll make it up to you."

"That would be nice."

"I didn't mean for them to be talking about funerals like that. Most of them write murder mysteries, so the talk gets kind of morbid," Dot explained.

"Not a big fan of morbid. Not a big fan of funerals, if you want to be honest."

"Well, of course you're not."

I found a largish twig and threw it into the trees. "Francie had three funerals. You know, one funeral is enough for most people. Not Francie, though. Had to have three."

"For pity's sake, why?"

"We had no idea where to bury her. We didn't have a plot for her in Atlanta, and we had too much going on with Trixie and her situation to arrange anything. Danielle's father offered her a spot in the family mausoleum in Philadelphia, but I didn't want to do that. Her fiancée's family had two adjoining plots in this cemetery outside of St. Louis, so that's what we decided to go with."

"So you had a funeral in St. Louis and, what, a memorial service in Atlanta?"

"There were two funerals in St. Louis, and I had to go to both of them by myself because Danielle was taking care of Trixie. The city had a memorial service for all the victims. That was a huge public thing in a big church. I think it was a cathedral, or maybe it was a basilica, something like that. I don't remember anything except that a lot of reporters with microphones were in my face afterward."

Dot twitched a little for some reason when I said that, but she didn't say anything.

"Then, the next day, there was the real funeral in the church that Paul's family went to. It was really his funeral; nobody said anything much about Francie. They wanted me to say something but I couldn't. I was the only one there who cared about her."

"That must have been terrible," Dot said. I knew that she didn't know just how terrible that kind of thing could be, but I didn't call her on it. It was the kind of thing that you say.

"So then we had to have a memorial service in Atlanta, for Trixie's sake. They let her out of the hospital for the day. It was mostly Danielle's family who was there, so she had to deal with them. I sat in the back of the church with Trixie. She was shaking the whole time, like a leaf, like she was getting ready to fall. Which I guess she was."

"I know this has been painful for you," Dot said. "But the best thing I can do for you is to listen. You haven't had anybody to listen to you for a long time, and I think that's something that you need."

"You can do something else," I said.

"I am not getting in that Goddamned hot tub, if that's what you mean."

"Not that," I said, "although that would be nice. All I meant was that you can take me out to dinner. I don't feel like cooking, and I don't think you do either."

"I can do that," Dot said. "You will have to drive, though. That was some tasty chardonnay."

33

We decided to have dinner at my usual restaurant in the grocery store parking lot. It was the most convenient place.

We got in my truck and drove down the Appalachian Highway to town. "How crowded do you think it's going to be?" she asked.

"Don't know. I come here for lunch, and breakfast sometimes."

"You sure you want to eat here? I mean, if you come here all the time?"

I wasn't sure either. I hadn't been there since I had driven Margie out of the dining room that time, but I didn't think she'd hold it against me. I wasn't sure that she worked Saturday nights anyway.

"It's a nice, friendly place," I said, "but stay away from the specials."

Margie came over with our mozzarella sticks. "Hi!" she said, more to Dot than to me. "It's a real pleasure to serve you this evening. I know I recognize you, but I can't recollect your name."

"No reason why you should recognize me," Dot said.

"Are you sure? You look so familiar. I mean, I know Mr. Morse here, but I know I know you from somewhere."

"I don't think you do."

"Weren't you on TV?"

193

"I was on an episode of *Cold Case Files* about five years ago," Dot said. "I didn't think it was that memorable, but I guess maybe it was."

"I guess I could have seen that at some point," Margie said. "Are you sure you weren't on *Sesame Street*? That's about the extent of my TV viewing these days."

"Do you have a little one?" Dot asked. "That's so sweet."

Margie fished a phone out of her pocket. "Here she is," and showed us a picture of a very cute little girl. "I'll go check on your dinner."

"You'll have to leave her a big tip," Dot said.

"I always do," I said. "Were you really on TV?"

"It was just one episode. They were filming something about a case I had written a little something about, and they did an interview with me and it ended up as part of the show."

"What did you write about?"

"It was a criminal case. Honestly, at this point, I couldn't even tell you what it was about; it's been that long ago."

"I guess I should be asking what you write about in general," I said. "I know you teach writing, but I never really thought about you doing any writing."

"I don't think I've written anything you would have read."

"Try me."

"It's not that interesting," she said.

"If you like, you can sit here and listen while I tell you about my high school football career."

"Dear God, no. I shouldn't be going into this, but I was just talking about it with the girls, so here goes. Does the name Carissa Buckley mean anything to you?"

"No."

"No reason why it should. Carissa Buckley is a sergeant in the Army. She's stationed down at Fort Benning—she's an instructor at the airborne school."

"With you so far."

"Last April, Sergeant Buckley is at her house in Columbus. Her husband is deployed to Afghanistan with the Rangers. So one night, a maniac breaks in to her house with a knife. It's dark, and he's wearing green camouflage paint on his face, so she can't recognize him—doesn't even know if he's white or black. She tries to fight back, but he knocks her out and rapes her. She's left with a severe concussion."

"That's terrible," I said.

"Fortunately, one of her neighbors sees him leave. The neighbor can't identify who it was, but he does call the police, and they're able to find Sergeant Buckley and take her to the hospital and get her treated. It's a good thing they did, because she might have died. She's in the hospital for three weeks."

"How did you get involved?"

"Carissa's husband Tim was one of my students. They sent him home to take care of his wife. He was getting frustrated with the Columbus police and the military police, and he needed to talk to somebody. Tim was thinking that if the police thought a writer was poking around the case, it might stir up something."

"Did it work?"

"No, because the whole thing was a mess. Carissa, bless her heart, couldn't give the police anything useful. On top of that, there wasn't any evidence other than the DNA, and that didn't lead anywhere. Whoever the rapist was, he wasn't in the federal or state or Army DNA databases. They didn't have a thing to go on, and it looked like nothing was going to happen."

"You were just there. Something must have happened."

"Tim found somebody who he thought was a possibility. It was someone who had been in his unit but had been given a dishonorable discharge for drug abuse. He still lived in Columbus. Tim ran him down, found him in a bar, and got into a huge fight with him. I went down to check out the story."

"Was it him?" I asked.

"Not even close. The DNA didn't match. And the Army gave Tim a reprimand—he was lucky that they didn't throw him in the stockade."

"So are you writing about it?"

"I wish I could," she said. "There's nothing to write about. It's just an unsolved crime that probably never will be solved, with a beautiful, strong young woman who is in physical therapy for a head injury, and a husband who can't stop beating himself up about not being there to protect her."

"It's tragic."

"It is tragic, but it's also incredibly frustrating. I wish there was something I can do, but I can't. All I can do is hope that there's some kind of break in the case."

"I think our dinner's here," I said.

Margie came over with a big tray and set it down on one of those folding stands. "You had the chicken-fried chicken, and you had the Cobb salad."

"Thanks," Dot said.

"So, are you going to write a book about this?" I asked.

"Well, I didn't really plan on doing that," Dot said. "I mean, it started out as a favor for a former student. And usually, with this kind of crime—well, it can be hurtful for people to bring it up."

"I know what you mean," I said.

"Do you write books?" Margie asked.

"Excuse me," Dot said. "We're trying to have a conversation here."

Margie turned red and went back into the kitchen.

"Nice, friendly place you have here," Dot said.

"That was a little abrupt," I said.

"Eavesdropping is a little rude."

"Margie wasn't eavesdropping. She just heard what you said and was trying to make conversation. She's a nice person."

"How's your chicken?" she asked.

"It's fine. Do you want a bite?"

"No."

Margie waited until Dot went into the ladies' room to bring the check. "I am so sorry," she said. "I should have kept my mouth shut. It was just so odd, because I know I've seen her on TV somewhere."

"I don't know why she was rude to you just now," I said. "Do you have any idea what you might have seen her in?" Maybe Dot had a second life as an actress in bad TV movies.

"She just looks so familiar. I'm sure I'm just not seeing her in context. You know, if I saw you in Home Depot, we might not recognize each other."

That made sense to me. You could recognize someone on TV and not know them if they showed up at your door the next day. Come to think of it, that's exactly what Dot had done—she'd shown up at my door, in the middle of nowhere. And Alicia had seen her, and Alicia thought she looked familiar too.

There was a perfectly reasonable explanation for all this, I thought, and there was a simple way to figure out what that was.

"Would you mind doing me a favor, Margie?"

"Sure."

"Can you look up someone on that phone of yours?"

"On what? Google? *Wikipedia*?"

I don't like *Wikipedia*, not one little bit. I've been around and around with them on some of the nonsense they've put on their website, stuff related to me and Trixie, some of it horrible. But it would be the fastest way to find out something.

"Try *Wikipedia*. Put in 'Dorothy Crawford.' That's her name. See if she's written a book or been on TV in some other way."

Margie punched the name into her phone. "It's not coming up with anything. It's coming up with somebody different."

"Who?" I asked.

"Oh, my God," she said. "I was right. I did recognize her. I knew she was on TV, I just knew it."

"She was on TV?" I asked.

Margie handed me her phone.

DOROTHY LARSON
From Wikipedia, the free encyclopedia

Dorothy Larson, born Dorothy Crawford (born March 30, 1957) is an American true crime author, based in Atlanta, Georgia. She was also a reporter and news anchor for ABC affiliate WJCL-TV in Savannah from 1986–1990, ABC affiliate WPTY-TV in Memphis from 1990–1996, and NBC affiliate WXIA-TV in Atlanta from 1996–2007. She was nominated for the 2008 Southern Writers' Circle Award for her debut book, *A Murder in Sandy Springs*, about the carjacking and murder of a Kennesaw State University coed. She is also an adjunct professor of English at Georgia State University.

BOOKS
A Murder in Sandy Springs, 2008, Piedmont Books

A Murder in Alpharetta, 2009, Pendant Publishing

A Murder in Little Five Points, 2011, Pendant Publishing

"That is her, right?" Margie asked.
"That's her."
"I knew I recognized her from somewhere."
"I didn't." I knew I should have. I knew I shouldn't have been able to forget that particular face.

34

I couldn't say that Dot lied to me, not really. I never once asked her, "So, were you one of the reporters who covered my daughter's death? Did you tell the Metro Atlanta viewing audience that I was the one who stabbed her? Were you one of the ones who waited on the courthouse steps to stick a microphone in my face every day of the grand jury trial?" She just hadn't told me. She had let me think that she was who she said she was.

But everything she had done was a lie. When she knocked on my door the first time, it was a lie. When she got me a burger and a dog from The Varsity when I was worried about Alicia, it was a lie. When she had told me that she cared about me, it was a lie. It had to be.

The worst lie, though, was the one I had told myself. I had told myself that I didn't care about Dot, that I didn't have an emotional connection with her, that our relationship wasn't based on anything other than friendship and companionship. That had been a lie too, but I didn't realize it until that emotional connection had been replaced by something painful and sharp.

What I wanted right then was her out of my cabin. I wanted her to take her bag and leave. I wanted the relationship to be over and done with in the shortest possible amount of time, before she caused me anymore heartache and embarrassment than she already had. I didn't know what she wanted, but it didn't matter that much to me. I wanted her gone. I wanted my privacy back, and my solitude. I wanted to keep my memories buried as deep as I could bury them. Part of me knew I would miss her when she left, but that was a very small part.

I used to be able to handle confrontations. Living with teenagers will teach you how to do that. I had my share of tense standoffs with Danielle, of course, and the occasional dustup at work. It's a skill like anything else, knowing when to escalate the volume, knowing when to back off, knowing where the lines were so that you either crossed them or stayed away from them, depending on what you were trying to do at the time. I didn't always win, of course—you shouldn't want to always win everything, every time.

I knew there had to be a confrontation with Dot. I couldn't control that. All I could control was where it would take place, what I would say, and how far I was willing to take things.

I thought about saying something at the restaurant, but I would have had to give her a ride back to the cabin regardless. I thought about saying something when we were sitting in my truck, out in front of the cabin, but I would have had to let her go in and get her things. I didn't want to keep anything of hers, and I didn't want to give her an excuse to come back. So I waited until we got inside. I knew what I wanted to say first.

"Why did you lie to Margie?" I asked.

"About what?"

"Being on television."

"I don't know what you're talking about."

"Dot Crawford doesn't know what I'm talking about. But I bet Dorothy Larson would."

She had the good grace to look embarrassed. "That means she either finally figured it out, or she looked it up on her phone. Do you know which?"

"I gave her your name, and she did a search on *Wikipedia*."

"Well, that's modern technology for you. I hope you're not unhappy with me."

"That's not a big enough word. Incredibly angry and disappointed is more like it. I think you should go."

"Are you going to let me explain?" she asked.

"I just want to know if you're doing a book about me. *A Murder in Buckhead.* That's a good title. Nice and snappy. That'll sell a lot of copies, I'm sure. Either that or *Double Fault,* because of the tie-in with the tennis."

"Will, for God's sake. Do we have to do this right now?"

"We're not going to do anything right now. You're going to go upstairs and get your bag and leave. I am going to stay here, and you are going to leave me alone."

"All right," she said. "I'll admit it. I was a TV reporter. I covered your daughter's case. I covered the trial. Maybe I should have explained all that to you; I wish I had, now. But you don't have to be angry with me. You certainly don't have to kick me out of the cabin."

"You told the entire city that I killed my daughter, and then lied to me about who you were. For all I know you're writing a book about Trixie. Of course I'm angry."

"Why do you assume this is about a book?" she asked. "Is it too much to think that I might be interested in you? Care about you? Be interested in your welfare?"

"You might be. But I know it's not true. You wouldn't be asking me all these questions if it were. You wouldn't keep pushing me. It's the only thing that makes sense."

She put her handbag on the kitchen table. "I can explain if we can manage to sit down and discuss this like reasonable adults over a cup of coffee."

"I don't want to make any coffee." I decided it was time to escalate the volume. "I don't want you hanging around here, trying to charm me, trying to convince me that this was all a mistake."

"If you want to keep yelling at me, then by all means do. But if you want to throw me out, I had a lot of wine at lunch and there's no way

201

I'm going to be able to drive out of here without a cup of coffee first. I can go upstairs and get my bag while you make it."

"That sounds reasonable," I said. I wasn't that interested in being reasonable, but I was not going to be able to go up the stairs and get her bag myself.

"If you can give me ten minutes to explain while I drink my coffee, I will try to explain. If you're still mad at me after that, I'll go."

"I'm going to start at the very beginning," she said. She was still wearing her parka and sipping her coffee out of a paper cup. She sounded calm and composed, the way she always had done on television. "Do you remember me telling you that there was a story about your daughter in the Athens paper two months ago?"

"Yeah."

"The reporter is one of my former students. Barry Wright is his name, and he did a good job. I sent him an e-mail to congratulate him, and he asked me if I thought he might get a book out of it."

"And you told him yes," I said.

"I told him no. It would be too difficult. Do you read true crime books at all?"

"I read *In Cold Blood* in college."

"That's a good start. Did you see the movie? Not the one they made in the '60s, the recent one."

"No." I try to avoid movies with brutal, violent scenes, for the obvious reason.

"OK, good enough. So Truman Capote goes out to the back end of nowhere and sits in on the investigation of this horrible crime. He writes a brilliant book about it. But he can't finish the book. They've caught the murderers, but he delays until the murderers were hanged. He couldn't write the end of the book any other way. *In Cold Blood* not only started the genre, it set the rules you have to follow."

"Oh. There are rules. That's nice."

Dot ignored my sarcasm. "True crime does two things: it sets up an awful event with terrible consequences, and then it tries to put

202

things right at the end by punishing the guilty party. It's all about balance. You have a great crime on one end of the scale and a fitting punishment on the other side, and that's the story you tell. That can only happen when the killer gets caught and punished."

"That's not true. People still write books about Jack the Ripper, and Lizzie Borden, and justice wasn't done on either of those cases."

"That's right. Those are the harder cases to write about, because there's an unsolved mystery at the heart of them. Nobody knows who Jack the Ripper really was, or who killed Lizzie Borden's parents. So if you're writing a book about that kind of case, you have to resolve the mystery and explain what really happened, or what you think really happened. The book is still about the quest for justice; you're just making the case to the reader instead of the jury."

"What you're telling me, then, is that you've been trying all this time to get me to confess to killing my daughter. Why would you do a thing like that?"

"Not confess," she said. She was talking a little faster now, and acting a little more nervous. "Explain. Clear things up. That means you have to be willing to cooperate or at least talk. And if Barry had approached you, he would never have gotten a foot in the door. You wouldn't even talk to him when he called."

"So you did it. You came up here. You got me out of the house, and you got me to talk about Trixie. You did what he couldn't."

Dot pulled herself into her parka. Her voice lost the assuredness of the TV anchor and became quiet and sad. "I did. And I'm sorry. I misled you, and I used you, and that's a terrible thing. I understand that you're upset about it. I never meant for you to find out, not this way."

The apology wasn't enough—I didn't see that any apology could be enough. But it wasn't an explanation, and that's what I wanted.

"What I don't understand is *why*," I said. "I mean, why me? You could write about a hundred different things that wouldn't hurt anybody, but you came all the way up here to come after me. I don't understand why anyone would do that."

Dot pursed her lips and threw her head back a little bit. "This is so embarrassing," she said.

"I should hope so."

"I started working on the Carissa Buckley project last summer. I thought there was a book in it, I really did. But it didn't pan out. They never caught the guy. It got to be December, and I was depressed and unhappy, and I started thinking about your case. It wasn't hard to figure out where you lived, and I was in the area anyway. So I stopped by. To be honest, I thought you would recognize me and kick me out first thing. But you didn't. You were nice. You were approachable. I thought I could get to know you a little, and see if you wanted to cooperate."

I got up from my chair and walked over to the coffee machine. I picked up the mug. It felt warm in my hands, as I had thought it would.

"Have you ever told me the truth?" I asked. "About anything?"

"I have been as honest with you as I could be. I never lied to you, not once. I may not have told you all of the truth about me and what I do, but none of it was a lie. I like you."

"Stop."

"I care about you."

"Get out."

"I think your daughter killed herself. I don't think you did anything wrong. I think the grand jury did the right thing by letting you out. I am not trying to put you in jail or cause you problems. But it's a powerful story, and I think if you let people know your side, it could go a long way toward reconnecting you with the world."

"I don't want to be reconnected. I want to stay here and live my life and not have anyone bother me. I want to handle my own problems, my own way, in my own time. I don't need your help, and I sure the hell don't need you to let people know my side of things. My side of things is that I didn't do anything to make Trixie kill herself. That's all people need to know."

"The First Cut is the Deepest," she said.

"What?"

"You asked about the title. That's the one that I decided on. *The First Cut is the Deepest.* The working title, anyway. It's from an old Cat Stevens song, but you probably know that."

"I want you to leave now."

"Because of the autopsy. That's what they said. That first cut was the one that killed her."

"Get out."

It didn't take her long to go. I stood at the front door and watched her taillights recede down the driveway. I went out on the back porch and felt the cold Arctic air blowing in. I watched her car wind its way down the mountain, headed for the far-off Appalachian Highway. I kept watching until all that was left was a small pinpoint of light merging into the traffic headed south.

I threw the coffee cup into the night. It must have hit a tree because I heard it shatter. I thought about spending the rest of the night throwing things off the back porch to hear them break, but then I'd have to clean everything up and go back into town to get replacements the next day. So I did the next best thing and went inside and wrapped myself up in the blanket. It was the old familiar cocoon of sorrow and grief, but there was no small measure of regret and pain along with it.

35

I spent the next two weeks drinking Coke and Southern Comfort and watching the NCAA basketball tournaments. I'd gone to the store looking for Maker's Mark, but I saw the Southern Comfort on sale, and I bought several bottles and started working my way through them. I wasn't a big basketball fan, but the TV broadcasts were loud and energetic when I was feeling quiet and listless. I knew I was developing a problem when I started looking forward to the women's tournament, but it held my attention long enough to get as drunk as I wanted to get.

Every night before I drifted off to sleep, I wondered if I would dream about Francie. I know that she isn't really there in my dreams, that she isn't speaking to me directly, that she's not trying to comfort me from beyond the grave. I know it's just random electrical impulses in my subconscious that conjure her up from time to time. And it's not as though I want her there, or need her there, because I don't— it's always troubling to hear from her, because she has insights that I don't have and is honest enough to tell me when I'm wrong about something.

Francie was like that when she was alive—smart, and honest, and caring—which is a combination you don't run across every day. I miss her terribly, and having her show up in my dreams doesn't help that, because I know that's not actually her talking to me. At best, it's a faded carbon copy of her personality, filtered through my own fears and desires. But I know that if she could be here, she would try to comfort me. She would want me to be happy.

I didn't dream about Francie. I dreamed about basketballs rolling up and down the court. I dreamed of shot clocks running down. I dreamed of being in the stands, in a large crowd, jumping and cheering. Once, I looked over to my left, and I saw Dot there, but she was watching the game and I couldn't tell if she was happy or angry, and she didn't say anything. The next night, she wasn't there, and I didn't see her again.

The day before the final championship game, I got a fare alert e-mail about flights to Newark for Alicia's wedding. I didn't want to go by myself, but I couldn't see any alternative. I knew Alicia wanted me to be there, and I wanted to be the kind of father who would go without thinking about it, who would walk her down the aisle with a smile on his face. I would never be that kind of father again, but it was my one opportunity to try, and I didn't want to waste it.

I bought the airline tickets first. It would be an irrevocable step, one that I hoped was in the right direction. Once I had the electronic tickets in my in-box, I would have made the final commitment. I wouldn't be able to back out without difficulty, at least of the airline-related sort.

I decided to fly out on the Thursday before the wedding. I could have taken the first flight out on Friday morning, but the Thursday afternoon flight wasn't that much more expensive. I wouldn't have to make the drive down the night before and stay at an airport motel, so it worked out about even. I picked out a flight that didn't look that full so I had a better chance to either score an upgrade to first class or at least a row in coach to myself. The flight back the next Monday looked more crowded, but I didn't want to spend the extra day in New Jersey if I didn't have to.

After I determined that the travel costs wouldn't blow a bigger hole in my budget than I expected, I loaded up the truck and made the drive up to Chattanooga to buy a nice outfit for the rehearsal dinner. I found a decent barbecue place for lunch near the mall and then drove to the Men's Wearhouse. I tried on a tan corduroy jacket, and I bought that along with a blue dress shirt with French cuffs. I have a pair of vintage cufflinks that Francie had given me for Christmas the year before she died. I'd never worn them, and this seemed to be a good time. I thought about buying a tie but couldn't find one I liked.

It was raining when I left the store, hard enough that I decided not to drive back home right away. I went over to the movie theater by the mall and got a ticket for some romantic comedy that was at the end of its run. I hadn't been to a movie since right before Francie died, and I wasn't sure if I would enjoy it or not, but the theater was dark and empty on a Thursday afternoon, and I found myself liking it more than I thought. The rain had let up by the time the movie was over, so I made the uneventful drive back home. I felt I had accomplished something.

I went to the library in Blue Ridge that next day. I'd seen the new Laura Hillenbrand book at one of the bookstores in the Chattanooga mall, and decided to see if it was at the library in Blue Ridge. It was checked out, so I got the new Jack Reacher book, and one of Bernard Cornwell's books about Richard Sharpe. The Sharpe books all have similar plots, which I don't mind, but I enjoy them more if I space them out a bit so they don't run into each other.

I decided to check and see if they had one of Dot's books. I had looked them up on Amazon, but I didn't want to give her the satisfaction of buying one. The only one they had was *A Murder in Alpharetta*, which appeared to be about two high school students who left one of their classmates to die in a ditch after a night of heavy drinking. The cover art was lurid—bold red lettering, and a close-up photo of what looked like a dead body. I put the book back on the shelf. I thought about putting it on a different shelf so other people couldn't find it, but that seemed a bit too petty.

I didn't see Sharon anywhere, which was unusual. I didn't want to talk to her, but I didn't want her to think that I was avoiding her either. There were a couple of times, after I had a little too much Coke and Southern Comfort, that I thought about calling Sharon and seeing how things were going in whatever relationship she was having. I didn't give in to that temptation, and I was glad that I hadn't. But there wasn't any reason we couldn't still be friendly, as we were before. I asked the librarian behind the counter if she was in her office.

"You mean Miz Lumpkin?" she asked.

"Excuse me? Who?"

"Miz Lumpkin. She got married last week. She and her new husband, they went down to Savannah for the honeymoon. She won't be back 'til Monday. You need her for something?"

"No, not really. Lumpkin?"

"He was her landscaper. Mowed the lawn, trimmed the trees." She leaned across the counter and stage-whispered the last word. "Twenty years old."

"Oh."

"He's cute, though. Very strong. Not the reading type, though."

"Oh." Sharon had said that she had an unconventional relationship, and that sounded about right.

There were moments when I felt I had made a mistake, when I would have been happy to see Dot again, but there weren't many of them.

She didn't try to contact me, which was a bit of a relief. I had worried that she would come back, that she would follow me around town, or that she would camp out in front of the cabin, waiting for me to come out, the way that people wait on that groundhog in Pennsylvania to come out to see his shadow. I heard from her only one time, in early April. It was the 5th, which was Trixie's birthday— she would have been thirty-one if she'd lived. The FedEx guy came by with a package that turned out to be a small bouquet of white orchids. No card. I didn't know anyone else who would send something like that except Dot—if she'd done any research at all, she'd have known when Trixie's birthday was.

The last birthday present I gave Trixie was the knife that killed her. She had turned fifteen and had been out of the psychiatric hospital for a little over a month. She was on three different medications, which had the advantage of keeping the screaming and cursing to a minimum, but had the disadvantage of leaving her dazed and listless. We were keeping her out of school until the fall. Danielle had shuttered her home-decorating business for a while and was staying home with her all day, trying to slog through a homeschool curriculum. All of us were miserable, and I decided to do something about it.

I brought the knife up to Trixie's room that night along with a bagful of cotton balls, antiseptic, gauze, and tape. She was lying on her bed, listening to Alanis Morissette sing about living and learning. She was wearing heavy flannel pajamas and thick wool socks, although it wasn't cold out. I knew why.

"Got a minute?" I asked.

"Go away," she said. But it was only a Level One go-away, so I didn't. If she actually wanted me to go away, she'd have ramped it up to Level Eleven and kept the volume there.

"I have something for you," I said.

"I don't want your lame birthday present. I don't want your sympathy or your pity. I don't want anything to do with you as long as I live."

"You'll want this."

I hadn't wrapped it—I'm not good with paper and scissors and suchlike. I had gone to the trouble of buying a nice presentation case, one with a lock on it. It was a solid wooden box with a crushed purple velvet inlay. I kept the box in my hand and opened it so that Trixie could see the knife inside.

She reached over and turned off the stereo. "Can I hold it?" she asked.

"Not yet."

"Did you bring it up here to mess with me, or can I really have it?"

"You can really have it. But there are rules. We need to discuss them first."

211

"It looks old. That's not a complaint, Daddy, but it does. Whose was it?"

"This was your Uncle Charlie's. He gave it to your grandfather before his last tour in '71. I got it when Grandpa died."

"Did he kill anyone with it?"

"I'm sure not." I knew he hadn't, because I had bought this particular knife at an army surplus store in Columbus. Charlie had kept his knife with him, and it had rusted away in the Laotian jungle by the time they found his body in '89. It was a lie, but not a lie that could hurt anyone.

"It's a combat knife."

"It's a KA-BAR. That's what it's called. It's got a seven-inch blade, chromium steel."

Trixie got off the bed and stretched out one finger. I let her touch it, and she traced a line starting from the hilt, along the side, stopping short of the point. Then she pulled back, like the surface of the knife was hot.

"I don't want it," she said. "It's too dangerous. I could cut off a finger by mistake if I wasn't careful."

"Careful is the key word. I want you to have it, but I want you to be careful. That means that it stays in its box, and the box stays in my closet—in the wall safe—unless I get it out for you. That also means that you turn over whatever it is that you're using to cut yourself."

"I'm not cutting myself."

"I know you are. It's OK. I understand that you need to."

"I'm not."

"I saw the socks that you tried to throw away. What are you cutting, the soles of your feet? That's got to hurt like hell."

Trixie's face tensed up, and she tried to take a step backward but miscalculated and landed on the bed. "Don't send me back there, Daddy," she said. "Please. I've been trying so hard to be good, and I don't want to go back."

"I don't want to send you back," I said. I spoke as calmly and as evenly as I could to keep her from being any more nervous than she was. "I don't want you to spend your high school years in a psychiatric hospital. I want to help you, but you have to help me. I know you're still cutting yourself, but you're not doing it in a safe way, not if you're using some random piece of junk. What are you using, anyway?"

She looked at me with suspicion. "Are you going to narc on me to Mom?"

"I won't. I promise."

Her backpack was at the end of her bed; she dug into it and produced a small piece of yellow plastic from a hidden pocket. It was a bottle cap, or part of one. The broken part was jagged enough that a patient enough person could use it to cut her skin.

"This is not safe," I said. "I'm not trying to be judgmental here, OK, sweetie, but it isn't. You can't sterilize this. You could get an infection and die."

"I'm careful," she said. "I'm always careful."

"Not careful enough. Look, I don't understand why you need to do this. All I know for sure is that it helps you keep a handle on things. I don't want you doing it, but if you're going to do it, at least let's do it in a safe way so that you don't get sick from an infection, and so your mother doesn't find out."

Trixie looked hopeful for a moment, the first time I had seen her look hopeful for a long time. Then her face turned grave. "This is crazy. We're never going to get away with it. I'll get caught. You'll get caught."

"I'm willing to take that chance, if this is what we need to do to help you. You want to go over the ground rules or wait until tomorrow?"

"I think I want to think about this for a while."

"OK, Trix. Good night. And happy birthday."

"Dad? Thanks. For the knife."

"You're welcome, sweetie."

She looked at it for a long minute as I held it in its box, and then she smiled—a smile that lit up her face in a way that I hadn't seen in a while. "It's…beautiful."

She didn't cut herself that night, and truth be told, she didn't cut herself that often—only when she felt she needed to, and never more than a few strokes. She knew what the knife could do and took care to stay away from nerve junctions and muscle fiber. I can still see her sometimes, sitting on that bed, running the knife slowly through the sensitive skin of the inside of the upper arm, watching the blood drip down, her face a mask of ecstasy and torment. I got her a rubber mouthpiece, like boxers use, so she never cried out from the pain of the antiseptic. And I was there, every time, watching her, making sure that she never did more than superficial harm to herself.

At the time, I thought it was a good decision. I thought that having a special knife, a knife with a history, although a phony one, would keep Trixie from using broken glass or plastic shards or something else unsafe that could cause permanent damage. By keeping possession of the knife, I could control when Trixie used it, and by withholding it from her when she was acting manic or upset, I could ensure that she used it only when she was calm enough not to seriously injure herself.

Giving Trixie permission to cut herself was one strategy among many. We used medication and therapy. We used Trixie's own determination and competitiveness to help her apply herself to her mental health as well as her studies. Danielle and I played tennis with her for hours to help give her a focus and a goal for getting better. When that wasn't enough, we brought Francie home—and that turned out to be decisive. Trixie graduated from high school, got a tennis scholarship, and went to college. We thought she had a good chance at having a stable career and a real life, and I still think she might have if Francie hadn't been killed.

Do I regret what I did? Yes, every single minute of every day. But at that place, in that time, it seemed more hopeful than desperate. I can recognize the desperation now for what it was, but it was at least a desperation rooted in empathy, and love.

I kept the flowers around for a few days. They were nice flowers, and it wasn't their fault. They did look pretty on my kitchen table. But they died in time, and I threw them out, and that was that.

36

The Newark airport has moving sidewalks, which makes it about one hundred times easier to deal with than the Atlanta airport. I made my way to the rental car counter and stood in line. I felt something uncomfortable in my pants pocket, and then I remembered that I had brought my cell phone with me. I picked it up and called Alicia's home number.

"Hello?" It was Toby's voice.

"Hi. This is Alicia's dad. Is she around?"

"No. Where are you?"

"Newark airport, waiting for them to find my luggage. I go to the rental car counter after that, and then I guess to my hotel."

"Oh. OK. Um, Alicia isn't here right now, but she said you needed to swing by here when you got in. I have your tuxedo for you."

"All right. I should be out of here before too much longer. When will Alicia be back?"

"Not tonight."

I felt the first little twitch of fear run up the back of my spine. "Did something happen? Is everything OK?"

"Don't worry. She went into the city—Manhattan, I mean—with her bridesmaids. Bachelorette party. She'll be back tomorrow morning."

"Oh. You had me worried there."

"Sorry. Hey, you want to have dinner? I don't have anything else going on, and there isn't any food in the house."

Toby was sitting on the front porch when I got there, noodling around with his guitar. He seemed to be playing one note over and over again, like he was tuning it.

"Not much of a song," I said.

"You don't know this song? Figured you might."

"Doesn't sound familiar."

He sang a couple of bars, something I recognized from one of Johnny Cash's last albums. Toby's voice was uneven, a little quivery—a world away from Cash's harsh baritone. He was singing about hurt and suffering and pain, and this did not seem to be a good sign. I wondered whether I had made a mistake in coming over.

"I'm having trouble with that chord," he said. "Simple enough song; you'd think I'd be able to play it. I can do it on the piano easy enough—you have to bang on that G all through the chorus. But it's not that easy on the guitar."

"Guess not. Sounded good to me, though. I didn't know you were a Johnny Cash fan."

"I'm not. It's a Trent Reznor song. Cash's song was a cover. Good cover, though."

"You doing OK?" I asked.

"Ask me on Sunday when it's all over."

"Well, you have a bachelor party to look forward to." I didn't want to be the one to encourage debauchery in the young, but anything had to be better than sitting around singing about death and pain.

"That was last weekend," he said. "Flew out to Chicago, spent two days with a bunch of my college friends, eating greasy food and drinking cheap beer. Nearly froze my ass off at Wrigley watching the Cubs with my dad. Hell of a time."

"Well then, nothing to look forward to except a lifetime of wedded bliss."

"If you say so. Hey, are you hungry? You probably had a long flight."

"I could eat."

We ended up at an Italian greasy spoon near the Rutgers campus. I got a pepperoni stromboli, which was more than I could ever eat by myself. I figured that Toby would eat anything I couldn't finish, though, and I was right about that. He got a bigger version of what I got, but with ham and brie and ancho chipotle something-or-other. He ordered a Blue Moon, which I thought at first was a cocktail but turned out to be a beer. I got a Coors, which tasted good with the greasy pepperoni. Toby downed his and ordered another.

"Slow down, tiger," I said, trying to sound avuncular. "Pace yourself. You got a big wedding ahead of you."

"You don't have to tell me. I'm right in the middle of it. I want to push past it and have it done with, like you do with final exams or dental work or something."

"Is it that bad?"

"I don't want to deal with 99 percent of this stuff. Mrs. M wants to handle everything, and I'm happy with that. I don't care what cushions are on the chairs. I don't care what the centerpieces look like. I don't care what kind of champagne we have. Do you care what kind of champagne we have?"

"I don't know anything about champagne."

"Me neither. Alicia—she gets worked up in knots over this stuff, but she shouldn't. She's having it out with her mom. That's OK; that's what they do. I don't want to be part of it. I don't want them asking me for opinions about stuff I don't care about. There's one thing I wanted, and I didn't get it."

"What happened?"

"Aunt Lucinda happened."

She was Danielle's oldest sister, if I remembered right. "The one who gets terribly, terribly hurt when things don't go her way?"

"You sure about that? I think that describes most of them."

"Lucinda has it down to an art form. What did she do this time? Insist that the chicken be free-range?"

"It's not chicken, it's quail. I think it's quail. Anyway, that's not what it was. It was about the music. All I wanted was a cheap band that would do cheesy eighties songs. Something light, something fun, something everyone could enjoy. I wasn't asking for Swedish death metal or Renaissance harpsichords or anything weird or different. Basic, standard American pop music. Nobody could possibly object to that."

"You'd be surprised what these people can object to. What did she want? Classical? Chamber music? Baroque quartet?"

"Oh God, if only. Turns out that her grandson is the drummer for a Coldplay tribute band."

"Is that good?"

"You listen to a lot of music? Contemporary music, I mean?"

"I bought the new Alison Krauss CD. Listened to it once or twice so far. It's pretty good."

"I love bluegrass. Is there a lot of Dobro in there? Or is it mostly mandolin and banjo?"

"I couldn't tell you."

"OK. That's not important anyway. Let's just say I'm not a Coldplay fan. In fact, you take my entire musical taste and make something that's the total opposite of it—well, you do that, you get Nickelback. But right past that is Coldplay. So I tell Mrs. M that I don't want them to play at the wedding, and Alicia agrees with me."

"But it turns out that Aunt Lucinda is terribly, terribly hurt and extremely put out," I assumed.

"Worse than that. She makes a deal with Mrs. M that the band is our wedding present, take it or leave it. I still don't want them. Alicia steps in at that point and convinces me to at least listen to the band, give them a shot."

"Sounds fair enough so far."

"They have a gig out in Allentown at this dive bar. We drive out there—it takes us a half hour to find the place, it's so far off the beaten path. By the time we get there, people had started throwing things at them. Alicia decides not to stick around, so we take off. "

"But you're still stuck with them."

"Yeah. The grandson said we never showed up, never gave them a fair chance, and Aunt Lucinda was furious about the whole thing. So we're stuck with them. Alicia wanted "Wonderwall" as our first song, and they agreed to play it, although they got all huffy about it being an Oasis song. But they're going to do only Coldplay the rest of the time, which is going to stink on ice."

"It's one night, and you'll have the rest of the marriage to gripe about it. It'll be fine. Having said that, you should have done the smart thing and eloped."

I said that last word when he was inhaling the last part of his stromboli, and he started coughing. I thought he might have had an olive go down the wrong way or something. I got up to give him the Heimlich maneuver.

"I'm OK," he said.

"Thank God," I said. "I had visions of you dying right here and my ex-wife killing me in the morning."

"I'm fine. But…"

"What?"

"We already eloped."

"You did?" I asked.

"Two weeks ago. Alicia was depressed and unhappy about all the wedding stuff, so we took off and went down to Virginia Beach for a long weekend. She drove the whole way; you know she loves her car trips."

"You got married in Virginia?"

"They don't have a blood test requirement or a waiting period. We found a minister who did the ceremony on the beach, at sunset. It was great. But don't tell anyone."

"Very romantic. I can't think why you went to all the bother, though. You can't back out of this shindig now."

"I want to be married to your daughter. I don't care how that happens. I didn't want to lose her because of all this wedding nonsense. I love her, and I want us to be together."

"I know, son. You did fine."

"Thanks. You know, I've been thinking about you a lot lately."

"How come?"

"Well, don't take this the wrong way, but at first, I thought you were kind of weird."

I could have said the same about him, although I didn't point that out. "But now?"

"Now I've had the experience of losing a child. I know it's not the same thing as what you and Mrs. M went through. It can't be. But every time I think about what we did—the decision we made—I feel all empty inside, and sad. It must be that way for you, a little bit."

"More than a little bit, but I get what you mean."

"Anyway, I guess I understand why you live like you do. It's not easy dealing with the pain."

"It's not. But it gets better over time. You're young, and you have each other, and that counts for a lot. Have a nice wedding, have a good honeymoon, and get on with your life."

Toby eyed the uneaten half of my stromboli. "Are you going to finish that?"

I slid it over to him. "Enjoy."

"Thanks. Oh, I have two messages for you."

"Messages?"

"One is from Mrs. M. Says that you had better be sure to be early for the rehearsal, like five thirty or so. You have the directions?"

"I do."

"The other one is from your friend, Ms. Crawford. She called and told Alicia that she couldn't get the earlier flight she wanted to make it in time for the rehearsal dinner but that she'd be there for the wedding."

"I'm sorry," I said. "It's a bit loud in here. I thought you said that Ms. Crawford was coming to the wedding."

"Well, yeah. She's your date, right? I mean, when you were up here last time, you said she was coming."

I felt that little twitch of fear running down my spine again, but at least I knew which direction the emotion was coming from. I cursed myself for being so stupid that I couldn't predict something as obvious as Dot showing up at the wedding. Of course she would. Anyone who could walk in to my cabin and convince someone as reclusive and suspicious as I am to go to a dinner party would have no problem whatsoever in crashing a big fancy wedding. Even if I ignored her, she'd be able to talk to Danielle and everyone in her family, and they all would be more than happy to dish all kinds of dirt about me. I didn't think that Dot would do anything—at least intentionally—to wreck Alicia's wedding, but she wouldn't have any trouble making my life miserable.

On top of all that, there was no way I could explain this to Toby without coming across as some sort of idiot. "You about done with that beer?" I asked.

"Yeah. We better go." He took a last swig out of his bottle. "Here's to single life."

"Hear, hear," I said. The single life has its disadvantages, but presents nothing so complicated as women showing up at weddings they're not invited to in order to harass you for no good reason.

37

"OK, you're the dad, right?"

"That's me."

"You stand over here, next to the bride, on the lip of the green here. You go last, understand?"

"Got it."

The young man whom Danielle had hired to be the wedding coordinator was short, with gelled-back blonde hair and pale skin. He was wearing a polo shirt and neatly pressed khakis but looked like he would be uncomfortable in anything less than a tuxedo. He scurried off to the front of the line to coordinate the rehearsal procession.

It was early in the evening, with enough light to do the rehearsal. The air was still around us, a little heavy, a little humid. We were outside, underneath the terrace of the restaurant, on the practice green of the golf course. They had three different functions at the Palace that night, so the rehearsal had to happen somewhere else, and this was the most convenient place.

"What I don't understand is, if you're doing an outdoor wedding, why you had to do it at the Palace?"

"The reception is going to be inside, that's why," Alicia explained. "They do the actual wedding ceremony as a throw-in. It will be nice to have it outside."

"If the weather stays nice."

"It will. The alternative would be to have it inside and you walk me down the grand staircase."

"That would not be my preference," I said.

"We can get you a cane."

"I feel old enough as it is." The first cadre of attendants started moving to the other side of the green.

"Don't worry about it. We won't go down the stairs. I don't want to trip on my train either."

"That's a relief. How are you making out with your mother?" I asked. I wanted to know if Danielle was on the warpath, or if she had calmed down after what had happened the last time I was up here.

"Things are fine," she said, in a tone that made me think that things were not as fine as all that. "She let me have my way about a few things, so it's been running smooth. The only thing she's worked up about right now is Ms. Crawford being here."

"About that," I said.

I spent the morning trying to call Dot and getting only her voice mail. I had tried her university number, and her cell phone number, but she hadn't picked up. I thought about calling Hartsfield and asking them to do an announcement over the PA to tell her to stay home, but that seemed like overkill. I didn't think she'd listen to me anyway.

There was going to be another confrontation. I knew that. This time, though, I couldn't control the place or the time or the outcome. That worried me more than I was willing to let on.

"I'm so excited to meet her," Alicia said. "We've been exchanging e-mails for weeks. But you probably knew about that."

"I don't know what she's told you. I haven't talked to her myself lately. I didn't know she was coming, to be real honest with you."

"I know you're on the outs right now. I don't know why. But I'd like her to come, and whatever it is, I hope you can work it out, at least for one day."

"It's not that easy."

"It can't be harder than being nice to Mom, and you seem to be doing OK with that."

"It's not the same thing."

"You'll be fine. Dot likes you. She told me to tell you she was sorry about what happened—whatever it was, I didn't ask—and that she wants to work things out. That doesn't sound unreasonable to me. Anyway, it can't hurt to talk to her."

"Sweetie..." I thought about explaining, about telling her why I had broken off things with Dot, why I didn't want her at the wedding. But I couldn't bring myself to do that. I didn't want to talk about Trixie, not then. I didn't want her death to overshadow Alicia's wedding. She didn't deserve that, and I wasn't about to do anything to make her sad and miserable. "It's complicated, and I don't want to go into it, but I don't see it happening," I said.

"Please. Talk to her and give her a chance to explain. For me."

The couple ahead of us marched down the imaginary aisle, and the wedding coordinator held up his hand for us to wait. "OK, bride, OK, Dad—you're the end of the procession. What you do is wait for the last couple to clear, then you listen for the musical cue." He pulled his phone out of his pocket and pushed a button. It played the trumpet notes of the Wagner wedding march.

"OK, you wait for that, and then everyone stands up, and that's your cue. Walk down the aisle, slowly. Take your time; you only get to do this once."

We walked across the green, with all eyes on us, taking our time. Toby was waiting by the imaginary altar, looking loose and comfortable in jeans and a wool blazer.

"OK, Dad," the wedding coordinator said. "The minister asks who gives this woman in marriage. What's your line?"

"Her mother and I do," I said.

"Nicely done. You hand the bride over to the groom, a little kiss for good luck, and then you get to sit down."

I gave Alicia a quick kiss and stepped back. It didn't take them long to complete the rehearsal, which was fine by me.

The dinner itself was fine—Caesar salad, steak, strawberry cheesecake, the sort of food that most people will eat. There was a bottle of wine for each of us, compliments of the bride and groom, complete with engraved corkscrew. I didn't drink any of it; I wanted to be sober for the drive back to the hotel. The country club served Pepsi instead of Coke, so I ended up drinking iced tea, which I don't like that much. I entertained the thought that Danielle had chosen this particular country club because they didn't have Coke, but that seemed overly petty, even for her. If she was going to make a point about something I'd done or not done, there were much more direct ways for her to do that.

I was worried that I wouldn't have anyone to talk to at dinner, but Alicia had done me the favor of sitting me next to Toby's mother. She was short, Italian, and voluble, and I didn't have much work to do to hold up my end of the conversation. I got an earful of stories about what Toby was like when he was young, which I filed away for future reference. She finished half of my cheesecake, which explained where Toby got his metabolism. I liked her but was glad that we wouldn't be doing Christmases together anytime soon.

Danielle was waiting for me when I walked out of the restaurant.

"Well, you made it, I see," she said. "Did you have a nice dinner?"

"Let's not make this ugly," I said. "There's no need for that, not tonight, not tomorrow. We can be pleasant to each other for the next forty-eight hours, at least."

"I have no idea what you are talking about," she said.

I wasn't fool enough to think that Danielle was happy to see me. She was playing the part of the gracious hostess, which allowed her to deal with equanimity to anyone and everyone, for at least a little while. I'd seen her do this a hundred times at dinner parties, or less formal occasions involving old football buddies or children's birthday parties. She could put on the mask for a while, and then take it off, and sometimes there would be something ugly remaining underneath after all the dishes had been cleared away. I wasn't going to be around to see that, though, and I was willing to be nice if she was.

"I'm looking forward to tomorrow," I said. "I know you've put a lot of hard work into the planning."

"I'm looking forward to it being over with and going home and putting my feet up. There are so many loose ends to tie up first. Speaking of which…"

"Yes?"

"I think we need to talk. Just for a few minutes. If you don't mind."

"I'd rather not," I said. "I'm tired, and I need to head back to my hotel."

"You're at the Holiday Inn, if I'm not mistaken," she said.

"You know me too well."

"Sometimes I wonder. I caught a ride over here with the wedding coordinator, and he appears to have taken off without me. If I could get a ride back to your hotel, I can get my car and get back to the Heldrich."

I had not lived as long as I had with Danielle not to recognize when she was about to drop a bridge on my head. This was a setup.

"I'm sure that you can get the country club to call you a taxi," I said.

"William Raymond Morse. For shame."

"Shame has nothing to do with it. Self-preservation is more like it."

"That's exactly why we need to talk," she said. "I am not taking no for an answer."

We drove back to New Brunswick in silence. I thought about turning on the radio, but I didn't know what the presets were or what a good radio station would be. There wasn't any traffic to speak of. At one point, I noticed a baseball stadium, all lit up off to the right, and I thought about how I'd rather take the exit and buy a ticket and get a hot dog and a beer and watch a few innings. I hadn't been to a ball game since the Braves choked in the '05 play-offs, but it seemed more attractive than driving somewhere with my ex.

"Penny for your thoughts," she said.

"I want to make sure I take the right exit," I said.

"Easton Avenue. You're almost there."

38

I got the key card out of my wallet and opened the door to my hotel room. She followed me inside; as though she was afraid I was going to slam the door on her. She made an appraising glance toward my tuxedo, hanging on the closet door. "So you did get your tux. I was worried."

I put the bottle of wine and the corkscrew on the chest of drawers. "I got it from Toby last night. Is that what you wanted? To check on what I'd be wearing?"

"That's not what I'm worried about. Why don't we sit down?"

"You want the chair? I'll sit on the bed."

"Fine."

"So," I said. "What do you want to talk about?"

"I don't want you to think that I'm spying on you. I was curious. I saw a name on the seating chart that I didn't know, and I did a little research. Just because I was curious, not because I care that much who you spend your time with now."

I breathed a quiet sigh of relief. This was about Dot. It was the one area where I knew we would agree. "I know who she is, and I know why you're concerned. I'm going to make sure she doesn't show up."

"So you do know who she is," Danielle said. "I wasn't sure."

"I found out. I didn't know at first."

"Then I was right."

"About what?" I asked.

"About you being a bigger fool than I imagined you to be. Why did you invite her? Why did you start talking to her? If she's writing a book—she must be—then there's no reason in this world for you to cooperate with her, much less invite her to your daughter's wedding. Have you taken leave of your senses?"

"Not entirely. I have been trying to talk to her all day, to make sure that she knows I don't want her here. Believe me, we agree about this."

"How did you get involved with her?" Danielle asked.

"She lied to me. She came by the cabin one day and told me she was lost, and we started going out. Dot—Dorothy Larson, I mean—is very clever and very manipulative. Once I found out who she was, I broke it off."

Danielle rocked back in her chair and rubbed her forehead with her fingertips, like I was giving her a headache. "You went out with this woman? On a date? Good Lord, Will, can't you be bothered to think about your *own* interests for one minute?"

"She used her maiden name. I didn't recognize her. If that makes me an idiot, then I admit to it. But I'm not responsible for her being here, and if I had anything to do with it, she'd be back in Atlanta right now."

"Did you talk to her?" she asked.

"Before I knew who she was and what she was doing, yes. After I left here the last time, she convinced me it would be a good idea if I talked through things with her."

"What did you tell her? Did she ask about how Trixie died?"

"No," I said. "I told her some things—things I should not have told her—but we never talked about that night. We might have, if I hadn't found out who she was and why she was asking and that she wanted to write a book. You have to believe me; I never would have talked to her if I knew who she was at the time."

"Are you going to tell her?"

"No, of course not."

"But you say that she's clever and manipulative, and she's determined. Is it possible that she might get back into your good graces?"

"No," I said, although I knew I wasn't being completely honest about that. "I have no intention of seeing her or talking to her again, at least not after tomorrow. She lied to me. She used me. I don't have any intention of telling her anything. Period. I know you're worried about that, and I understand, but believe me, she's not getting any more material from me."

"You have never told anyone the truth—the real, authentic truth—about what happened to Trixie. You lied to Alicia when she asked you. You lied to the grand jury. You may have lied to your lawyers, for all I know."

"I never lied to you," I said.

"You're only saying that you never lied because you never told me the truth in the first place."

"I don't have any answers for you. I don't understand why Trixie took her life. I can't explain it. But that's what happened."

"Why can't you explain it? Why can't you tell me what happened?" She was out of her chair now, and getting more and more agitated.

"Why now? Why, after all this time? Why on the day before Alicia's wedding?"

"Because you're going to tell her. Maybe not Dorothy Larson. But somebody is going to ask you, one day, and you're going to spill your guts. Maybe because you're lonely. Maybe because you're drunk. But it's going to come out, sooner or later. And if I have to read about it in a book or a newspaper or a magazine article, I'm going to be desperately unhappy with you, and that will have severe consequences for the both of us. Do I make myself clear?"

"I think you should leave," I said. "If I thought it would do any good to tell you, I would tell you. But it won't. It didn't then, and it won't now."

"You will tell me," she said, again with the sound like breaking glass in her voice.

"I'm not Alicia. You can't bully me into telling you everything."

"You will tell me what I want to know. You owe me that much. You owe me the truth."

"I don't owe you that."

She sank back down in her chair. I was afraid that she was going to start to cry, but no tears came. "You have no idea," she said in a slow, quiet voice. "You have no idea what you owe me. Telling me how my daughter died would be the smallest, tiniest part of all the things that you owe me. It's all I want, all I am asking for."

"I'm sorry, Danielle."

"I thought I would never see you again. That's the only reason I've been able to go so long without knowing. I thought you would stay in that little cabin and never come back down. But you came to see Alicia, and now you're here for the wedding, and if they are able to have another child, you'll be here for that. I can't stand it. I can't stand seeing you, knowing you're in the same room, knowing that you know what happened to my daughter, and that you won't tell me."

"I can't tell you."

"Why? Are you protecting me? If you are, stop it. I don't need you to protect me. If you're protecting yourself, well, you've been doing a damn poor job of that too."

She was right about that, and she was right about one other thing. I wanted to be part of Alicia's life again, and as long as Danielle was part of Alicia's life, I had to take that into account. I had thought that silence was the price I had to pay for having a relationship with Alicia. It turned out that I was wrong. If I wanted to make peace with Alicia, I had to make peace with Danielle, at least this far.

"What do you want to know?" I asked.

"Did you give her the knife?"

"No."

"But you got it out for her. It was in the safe. I know that. She didn't have the combination. You must have gotten it out."

"I did."

"Why?"

39

It was late, and I was tired, but I couldn't go to sleep because Trixie was taking a bath. We didn't trust her in the shower; she'd tried to break the glass door several times. We ran only an inch or two of water in the bathtub so she couldn't drown herself. Washing took forever.

Danielle always watched Trixie when she bathed, but Danielle was in Panama Beach, measuring curtain rods for a client. It was her first trip away from home since Francie died. She needed the work, and the break, so I got to stay home and watch our daughter.

I wanted to let Trixie skip her bath, but I couldn't. She'd spent a couple of hours on the treadmill—working out was one of the few things she was allowed to do—and she smelled like a goat. So I didn't have a choice. I couldn't leave Trixie alone in the bathroom. It would be too easy for her to slam her head on the edge of the tub. I didn't think she would do that—she'd been calmer and more relaxed over the last week—but I wanted to be careful.

"This is stupid," Trixie said. "You shouldn't have to watch me."

"It's just for a while. Soon we won't have to."

I didn't know which of us was more uncomfortable. I kept one eye on Trixie and one eye on a magazine, trying to respect what little privacy she had. She crouched in the center of the garden tub, cold and miserable, like a small, wet animal looking for shelter.

"I've been home a month now. I haven't tried to do anything since I've been here. I've been good. I'm taking my medication. I don't want to go back to the hospital."

"I know you don't. The more you can do to make us trust you, the more you're going to get to do. It's a slow process." Only that week we'd decided to trust her around plastic utensils.

"I'm better now."

"But you were a very sick girl for a very long time." She had spent eight weeks in a private psychiatric hospital outside of Macon after Francie's death. There had been only three suicide attempts in that time, but they were all serious. She still had the stitches from the stray ball-point pen that she had managed to jab into her thigh. She'd tried to swallow bleach, and had tried to choke herself on a helium balloon that some well-meaning friend had sent her.

"I understand what happened now. It wasn't my fault. I thought it was for a long time, but now I know that I didn't do anything wrong. I know I'm not ready to go back to school next semester, but at least I'm together enough to take a shower."

"Maybe we can talk about it when your mother gets back. Why don't you get out and dry yourself off? Then we can go to bed."

She opened the drain and got out of the tub. I handed her a towel.

"Checking for fresh scars?" she asked.

"Yes," I said. "You look fine." Large patches of her skin were criss-crossed with faint white lines, but there wasn't the angry slash of red anywhere except for the healing wound in her thigh.

"Can I have my robe, please?" She sounded miserable and defeated, and I wanted to give her a hug, but I knew she didn't want that. Trixie wouldn't let anyone touch her.

"Sure."

She got out of the tub and walked through the master bedroom into her room. We'd taken the restraints off her bed—they did more harm than good, we had thought—but we had removed every-thing that we thought she could use to hurt herself, and kept the

236

door locked. The only other pieces of furniture in the room were two bookshelves. One held books, the other had her clothes—we couldn't allow any wire hangers for the obvious reason, and we thought she might try to jam her hand in a chest of drawers. The bookcases were screwed to the wall. It was as safe as we could make it.

Trixie asked me for the knife. She had done so every night when I had put her to bed.

"How do I know you haven't thrown it out?" she asked.

"Because I would not do that."

"Mother could have. She knows it's there. She could have chucked it."

"She knows about the knife, and she knows what it means to you. She would not do that."

"I want to see it," she said. "I don't need to cut myself. I don't want to cut myself. Dr. Carter would find out about it and send me back to the hospital anyway."

"That's a good reason not to pull it out of the safe. It's OK where it is. You need to get some sleep."

"I can't sleep. I worry. What if something happened to my knife? What if a burglar got it?"

"You're being ridiculous."

"Haven't I been good? Haven't I done everything I could do since I've been home to make things better? To be better? Haven't I shown you anything?"

"You have, sweetie. You've been fine. You're doing so much better. Let's not risk that."

"I want to see it for one minute. You can go get it out of the safe. I'll wait here. You can hold it. You don't even need to take it out of the box. Just lift the lid for one minute so I know it's there. Please."

"No."

"It will help."

"I'm sure it would."

"You know I'm worried about this. You know it would help. I'm begging you, Daddy—just one minute."

"So that's why I got the knife out of the safe," I told Danielle. "Because it meant something to her. Because she was trying so hard. Because she was just so anxious, and because that was making her so miserable."

"You didn't want her to cut herself," Danielle said. "Not that night."

"No. Definitely not. I wanted to talk to you. I wanted to talk to Dr. Carter. I wasn't sure it was a good idea. I thought it might help her, the way it did when she was in high school, but I wasn't going to make that decision on my own. But to look at the knife, for one minute? That sounded reasonable."

"You left her alone in her room while you went to get the knife?" she asked.

"I locked the door. I went to the safe and opened it, and I got out the box. The key was sitting next to it, so I unlocked the box and put the key back in the safe. I closed the safe, which locked it. I remember thinking it was stupid for me to close it, because I would have to open it again when I came back."

And it was a good thing I closed the safe, I didn't say, *because if I had left it open, the police would have known where the knife was hidden, and then they would have known for sure that I gave Trixie the knife, and I would be in prison right now.*

"I took it down the hall and unlocked Trixie's door. I opened the box and told Trixie to sit down on the bed, which she did. I took out the knife and showed it to her. I thought that would be enough, that she would go back to bed, and we'd have the same discussion the next day."

"What did you do? Did you give her the knife? Did you think she was just going to cut herself and that would be it?"

"No. I didn't. I wouldn't have."

"But she got it anyway."

"Yes," I said. The word was an effort. I could feel the blood in my veins running warm, pounding through my temples with an almost concussive force.

"How? How did she get it? Goddamn it, Will! Don't sit there and stare. If you're going to tell me, tell me."

"I want to hold it," Trixie said.

"I don't think that's a good idea."

"Why not?"

"I'm going to put it back in the safe now. You've seen it. You know it's still here."

"I don't know it's the same knife," she said. "It could be a different knife. If I can just hold it, for a second, I'll know."

"Don't be silly. It's the same knife."

I expected her to keep arguing with me, to wear me down, but I wasn't going to let her. Besides, I was tired and ready for bed. I closed the case and turned for the door.

Trixie sprang off the bed and punched me in the gut. All of her momentum and all of her pent-up anger was concentrated in that punch. She hit me right in the solar plexus. I bent over, all but paralyzed with shock and loss of breath.

Somehow I held onto the case. She took it away from me, and held up the knife. I staggered for a moment, and then fell backward into a bookcase.

Trixie got back on the bed. She got on her knees and took off her robe. Her hair was still wet. I don't know why I remember that. I was lying there in a heap, and I couldn't get up, but I could see her. She took the knife with both hands. It was like she was talking to it. Then she stabbed herself, deep in the pit of her stomach.

I tried to get up, but I was only able to stand up on my knees and shuffle toward the bed. Trixie took out the knife, and I saw the blood glinting on the blade. Then she stabbed herself again, finding a soft place between her ribs.

I pulled myself up on the bed and pulled the knife out before she could slash herself anymore. She grabbed at it and cut her hands, although I didn't know that because they were already so bloody.

There was blood everywhere, everywhere, everywhere.

"You know the rest of it," I told Danielle. "I tried to stop the bleeding, and I got her downstairs, and I drove her to the hospital."

I looked at her, and she was crying. Just a little, right at first, and then she lay on the bed next to me and started crying in earnest. I wanted to comfort her, but she didn't want that, at least not from me. I lay beside her and cried my own tears, the same tears I had been crying for the last five years.

I don't know when she left, but she did at some point, without a word. I don't know when I got out of bed, or how I managed to open the bottle of wine, but I did.

40

Daddy, you need to get up.

Don't want to.

You have to.

I want to lie here and be miserable a little while longer.

You're going to be sick.

Maybe so.

You're about to throw up. That's not good if you throw up in bed. You could choke.

Maybe I would be better off.

Not today. You wouldn't do that to Alicia. Not today.

Leave me alone.

Get up. You can make it to the bathroom; it's not far. If you can throw up, you'll feel better, and you can get back to sleep.

Don't want to.

Daddy, please. Just this once.

I did what she said. I pushed myself off the bed. I clutched at the wall to steady myself. I made it to the bathroom, one step at a time. I opened the lid of the toilet and threw up. I flushed the toilet so I couldn't smell it, but I felt the oily, foul taste in my mouth. I threw up again, and then a third time, my head bending low against the toilet. I was afraid to get down on my knees because I thought I wouldn't be able to get up again. I threw up one last time and then straightened up and ran the tap in the sink. I washed the taste out of my mouth and flushed the toilet again.

Good job, Daddy. I knew you could do it.

Thanks, Francie.

I'm not Francie.

Then who is it?

Daddy, don't play games. I came to help you. Are you feeling better?

A little.

Go back to sleep. It'll be OK in the morning.

Thank you, Trixie.

I'm sorry about all this. Sorry I did what I did. I never would have done it if I knew what it would do to you and Mom. But it's over now.

It's OK, sweetie.

Go back to sleep. I love you.

Love you too.

41

"*Con permiso*," I heard a voice say. "*Tengo que llegar mi lentes de contacto.*"

"I speak English," another voice said. "Is this your room?"

"Yes. Yes, of course. I left my contact lenses in there, and I need to get them."

"Sir? Sir?" the second voice asked.

"Go away," I said.

"Will? Are you OK in there? We're traveling together. I need to help him. He's not feeling well."

"Can you look up for a minute, sir? See if you know this lady?"

I was lying on the bed, still wearing my clothes from the night before. I had the tang of vomit still in my mouth. My throat was dry, and my voice was scratchy. I was able to open one eye and turn my head enough to see that Dot was trying to get past the housekeeping cart and into my room.

"I know her," I said.

"If you could come back a little later, after we've had a chance to clean him up a bit, that would be helpful. *Por favor.*"

"*No problemo*," the housekeeper said, with more than a touch of sarcasm.

"Do you know what time it is?" Dot asked me.

I turned my head and saw the sunlight streaming into the room. "Urp," I said.

"It's almost noon. You have to be there by four for the pictures and such. What have you been doing in here all this time?"

"Nothing much," I said.

Dot's eyes darted over to the nightstand, where the empty bottle of wine was still sitting. "Did you have to drink the entire bottle?" she asked.

"Yes," I said.

"Well, I'm not your mother. Into the shower with you, now. Do you have your key? I'm not going to be able to get that housekeeper to let me back in again."

"In my wallet."

I got in the shower and turned the hot water up as far as it would go. I breathed in the steam, which made me cough. I spit up a couple of greenish globs. I found the soap and got as clean as I could. I used the hotel shampoo to wash the grease and oil out of my hair. When that was done and the shampoo was out of my eyes, I got out and cleared off the mirror and started the shaving process. I took a little more care than I otherwise would have because I knew there'd be pictures to take.

I got on a T-shirt and underwear before Dot came back. She had a cold bottle of red Powerade. Not Gatorade, mind you, which most people would have gotten, but Powerade, which is a Coca-Cola product. "Drink this. You need the electrolytes."

"Thanks. I appreciate it."

"Not a problem."

"So, how did you figure out which room I was in?"

"I was a reporter for twenty years. You don't get to be a good reporter without having good investigative skills."

"No, seriously, how did you figure out which room I was in?"

"I asked your daughter. She'd tried calling you to see if you had plans for breakfast, and you didn't pick up. She called me and asked me to check on you. Are you going to be all right? You look like hell."

"I feel like hell."

"Do you have regular clothes to wear?" she asked.

"I can put on some jeans. Why? Are we going somewhere?"

"I am going to absolutely lose my mind if I don't get some decent coffee. And you need to eat as many carbohydrates as you can to soak up all that alcohol in your system, so you can walk down the aisle without staggering."

"I know the perfect place," I said. "If you don't mind driving."

"It's not a problem. I'm happy to help. Why don't you get dressed and I'll pull the car in front of the lobby, so you don't get wet."

"Dot?"

"Yes?"

"Why did you come here?"

"To help you. And it was a good thing I did. From the looks of it, anyway."

"I appreciate it. More than that, I needed it."

"Don't worry about it," she said.

"One question, though."

"Shoot."

"What did you mean a second ago? About getting wet?"

It was raining when we left the hotel, a few drops, but enough that I guessed the wedding would be moved indoors. Before we left, I had turned on the Weather Channel to catch the local satellite feed, and there was a line of storms moving across the Appalachians into central New Jersey. This was the leading edge of it. They didn't say anything about there being a severe storm warning or the possibility of tornadoes, which you'd worry about in the South. It was going to be a little precipitation, but I hated that it was raining on Alicia's wedding day.

"They say it's good luck," Dot said.

"Let's hope so."

"It'll move out by morning. It shouldn't affect your flight home on Monday."

"Did Alicia give you my entire itinerary, or just the highlights?"

"She's a very nice girl, your daughter. I am looking forward to meeting her in person."

"She told me the same thing."

"What do you know about your new son-in-law?" Dot asked.

"He's an ethnomusicologist."

"Of course he is."

I was able to give her directions to the diner where Toby had taken me the last time I was up here, and we got big plates of hash browns, bacon, and French toast. "You know they're going to be serving dinner after the wedding," Dot said. "There's no way I can eat so much as 10 percent of this and still have room for a big meal."

"About that," I said.

"About what?"

"It sounds like you're planning on coming to the wedding."

"Of course I'm coming to the wedding," Dot said.

"But you're not invited. Or, at any rate, I didn't invite you."

"You did invite me. I specifically remember this." She took a big bite of French toast. There was a playful look on her face, and I knew she was baiting me. "Besides, even if you didn't invite me, your daughter wants me to be there. So I am going to be there. You can ignore me if you want, but I'm still going to be there. And there's going to be pheasant. I love pheasant, don't you?"

"I'm not crazy about it. Look, this is my daughter's wedding we're talking about."

"And she invited me. What's your problem?"

"What's my problem? What do you think my problem is?"

"I am glad you mentioned that," Dot said. "I have news for you."

I wanted to look over my shoulder to see if yet another bridge was going to fall on me. They had been coming fast and thick this weekend.

"They made an arrest in the Carissa Buckley case."

"What? Who?" I asked.

"You remember. I told you. She was the Fort Benning soldier who was raped, and I was researching the case."

"That's good, I guess, but what possible difference could that make for you going to the wedding?"

"It's not just an arrest. They caught the guy, for-real this time. He'd raped another girl, over in Milledgeville, and they made a DNA match. Got him dead to rights as far as I can tell."

"The system works."

"Don't be sarcastic. I'm going down there for the arraignment as soon as we get back. Best of all, I know the defense lawyer—he went to school with Hal."

"Well then," I said. "Good for you. I guess. Grist for the mill." I picked up the saltshaker and put a bit more salt on my hash browns, to help the electrolytes.

"You don't understand. I can write that book now. *Assault at Fort Benning*, which isn't the greatest title, but I think it could work. I'm mostly hoping at this point that the suspect pleads insanity—that would add a different dimension."

"I'm sorry," I said, "but I still have absolutely no clue whatsoever about what this has to do with you not going to my daughter's wedding."

Dot looked at me for a long moment and then stamped her foot, like she was five years old and I was telling her she couldn't have another cookie.

"Setting aside the fact that you don't seem to be able to be happy for me, at least a little bit, I would think that anyone would understand the basic principle involved here. The only reason I was even thinking of writing about you was because I wasn't going anywhere with the other project. Now it looks like I'm going to finish it, which means I won't have any time to spare on anything else. So there's not going to be a book about your daughter. You don't have to worry about that. If you want to hold it against me that I thought about writing it, fine. And if you want to hold it against me for the rest of your life that I misled you about it, fine too. "

"You can't expect me to forget what you did," I said.

"No. I am not. Believe me, Will, I have had plenty of time over the last few weeks to think about what I did, and how I treated you.

I apologized to you that night, but it wasn't enough. I understand that. But I don't think you understand how I feel."

"So explain." I wasn't going to argue with her, because she was right. I had not spent one minute since the night she left thinking about how she felt. I assumed she felt guilty for lying to me, but that was the extent of my empathy.

"Do you remember when I told you about my ex-husband?" she asked.

"Sure."

"When he left, I told myself that I didn't care. Then I told myself that I wouldn't care. I didn't have to care about anything or anyone other than myself and what I wanted. It was easier to live that way, it was easier to teach that way, and it was so much easier to write that way. When I started my research, I didn't care about you or your daughter. All I cared about was writing a book that I could sell to a publisher. And that's why I could lie to you, because I didn't care. I didn't expect to care. Will, if you put any more salt on those hash browns, you are going to give yourself a heart attack sitting right here."

I put the saltshaker down and took a bite of French toast.

"Did you see what you made me do there? You made me care. I didn't think I was going to care about you. It surprised me. It shocked me, if you want to know the truth. I imagined you as this big, overbearing jock, and then I met you, and you were sweet and kind and lonely. I responded to that. I don't know why. It didn't make any sense to me. It still doesn't. But I care about you, Will. And I care that I hurt you, and I'm sorry, and I want to make it up to you. All I am asking you to do is to let me do that, just for today."

I wanted what she said to be true. I wanted to know that someone who was alive and present and in my life cared about me and wanted me to be happy. I'd missed Dot, and I couldn't think about her without a pang or two of regret. But I didn't trust her, and worse, I didn't think it was smart to trust her.

"I understand what you're saying," I said. "Our relationship was important to me too. I cared for you too, and I didn't realize exactly how much until you weren't there. But don't think it's a good idea for you to be at this wedding. It's my daughter's big day, and I don't want anything to happen that could ruin it."

"Do you really think that about me?" Dot asked. "Can you sit there and tell me that you seriously, honestly think that I would do anything to ruin your daughter's wedding? Why do you think I came all the way up here? Did you think I was going to interrogate your daughter about you and Trixie? Or your ex-wife, or her family?"

"I don't know what to think," I said.

She got up then, and left, and made her way toward the front door. I was worried for a moment that she was going to drive off and leave me stranded, but she went inside the ladies' room and slammed the door behind her.

The table was still piled high with food. When the waiter came over with the check, I asked for another cup of coffee and a couple of Styrofoam containers. I wasn't hungry anymore, and putting the food into the containers gave me something to do while I considered the predicament I had gotten myself into. I had exactly one person, besides my daughter, in this world who cared for me at least a little, and I was trying as hard as I could to push her away when I needed her, and I had pushed her hard enough that she might not want anything to do with me.

I sat there for a long time and finished my coffee, cursing myself for being so stupid. It was bad enough that I had let Danielle bully and cajole me into retelling the story of Trixie's death, but I had gotten myself drunk in the bargain, and now I was risking the chance of disappointing my daughter and alienating Dot. All I had to do was try to forgive her, and maybe we could make things up down the road. It would be painful to forgive her, I knew, but life without her had every possibility of being more painful than that.

She came out of the bathroom after what must have been a good twenty minutes. Her eyes were red and puffy, but her face looked grim. She didn't sit down.

"Did you pay the check?" she asked.

"No. You pay the cashier, up front."

"You're paying. I've done enough for you for one day."

"I don't mind," I said.

"Good. This is what's going to happen. I am going to drive you back to the hotel. You are going to get into your tuxedo, and I am going to drop you off at the Palace so they can take pictures. With me so far?"

"That'll work." At this point, I was willing to go along with whatever she had in mind.

"I am going back to the hotel. I am going to change clothes. Not only did I pay for my airfare and hotel, I went to the trouble of buying a new dress for this wedding, and I am going to wear it. I don't care what you think about it, and I don't care what you think about me being there. I am going to this wedding, I am sitting at your table, and you are going to be nice to me while we are there. Is that asking too much?"

"No," I said.

"After this is over, if you want to hate me, you can. If you don't want anything to do with me, fine. It's up to you. I've told you how I feel about you. You can decide how you feel about me. If you want to tell me, fine. If you don't, fine. But I made a commitment to be here, today, for you, and I am going to keep that commitment even if you still hate me."

"I don't hate you," I said. "I never hated you."

"Then we're off to a good start. You're not seriously taking all that food with you, are you? That's going to be disgusting in the morning."

"I guess not."

"I don't know what I'm going to do with you," Dot said. "Come on. Let's get you ready for the big day."

42

The Palace was large and airy and had huge staircases everywhere. I got someone to show me to the elevator. The plan, as I understood it, was to take the pictures upstairs before the wedding. I walked down the corridor and found Toby lounging on a leather sofa.

"You're early," he said. "She's in there getting ready. It'll be awhile. The photographer just got here; he's setting up."

"Might as well relax, then."

"Might as well. It's going to be a long day."

I spent the next half hour talking baseball with Toby and his dad. He was a Cubs fan, so that meant he was ticked off about Greg Maddux, Alfonso Soriano's contract, Ron Santo not getting into the Hall of Fame before he died, night games at Wrigley, and Carlos Marmol's control problems, although not in that specific order. He was making the case for Starlin Castro for Most Valuable Player when the photographer poked her head out.

"I need the groom," she said, and Toby obediently trooped over.

"You get along with your ex-wife?" Toby's father asked. I hadn't talked to him at the rehearsal. He was tall, with a gut that was straining his cummerbund.

251

"Not so much lately."

"It will be better when the grandchildren come. Or that's what I keep telling myself."

"I guess we'll see," I said.

I hated the thought of seeing Danielle. I knew that she hadn't wanted me here at one point. Could confronting me about Trixie have been part of a plan to make sure I didn't show up? I hated to think that. She'd been as upset about the whole thing as I was. She went into the bathroom at one point; I remember that, but I didn't remember when she left or what she'd said to me on her way out, if anything. I was too wrapped up in my own grief to comfort her, which was part of the reason we ended up divorced.

If I hadn't shown up, I was sure that Danielle would have been pleased—if nothing else, she would have been able to hold it over my head for the rest of my life. But I was here. That made me something of an annoyance, like the rain.

The wedding coordinator called me in to get my picture taken a few minutes later. Alicia was there. She was wearing her white dress—a satiny fabric, with lacy trim, and that's as much as I can do to describe it. She looked glorious. Her train was so long that she couldn't maneuver, and she was holding a bouquet of purple and white roses the size of a basketball, so I had to come over to where she was standing in order to give her a kiss.

"Be careful of the makeup," she said.

"You look beautiful," I said. "Just beautiful."

"I have to look beautiful for only a couple more hours."

"You'll always be beautiful to me." I noticed that she was wearing a pendant on a thin gold chain around her neck, and there was a diamond in the pendant that looked familiar. "Are those the rings I gave you?" I asked.

"They are. I had a friend of mine make them into a pendant. She did a great job."

Alicia's friend had hammered the gold band into a wide circle, and fashioned the other ring into spokes that supported the diamond setting in the center. There was engraving on the outer ring, three words, but the letters were too small for me to make out.

"What does that say?" I asked.

"Ask me later," she said. "I can't tell you now."

"Why not?" But the photographer had finished fiddling with the lighting, and she demanded our attention.

"OK, Dad," the photographer said. "You need to get over on the other side. Stand up straight, and smile."

The pictures took an age. All I had to do was stand there and smile, which was easy enough. Danielle stood beside me in a couple of the pictures and stared daggers at me, but she didn't say anything and I wasn't about to say anything.

I have never liked getting my picture taken, and I have never liked wearing a tuxedo, so it wasn't pleasant, but I knew it had to end soon. The whole process seemed to take longer than it should have because the wedding coordinator kept sticking his head in the door, wanting to know what Danielle thought about this or that detail of changing the plans for the ceremony for indoors rather than outdoors. But soon enough, the last picture was taken, and everyone moved downstairs. Alicia took the elevator because of her dress, and I followed her because of my knees. Everyone else got into position, and the wedding coordinator checked to make sure that no one had an unzipped fly or anything.

"You ready?" I asked Alicia.

"This is the easy part."

"Of course. You've done this before."

"Did Toby tell you that? Oh, he is in *so* much trouble. That was a *secret*."

"Don't worry. I'm not going to spill. But if this is the easy part, what's the hard part?"

"Dancing in this dress and with these shoes. You are going to dance with me, right?"

"Of course."

"Then everything will be fine. You say your line, I'll say my line, and we'll go dancing and eat some pheasant."

"I love you, sweetie. Thank you for having me at your wedding."

"Thank you for being here. It means so much to me. I know it was hard for you."

"I'm glad I came."

"I didn't tell you what it said on the pendant," she said. "It says *Hope, Believe, Love.*"

"Francie always used to say that."

"It was the last thing she said to me, right before I left to get on my plane when we were in New York for the tennis tournament. I was so upset—worried about Trixie, worried about you and Mom. She told me not to worry, and then she said those words. Hope. Believe. Love. I've never forgotten that."

"I know. I wish she was here."

"I do too. I wish Trixie was here, and Junior. But they're not. All we can do is hope, believe, and love."

"I love you, sweetie," I said.

"I love you too, Daddy."

"Let's go get you married."

We walked together to the back of the room, where the ceremony would take place. I looked down at every step to make sure I wasn't stepping on Alicia's train. The string quartet struck up the notes of the Wagner wedding march, and everyone stood up. I walked Alicia down the aisle, one step at a time, feeling the pressure of her hand clutching my arm.

I have lived a long life, and I have lost most everything I once cherished, but not everything. Not my daughter Alicia, and not the moment when I walked her down the aisle and handed her over to her husband. I have that now and I always will.

The preacher was tall and thin, with wire-rimmed glasses and a bald spot. "Who gives this woman to be married?" he asked.

"Her mother and I do," I said, and then I sat down next to Danielle. She squeezed my knee for a second, and then folded her hands.

43

At the close of the ceremony, I gave Danielle a quick hug and looked around for the nearest men's room. I knew I needed to be alone for a few minutes. I knew there would be a wave of emotion, but I didn't expect it to last very long, not after what I'd gone through the night before—like how a small aftershock accompanies a big earthquake. I could have found some other quiet place to go, but I wanted the men's room because I figured Dot would not follow me there. I was able to pull myself together after ten minutes or so, and then I ran some cold water over my face and got myself looking presentable.

Dot was waiting in line for what I guessed was the sushi bar. She was wearing a cocktail dress in a shimmering navy fabric. She had her hair pinned back and looked smashing. I wandered over in the other direction and found a different station that was giving out mini-hamburgers. The server said that they were made from Kobe beef—don't know about that, but they were about ten thousand times better than what they serve at Krystal.

Dot came over with a plateful of sushi. "Do you want to try one of these?" she asked. "They call them Philadelphia rolls."

"I didn't know they had sushi in Philadelphia. What's in them?"

"Salmon, cucumber, and cream cheese. Hence the Philadelphia."

"Raw?"

"It's not good any other way."

"I'll pass."

"Your daughter sent me an e-mail last week and told me to make sure you went over to the bar and tell them you're the father of the bride."

"Why?"

"It's a surprise."

I crossed over to the bar—gingerly, because people were packed in to get the free hooch—and the bartender produced an old-style glass bottle of Coke from an ice bucket and popped the top. He handed it to me, and the cold stung my hand. I tasted it, and it was bracing, just what I needed, but a little different.

"From Mexico," the bartender said. "The bride told us to save it for you, special. They still make it with real sugar down there."

"Thanks. Thanks so much."

"There's plenty more if you want."

I hung around Dot for the rest of the cocktail part of the reception, sipping the Mexican Coke and listening to the people come up to her and ask why she looked so familiar. I was kicking myself for not recognizing her sooner. She looked much more like the Channel 11 anchorwoman she had been than she ever had in Blue Ridge.

"What do you know about the band?" she asked.

"It's a Coldplay tribute band. If you know what that is, you're ahead of me."

"Can you dance to that?"

"I'm going to try. With Alicia, I mean."

"You're not going to dance with me? Not once?"

I wasn't crazy about the idea of dancing with Dot, but I had agreed to be nice to her, and dancing with her was probably part of that. We stood there, silent, for a long time, while the press of wedding guests moved all around us. I saw Alicia standing over by the ice sculpture, and she gave me a little wave of encouragement.

"I'll think about it," I said.

"Good. I'm going to get a little more sushi. Sure I can't tempt you?"

"You can try," I said. "But you'd be better off doing it with another one of those Mexican Cokes."

The little wedding coordinator guy clapped his hands just then, and we were all herded in to the ballroom.

44

I didn't know the song the band was playing, but it was slow enough that Alicia and I could dance together without either of us embarrassing ourselves too much.

"You and Toby looked very nice together," I said. They'd danced the first dance, and nobody had tripped over anything, which made it better than my wedding, when I'd almost sprained my knee tripping over Danielle's dress.

"You look very nice with Ms. Crawford. Thank you for bringing her."

"Thank you for inviting her."

"My pleasure. Did you get things straightened out with her?"

"Let's dance."

And we did, but not for long enough. Six months before, I would not have thought that I would ever have gotten the opportunity to see my daughter again, much less dance with her at her wedding. The song only lasted a couple of minutes, and then she hugged me and gave me a kiss, and I sat down at my table while the band started a fast-paced song. It wasn't enough. But it was far better than being alone and grieving on my mountain. I had my daughter back, and one day there might be a grandchild for me to hold. If my heart still ached for the children I had lost, it was at least lighter than it had been in years.

"It almost looks like the napkins were set up to match the cabbage in the salad," Dot said.

"You have to hand it to my ex-wife," I said. "Great eye for color. The ribbons on the centerpieces are the same shade too."

"Very observant of you."

Someone on the other side of the room clinked their fork against their water glass, and a few other people started doing it, and they kept it up until the groom kissed the bride.

"They're going to do a couple of slow dances after dinner," Dot said. "I checked." The music had been fast and discordant, although I couldn't tell if the discord was because that's how the music was supposed to sound, or because the musicians weren't playing it the right way. Either way, I hadn't tried to get out on the dance floor. I'd been sitting at the table guzzling Mexican Cokes and listening to Dot try to make small talk. It was not that interesting, but it was instructive—I was never much on small talk, and hadn't had any recent opportunities.

"How slow?" I asked.

"I know they're doing 'Lovers in Japan,' and you ought to be able to dance to that one. You owe me, anyway."

"You listen to this stuff?" I asked. I couldn't imagine that anyone did.

"Coldplay is one of the most famous bands in the world. Their lead singer is married to Gwyneth Paltrow. She was in the *Iron Man* movie."

"I'll take your word for it."

"No stalling. Are you going to dance with me or not?" she asked.

I thought about it. I was no kind of dancer. But Dot was right. I did owe her, at least something.

"Sure. Let's cut a rug," I said.

The song wasn't that slow, but it wasn't that fast, and we got down and boogied as best we could. When the band took a break, Toby got up on the stage, picked up a guitar, and started to strum a little. What came out had a very close resemblance to "All Shook Up," and Toby, as it turned out, did a decent Elvis impression. He got a nice round of applause, and he started singing "Jailhouse Rock." Alicia sat at her table and looked embarrassed at first, but soon she was out on the dance floor herself. I got to dance with her a little more, and I can say I hadn't had that much fun in ages.

Toby called Alicia up to the stage then, and then launched into an a capella version of "Love Me Tender." Dot grabbed my arm and pulled me in, and we danced close together.

"That's a great song," Dot whispered.

I didn't say anything, and she didn't press the issue.

We stayed until the last guests were straggling out the door and the band was packing up. I would have left earlier, but I wanted to talk to Danielle before I left. I wasn't sure what I wanted to say, or why, but I felt I needed to say something, even if it was as simple as good-bye.

I asked Dot to get her car keys from the valet, and she agreed. I got to my feet—slower than I would have liked, as my knees were a little stiff from the activity of the day. Danielle was involved in a deep conversation with the wedding coordinator on what appeared to be the final disposition of the centerpieces. She saw me out of the corner of her eye and gave me a dismissive flip with her hand, which I interpreted as *I see you there, but you'll have to wait one moment.*

I sat down at an adjoining table to wait. Whoever had been sitting there had taken only a bite or two out of his or her slice of wedding cake. I thought about taking a bite but decided against it. It was good cake, but I didn't need any more to eat.

The wedding coordinator finally took off at high speed and retreated into what I guessed was the kitchen. My impression was that he'd had a long day, but so had I.

Danielle got up and sat across the table from me, like she didn't want to get too close. "You're still here," she said.

"You did a great job with the wedding. It was lovely. I know Alicia appreciates it."

"I'm sure she does. She may even tell me that herself one day. Did your friend Ms. Larson enjoy herself?"

"I know what you're thinking. The whole thing with her doesn't make a great deal of sense to me either. But she's not going to write the book she was planning, and she helped make sure I got here in one piece."

"I should be unhappy with you about bringing her here, but I am exhausted, and I need to take off my shoes and lie down in the worst possible way."

"Well, then. Good night, Danielle."

"Can you stay a moment?" she asked.

"Of course."

"It won't take long." She found a chair closer to me and sat down. "I should have let your daughter talk me into flats."

"She was beautiful, wasn't she?"

"She was indeed. I'm glad that she's happy. She deserves it."

"I think so too," I said.

"I wanted to ask you one thing, before you go. I wanted to ask you last night, but we were both too upset, there at the end."

"It was kind of emotional for me. For both of us, I know."

"You've had a hard time. We've both had a hard time. And when you're having a hard time, it can be difficult to acknowledge that other people are having it as bad as you are."

"I guess that's true." It was as close as I was ever going to get to sympathy from Danielle, and I was ready to accept that.

"I want to know one thing," she said, "and then we can let things lie for now. Did you do everything you could to protect our daughter?"

I closed my eyes and thought for a long moment.

"No," I admitted. "I fucked up. I wish I hadn't, but I did, and now she's dead, and it's my fault. I never should have let her get anywhere close to that knife, but I did. I believed she was getting better. I hoped that she had decided that she wanted to live. I was wrong about that. I shouldn't have trusted her, but I did."

I waited to see if she had anything else to say, but she didn't do anything other than blink back a couple of tears.

"Can you forgive me?" I asked.

"No," she said. "I can't do that. But I want to, now. More than I did before."

"I understand."

"You'd better go," she said.

I should have told Danielle that I still loved her and cared about her. I should have told her that she had been a wonderful wife and a great mother. I should have told her how sorry I was for not recognizing that, for not being faithful, for everything I did and didn't do in our marriage. But I didn't. I couldn't bridge the gulf, not then. We said good-bye, and that was it.

I didn't blame Danielle for not wanting to forgive me. I have not forgiven myself. I don't know that I ever will.

But there was one step I could make in that direction.

I walked out of the Palace and saw Dot, standing alone under the porte cochere, waiting for the valet to bring her rental car. She was wearing an elegant black cloth coat, and had her hands in her pockets against the chill of the evening. Her face was lit up by the floodlights. Behind her, the rain was falling in torrents.

I wasn't under any illusions. I knew what Dot had done—how she had betrayed me, how she had wounded me. No one could blame me if I turned my back on her and returned to my cabin and my solitude.

But I knew that if I did that, I would be turning my back on something more important.

The valet pulled up with Dot's rental car, breaking the spell. She saw me as I limped my way down the stairs, and smiled. "Would you mind driving?" she asked. "I've maybe had a bit too much champagne."

I made the short drive to the Holiday Inn. All the parking spots that were close enough to the door where we could walk in without getting soaked were taken. We sat in the car for a quiet moment, waiting for a break in the rain.

"Did you have a good time?" Dot asked.

"I did," I said. "Thank you. I couldn't have made it without you. I appreciate that."

"I'm glad I came. It was a lovely wedding."

"You were lovely too," I said.

"Well, thank you. A lot of effort went into looking this good. It's nice to see that it didn't go to waste."

"It didn't."

A gust of wind blew through, carrying a sheet of rain with it.

"It's a shame the weather had to be so miserable," Dot said.

"I need to tell you something. Not about the weather."

"Oh, good. Nothing more uninteresting than talking about the weather. It's always too hot, or too cold, or something, just enough for people to talk about it when there's nothing else to talk about."

"I'm serious."

"So be serious."

"I'm sorry," I said.

"Now that's interesting. What makes you say that?"

"I knew you cared about me, and I turned my back on you."

She reached over and took my hand. "Will, I understand. You were upset. It's not fair for me to expect you to trust me after I misled you the way I did."

"It's more than that," I said. "I care about you too. It's why I was so upset with you. Not just because you lied to me, and not just because you were going to write about me and Trixie. I cared about you, and I knew I was losing you, and that made it much worse."

"Can you forgive me?" she asked. "I know it would be hard for you. And I know I don't deserve it. But it would mean a lot to me if you could."

"I don't want to forgive you," I said. "But I do. I have to. I have to forgive you because I love you."

Dot just looked at me, mouth partway open, with her eyes registering a fair amount of surprise. It was the first time that I had ever seen her be at a loss for words. "For goodness' sakes, Will," she said at last. "If you're going to tell a girl something like that, there were about fifteen times today that would have been more romantic."

"I know this isn't the romantic way to do it. Hear me out, though. I was talking to my ex-wife, just before we left, and I asked her to forgive me. She said she wanted to, but she didn't. It wasn't just because I hurt her so badly, although I did. It was because she didn't love me enough anymore to want to try."

"I'm sorry that she couldn't forgive you," Dot said. "That must be painful."

"It is, but there was something even more painful. I can't live with myself this way. I have spent the last five years letting grief and shame and regret eat me alive. As long as I was alone and didn't have anyone to care about, or anyone who cared for me, I could live with that burden. But I can't do that anymore. It's not fair to me, and it's not fair to you. I have to try to forgive myself, if I can, and I have to forgive you too. If I don't do that, I won't do anything but suffer for the rest of my life, and I don't want that. Not anymore."

"You don't deserve to suffer any more, Will. It's all right."

"I love you, Dorothy."

"I love you too."

"I'm glad. I never thought I would get to hear that again."

"I think the rain is starting to let up a bit," Dot said. "Let's go inside. We can get some coffee."

We got out of the car. I took her hand, and she squeezed it, and we walked together, hand in hand, through the rain.

45

Hey, Daddy.

Hey, Francie.

It was a beautiful wedding.

I know. I wish you could have been there.

I know. How are you? Are you all right?

I'm fine. I'm just tired. It was a busy weekend, but it was a happy weekend.

Are you happy?

Yes, I am.

It's good to hear that. I was worried about you for a long time. But your friend seems to be taking care of you.

I need taking care of.

I wish I could be there for you, Daddy.

You are.

It's not the same.

I know.

Do you remember what I told you?

I remember, Francie.

Hope. Believe. Love.

I'm trying.

You're doing more than that. You didn't think you had hope, but now you do. You didn't believe in yourself, but now you can. You didn't have love, but you found it again.

I love her.

I know. I'm glad.

I love you too, Francie. And your sister, and your brother.

We love you too. Don't forget.

I can never forget you.

Don't be silly, Daddy. Don't forget. Hope. Believe. Love.

I won't. I promise.

"May I have your attention," the flight attendant said. "We are now making our final descent into Hartsfield-Jackson International Airport. All passengers must be in their seats with their seatbelts fastened. All carry-on items and all tray tables must be secured at this time. All portable electronics must be turned off."

I opened my eyes. We were almost there. I looked out the window and saw Atlanta rising to meet us. I looked over to my right and Dot was there, looking concerned.

"Are you going to be all right?" she asked. "I was worried about you falling asleep on the plane, like you did last time."

"I'm fine," I said. "I had a dream, but it was a good dream this time."

"Well, that's good. You know we're almost there, right?"

"Yeah."

Our plane circled Atlanta a couple of times, waiting for a clear runway. I looked out the window and watched the city roll past. I could pick out the white Coca-Cola building, standing alone on the edge of the Georgia Tech campus. Traffic streamed up and down the Connector. The glass towers of Downtown glinted in the late afternoon sun.

I left Atlanta five years ago, because the weight of memory, shame, and regret was far too great. I knew I would carry the burden of Trixie's death the rest of my life. But I knew I didn't have to let that burden destroy me.

I once thought I had lost most everything I once cherished. But in the course of the last few months, I had been able to restore my relationship with my daughter and find a woman whose love I hoped would sustain me through the rest of my life.

"So, what's next?" she asked.

"I don't know," I said. "I figure we take things one step at a time. Go slow. Figure out what it is that we both want."

"No, I mean after the plane lands."

"Oh," I said. "I have my truck parked at the airport. I can give you a ride if you like, or you can take the train back downtown. Your choice."

"Are you hungry?"

"I could eat."

"Good. I was thinking we might get a bite to eat somewhere, and then maybe we can swing by the IKEA in Atlantic Station."

"What for?" I asked.

"You've got that upstairs room in your cabin, which is very nice and everything, but the furniture is so tiny. If I had a regular-size desk, and a swivel chair, I could go up there and write, and I'd be out of your way. You wouldn't even notice I was there."

"I think I would notice if you were there."

"I was thinking I could pick out the desk and the chair today, and you could take it with you in the truck. I could drive up Friday night and we could put it all together over the weekend. We can carry it up in pieces, so it's not that much of a strain."

It sounded like a big job to me, but if Dot didn't mind doing most of the heavy lifting, I thought we could manage. "I don't know that I like the idea of you being upstairs writing the whole time when you're at the cabin," I said.

"I'm not going to write the whole time. But I'd like to make some progress on this book, at least for a couple of hours a day. We'll still have plenty of time together. And I'm not going to be teaching this summer, so I can spend some more time in Blue Ridge."

"I'd like that."

"I would too. Anyway, once I get the first draft done on this book, I can start doing some plotting on the next one."

"Which one is that?" I asked.

"I was thinking about doing something different. A historical romance novel, to be specific, about the doomed romance between a World War I nurse and the disgraced heir to the Duchy of Newcastle-on-Tyne."

"Are you sure that's a good idea?" I asked.

"Well, you've done most of the research. If you don't mind sharing that with me, I can start on the outline, and then it's just a matter of filling in the blanks."

"That's not what I mean."

"What do you mean?" Dot asked.

"It's an interesting story. I will grant you that. But it's a sad story, at least when I heard my mother tell it."

"The world needs sad stories."

"I know," I said. "But I prefer happy endings."

Dot leaned over and gave me a brief kiss. "I do too."

About the Author

Curtis Edmonds is a writer and attorney living in central New Jersey. His work has appeared in *McSweeney's Internet Tendency, Untoward Magazine, Liberty Island, The Big Jewel, Yankee Pot Roast,* and *National Review Online.* His book reviews appear on the *Bookreporter* website. Other short fiction appears online at his yet-to-be-award-winning website, http://www.curtisedmonds.com.

This is his first novel.

Acknowledgments

This book was written at night.

That is to say, it wasn't written the way that you might imagine that an author writes a book. It wasn't written in a book-lined study, with quiet, stirring music playing in the background, while a handsome, suave author nimbly pecks away at an antique typewriter. It was written at night, in my bedroom, with me sitting on the right side of the couch, tapping away at a Dell laptop perching awkwardly on a cheap Ikea stand. It was written amidst exhaustion, frustration, and about fifteen other words ending in "-tion" that would fit in this sentence. It hasn't been glamorous, and it hasn't always been fun, but it's over with. That means it's time to say "thank you" to the people who helped me get this book from my brain to my laptop to your e-reader.

I could not have written *Rain on Your Wedding Day* at all if it were not for the patience and forbearance of my lovely wife, who sat on the other side of the couch and waited for me to work through whatever depression or cussedness or anger that was driving me through the writing process--not to mention the editing process, and the querying process, and the self-publishing process. But her contribution is more than just being patient with me when I was thinking about something else, or forgiving me for those times when I'd snap at her for interrupting me when I was trying to finish a sentence. A big part of this book is about our need for love and acceptance, and I would never know anything about either if this beautiful, wonderful woman hadn't agreed to marry me.

The writing process was interrupted quite frequently--more frequently than you would comfortably want to imagine--by one (sometimes both) of my twin daughters complaining about the tyranny of bedtime. If the story, at times, seems unfocused or distracted--well, one doesn't like to *blame* one's children for one's narrative shortcomings, but at least, you know, there's a *reason* why the book is that way. Having said that, although this book may have been written badly, it could not have been written at all if two little girls hadn't decided that it was, eventually, time to lie down and go to sleep. If you're reading this, kids, thank you and I love you very much.

My mother passed away between the time that I finished this book and the time that I got it published. I think that she might have liked it, except for the swear words. Thanks so much to the rest of my family for the love, encouragement and support, and for not looking at me funny when I said I was writing a novel.

When I started writing *Rain on Your Wedding Day* in May 2010, it was for an audience of one. I had met literary agent Scott Hoffman of Folio at a writer's conference, and tried to sell him on a road-trip novel I had written. He asked to see something else that I'd written, and I sent him the first few chapters of the first draft. Without his encouragement, I never would have written the rest of it. Scott has been an invaluable sounding board on other projects, and I hope that this work lives up to whatever faith he once might have had in me.

Martin McHugh (http://www.linkedin.com/pub/martin-mchugh/19/8a4/7b0) and Eric Simpson (http://ericjsimpson.com) copy-edited the first draft of *Rain on Your Wedding Day* and provided loads of helpful insights. Martin took the time to show me why lots of things about the way I wrote the manuscript were wrong. Eric, an accomplished poet, helped bring out the emotional tone of the story.

I contacted Saladin Ahmed (http://www.saladinahmed.com), the talented author of the acclaimed *Throne of the Crescent Moon*, for a critique, largely because we were both raising twin toddlers, and because his book was so fabulous. I appreciate his willingness to take a look at the manuscript and help with some structural issues in the first few chapters. Thanks also to Pat Smith of Welkin Press (http://www.welkinpress.com), who helped me clear out some of the deadwood in the early part of the book as well.

Many thanks to Karen Dionne, who runs the Backspace Conference (http://www.backspacewritersconference.com) which is the best-run and best-attended writer's conference on the planet.

When I realized that I had reached my limit on what I could do with the novel, I asked Carin Siegfried (http://cseditorial.com) to help me get the manuscript to where it needed to be. I could not be happier with the job that she did. (She noted, early on, that a lot of people in the novel were dead, which you probably have figured out yourself.) Working through the edits took me two months of grinding agony, and I hope you will agree that it was worth it. I had to face up not just to my own shortcomings as a novelist, but as a human being. (I came to realize, just for example, that I had no idea about what clothes women wear and why, that things like baseball and 55-inch TV sets are not items of universal interest, and that it's maybe too much to ask a reader to read a whole entire book without any dialogue tags.) If this is a better book than it has a right to be, she is the main reason why.

Angelle Pilkington (https://www.elance.com/s/editor-pilk) proofread *Rain on Your Wedding Day* and helped me realize that I had absolutely no idea whether Will was carrying his cell phone at any given time. I thank her sincerely for making me appear less stupid than I actually am. Any remaining errors or stupidity are mine and mine alone.

The cover art is by the talented Canadian artist Anita Bezanson (http://www.flowersandmachinery.com), based on a photograph taken by Michael Novelo (http://wp.novellogic.de). I am a lawyer by trade, which means that I am not artistic by nature, and also means that I am kind of a wart. But Anita was very pleasant and willing to work with me during the process, and I think the cover is quite something. The calligraphy design of the dedication was done by Jacqueline Cozma (https://www.elance.com/s/jacquelinemc), who did a fabulous job.

Julie Csizmadia of CsizMEDIA, Creative Design Solutions (https://www.elance.com/s/jcsizmadia) produced the electronic eBook and print edition of this book and made it look much better than it perhaps has a right to.

I have so many friends that have encouraged me in this project. (Many of them encouraged me by not making fun of me, or at least not very much, and I appreciate that.) Cornelia Read and David Abrams allowed me to draw a little bit on their experiences in publishing, and you should read their books, of course. Thanks also to many friends from the dearly-departed Cantina for their support and advice.

Richard Biegen read an early draft, and helped convince me that I had handled the horrible decision that Alicia has to make in a sensitive manner. Ryan Garcia is a good friend and a better collaborator (and we'll get that bacon apocalypse book back on the best-seller list one day, see if we don't). Good friends like Deanna Slater, Iris Engleson, and Cindy Naas Stapleton who read my stuff and help give me the illusion that I know what I am doing are a pearl beyond price.

Carol Fitzgerald and Tom Donadio have published my book reviews for Bookreporter.com for ten years now, and have been remarkably good about the whole missed-deadlines thingy. I owe a big debt to Christopher Monks for helping me get various funny ideas out of my brain and into McSweeney's Internet Tendency and the wider world beyond. Thanks also to Matt Rowan at Untoward Magazine, Kurt Luchs at The Big Jewel, David Bernstein at Liberty Island, and everyone else who's had the foolhardiness to publish my stuff.

Special thanks to Alanis Morissette, whose song "Ironic" inspired the title of *Rain on Your Wedding Day*. (I put in a couple of references in the text, but I still need to say thank you.)

Will's cabin is based on a cabin that my wife and I have frequently rented through Above The Rest Luxury Cabins (http://www. abovetherestcabins.com). (I say "based on" because Will's cabin has a second story that "our" cabin doesn't have.) I've always enjoyed visiting Blue Ridge, Georgia, and greatly appreciate the Southern hospitality of its people. Blue Ridge has a lot more going for it than antique stores and brooding, unhappy retirees. Check it out (https://www.facebook.com/blueridgegeorgia).

Without going into the details too much, *Rain on Your Wedding Day* was rejected, along the way, by a lot of different people in a lot of different ways. The details don't much matter, and I don't want to single anybody out, but it was a painful experience.

There's only one person who can change that story, and that person is you.

I don't mean to bother you or trouble you any more than I probably already have. But you've read the book, right? (Please tell me you read the book and didn't just skip to the acknowledgements.) You not only read it, you finished it. You got this far. So do me a favor.

Tell somebody.

I don't care much how you do it. Rate it on Goodreads if you like that sort of thing. Write a review for your favorite online book-seller. Tell your Facebook friends, or your Twitter followers. (I am @Curtis_Edmonds on Twitter.) If you liked the book (please tell me you liked the book) let somebody know.

Thanks for reading. You're the best.

Curtis Edmonds
January 2013
Duckthwacket, New Jersey